DEAD MAN ON THE MOON

CHAPTER ONE

The itch was still there, right between Natalie's shoulder blades. It felt like a prickly feather brushing her skin. The more she tried to ignore it, the worse it got. Her skin twitched, and she shifted around, hoping the fabric of her shirt would scratch the spot. No dice. The slight whisper of cloth over the spot only aggravated the feeling. The itch screamed for relief, begged for a deep, satisfying scratch like a dehydrated man begged for water. Natalie Espinoza grimaced. A half-second scritching would take care of the problem, but no such thing would be available until she went through an airlock, disconnected all the tubes, and climbed out of her space suit.

Natalie knelt next to the core sampler, a machine that looked like a table lamp that had lost a fight with a micro-scope. She checked the hollow tube that pressed against the regolith—the moon's surface—to be sure it was positioned properly, then stood up. The push to her feet was a little too strong, and it sent her bobbing upward a little too fast. Her boots left the ground for a moment before she dropped back down to earth. Or Luna, she supposed.

Bill Hayes, her partner, reached out a gloved hand to help her, realized she didn't need it, and pulled back. Behind him, Earth had risen about halfway up the horizon, well over the lip of the crater. The oceans and continents of the Eastern Hemisphere glowed blue, green, and brown amid a backdrop of hard white stars. It was actually quite pretty. Or it would be, if the damned itch weren't spoiling it. Natalie wiggled again, but it continued to nag at her like a stubborn imp.

"Still adjusting to the gravity?" Bill's voice asked over the com-link. The darkened faceplate of his helmet hid his expression, but she read helpful concern in his voice. Lately Natalie had been wondering if he was harboring a small crush on her. When her thesis advisor had sent her out for yet more core samples, Bill had been quick to volunteer his help, even though such menial work was well beyond the purview of a doctoral candidate like him. And there were other signs—standing a little closer to her than circumstances required, offering small favors, looking at her when he thought she didn't notice. It was only a matter of time before he asked her out.

"I'm getting there," Natalie replied, her voice bouncing around her helmet's interior. "What's worse is the itching."

"Itching?"

"Every time I climb into one of these stupid suits, my back starts to itch," she complained. "It drives me crazy."

"Don't!" he begged, holding up gloved hands. *"You'll get me feeling it."*

Natalie smiled, though now her right cheek was starting an itch of its own. It was purely psychological. Had to be. But knowing this fact didn't help in the slightest. To distract herself, she gestured at the sampler crouching at her feet.

"I think this one's ready," she said. "Where should we put the other one?"

"Dr. Gu said he wanted the samples taken at least fifteen meters apart," Bill reminded her. *"And he wanted half of them*

taken from the shade. We've got three samplers in the sun, so let's start on the shade."

"Okay. You stake out a spot, and I'll get another sampler."

Without waiting for an answer, Natalie loped over to the crater wall. It slanted steeply upward, and the gritty slope was strewn with fist-sized gray rocks. The lip of the crater only came to the top of her head. Natalie leaped upward, bounding in a single leap to the edge of the crater and touching down in a perfect landing. A small smile crept across her face—maybe she was finally getting the hang of this. She strode toward the wagon, feeling like a child playing a game.

"Take three giant steps forward." "Mother, may I?" "Yes, you may."

The wagon, a larger version of the red flyers kids still used back on Earth, held three more samplers. Natalie lifted one without effort. On Earth it would have weighed about thirty kilos, but here it barely topped five. She headed back to the crater, which was exactly sixty-seven meters across. Natalie knew because she had measured it. Below, Bill had almost reached the thin crescent of the shady side. Overhead, the sun made a harsh, white disk that showered the landscape with deadly light. Without an atmosphere to blunt the sun, every rock and crater cast a shadow sharp as a knife. The comparison made Natalie shudder just a little. If her suit ruptured and failed to repair itself, she would be unconscious within ten seconds and dead within ninety. The itch between her shoulder blades flared again.

Natalie was just about to jump back down into the crater when Bill started shouting into the com-link. *"Oh my god! Oh Jesus! Shit! Natalie! Oh god—Natalie!"*

Natalie's heart jerked. She dropped the sampler and leaped into the crater, breath coming harsh within the helmet. Raw sunlight hammered down on her from above, and Bill had moved into deep shadow. Natalie couldn't see him. The metallic smell of canned air mingled with the sharper smell of her own fear.

"Bill!" she shouted as she dropped to the crater floor. "Bill, are you all right?"

"Oh god. Oh shit!"

Natalie hit the ground and tried to run, completely forgetting about the moon's weaker gravity. Her first step sent her bounding upward and she drifted back down with maddening slowness. Natalie's stomach lurched. When she touched down on the gritty surface, she forced herself into the careful lope she had only recently learned. A few more half-leaps got her into the shade of the crater's far wall. The light around her vanished as if she had thrown a switch. Ahead of her, she could make out Bill in his space suit. He was kneeling on the ground behind a small boulder. Natalie's stomach tightened and fear clawed at her chest. Emergency protocols flashed through her head—how to handle a small puncture in a suit, what to do if a victim vomited inside his helmet, which frequency to use for a distress call.

"Bill!" she shouted again. "Bill, say something!"

Harsh breathing came over the com-link. Then Bill said, *"I'm all right. Jesus. I'm just—shit!"*

Relief flooded Natalie's veins with cool water. "Don't scare me like that," she scolded as she came around the boulder. "You almost made me—"

The words died in her throat. Bill was kneeling next to a human head. It was lying face-up on the lunar sand. The skin had blackened and pulled away from the eye sockets and mouth, leaving behind a hideous mummy's grimace. Below the head lay a simple red shirt and pair of light brown trousers. Vague lumps inside indicated an emaciated, mangled mess of a body that occupied far too little space. No space suit. Natalie stared at it, not sure what she was seeing. It was like coming across a camel in a boardroom. Bill reached down to touch the corpse's neck, and for an insane moment Natalie wondered if he were going to check for a pulse. Bill's gloved hand brushed the blackened jaw. Tissue flaked away and trickled lazily into the collar.

4

Natalie's gorge rose and she tasted sour bile. Several deep breaths and hard swallows kept her from throwing up. Would Bill still want to ask her out if he saw her barf inside her helmet? The thought made her want to laugh and she tried to clap a hand over her mouth. Her hand hit her face-plate instead. She cleared her throat.

"I think," she said, "we need to call someone."

The itch was completely gone.

Chapter Two

The acceleration pressure abruptly ended. For a brief moment, Noah Skyler floated weightless in his harness. Then he dropped back to the chair as the shuttle touched down with a lurch and a bump. Noah's stomach lurched and bobbled in sympathy. The passenger in the chair next to him snatched up an airsickness bag and held it in front of her face. Noah's insides oozed with nausea, and he silently begged her not to throw up—it would set him off as well. The passenger, a dark-haired woman about Noah's own age, took two deep breaths and held a third. Finally she exhaled and set the bag down. Noah swallowed with relief and reached for the stiff release catch on his harness. In the passenger bay around him, other people were doing the same, filling the space with clicks, clacks, and murmured voices. Several were already up and opening the overhead bins to drag out shoulder bags and backpacks.

A chime sounded. *"This is Captain Shelly Mills, hoping your flight was just the way we like 'em—straightforward, uneventful, and boring. We've touched down in a perfect landing and it is now safe to unbuckle your harnesses, though I'm sure most of you have done so and are reaching for your carry-on."*

The passengers doing just that paused, then laughed and went back to their business.

"We just want to remind you," Captain Mills continued over the loudspeaker, *"that the moon's gravity is about one-sixth that of Earth's. Not only do you weigh less, your luggage does as well. So don't—"*

A yelp as a blond man in his early twenties hauled a bag out of the overhead bin with too much force. It wrenched the owner around, tore itself away from his grip, and crashed into the opposite bulkhead, narrowly missing a flight attendant.

"—pull too hard," Mills finished. *"We hope you enjoyed your flight, and enjoy your time in Luna City."*

The red-faced owner of the errant bag retrieved it. Several passengers hid smiles behind their hands, others laughed outright. Excitement fluttered in Noah's chest as he got carefully to his feet. He felt light and airy, as if he could leap to the top of a skyscraper. After six hours on a windowless shuttle, he wanted to. Every muscle screamed for exercise. Moving with a meticulous caution that belied his trembling hands, he retrieved his backpack, unable to avoid rubbing elbows and bumping into the people around him. The shuttle carried two hundred passengers, and every seat had been taken. Everyone looked rumpled, and the air smelled of sweat and stale clothes despite the hard-working filters and fans. Still, a sense of anticipation hummed through the compartment, keeping the mood light.

Noah forced himself to wait patiently in the inevitable crush to exit the passenger bay, though inside he was jumping up and down like a little kid. He had arrived safely on the moon, and he was going to study at Luna U, the most prestigious university on . . . Earth? He grinned. The term didn't seem to apply. Still, he was here, and on an all-expense grant to boot. He couldn't wait to get out and explore.

Ahead of him in line was a guy barely out of his teens. He was bopping his head up and down, apparently listening to music piped in from his onboard computer. Noah shook his head. Was the kid even old enough to study at Luna? Look at him. He was dancing in place like a child who had to go to the bathroom. And his clothes were—

The line edged forward, and Noah grimaced wryly. Only twenty-seven, and he was already thinking like an old fogey. He readjusted the bag on his shoulder and scootched forward, trying to see over the kid—okay, young man—in front of him. Noah was a little on the short side, with auburn hair, dark blue eyes, and a boyishly handsome face that often got him more attention than he really wanted. He had a whipcord build achieved partly from lucky genes and partly from hours spent clinging to near-vertical surfaces by piton, rope, or just his fingertips. Noah wondered if rock climbing on Luna was allowed—or a challenge. In this gravity, even free climbing would be a cinch, vacuum suit notwithstanding.

Vacuum. If he wanted to climb, he'd have to go . . . outside. Well, all right—maybe there was a climbing gym somewhere.

Eventually Noah filed past a smiling Captain Mills, through an airlock, down a corridor, and into the receiving gate at Luna City port. It looked rather like an airport, complete with a blue-carpeted waiting area and rows of hard plastic chairs. The crowd of rumpled passengers threaded their way through them, following an arrow-shaped sign that pointed them toward baggage claim and customs. The people walked with an odd, bounding gate. Occasionally someone leaped above the crowd and drifted back to the floor. Green plants bulged and arced out of pots and planters around them, breaking the cold monotony of white ceramic walls and floors. Voices and conversation bounced and echoed.

One entire wall of the waiting area was a window that looked out across the lunar surface, and Noah paused at it. The lunar outdoors looked like a dirty beach studded with rocks and boulders spread beneath an utterly black velvet sky. Stars, thousands of them, shone hard and unmoving as diamonds. It was stark, beautiful, and deadly. Noah stared, entranced. Pictures and holos didn't do it justice. He put a hand on the cold Plexiglas. Death lay only a few centimeters away.

Something cracked against the window like a rock hitting a windshield. Noah snatched his hand away and a jolt of fear touched his stomach. A tiny puff of dust spurted up from the ground a few steps from the window, leaving a tiny crater. The window wasn't even scratched.

"Micrometeor ricochet," said a woman standing beside him. She had long blond hair that reached almost to her waist, enormous brown eyes, and a round, merry face. Pretty. Very pretty. Noah's practiced eye picked out the fact that her matching beige blouse and trousers—raw silk—were hand-tailored to fit her well-toned body. She had a suntan, and her shoes were Italian leather.

"Glad we're in here and not out there," she continued, looking out the window with him.

"Yeah," Noah said. "The weather's gonna put a crimp in my workout schedule. Hard to jog when your lungs are getting sucked out of your chest."

She laughed and held out her hand. Her fingernails had been done by a professional. "I'm Ilene Hatt."

"Hi," he said, shaking. Her grip was firm and dry. "I'm Noah Skyler."

"I know. We're rooming together."

He blinked at her. "Say again?"

"A friend of mine works in the housing office," she said. "I got a copy of the assignment roster, and apparently we're rooming together."

"Oh. Um . . . hooray?" Noah said, feeling off-balance. "I mean—"

She laughed again. "It's obviously a mistake. We'll just have to go down there and straighten it out. Come on—the line at customs and immigration is going to be horrendous."

They stopped at baggage claim to pick up their single allotted pieces of checked luggage—Noah had a duffel bag, Ilene a leather suitcase—and followed more arrows down plant-lined corridors to customs, chatting along the way. Ilene, Noah learned, was a second-year graduate student at Luna University. She was studying chemistry, and she had gone home to visit her family for a couple months before the new semester started. Noah suppressed a small start at that. A trip from Earth to Luna City was a two-stage process. First step was riding the tether up to Tether Station. Second step was a six-hour shuttle trip to Luna itself. It was expensive as hell, and Noah had only been able to afford it because it was part of his grant. Then the penny dropped.

"Ilene Hatt," he said. "As in, Hatt Testing Laboratories?"

Ilene sighed. "Yes, that's them. Us. I'm rich, I'm wealthy, let's move on. What about you?"

"I'm not rich."

"Most people aren't," Ilene said with a touch of exasperation. "I mean, what you are studying?"

"Material science," Noah stammered. "You know that low-gravity orbital construction that just got underway—"

She cut him off. "Well, this is the place for it. So what were you back home? An engineer?"

"I'm a crime scene investigator."

"A cop?" she asked, brown eyes wide with interest. "What are you doing up here?"

Oh great, he thought. She's one of *those*. People like this really burned his butt with their ignorant assumptions about his world: I'm a cop, therefore by definition, I must be an uneducated and ineducable pinhead.

"I told you—getting my master's," he said with all the patience he could muster.

They joined the long line before the customs and immigration station. A hint of her perfume—something floral—hung in the air around her. "So why does a cop need a master's degree from Luna U?"

"That was arrogant," he said.

"No more arrogant than what you're thinking," she shot back.

"And what's that?"

" 'Why would someone with her kind of money need a master's degree?' "

"Well? Why would she?"

"I'll answer yours if you answer mine."

Noah paused and looked at her chocolate-brown eyes. "Are we arguing or flirting?"

"Not sure yet." She reached out to straighten his collar, and a cool fingertip brushed his neck. Noah swallowed hard. "If we're roommates, it'd be inappropriate and awkward for us to flirt."

"Then let's hit housing right after customs," Noah said, and managed a grin.

"You," she said, "have an amazingly cute smile, Noah Skyler. I can say that, since we've decided we won't be roommates."

"And you. . . you . . . ." He floundered. "You should probably move forward," he said. She gave him a questioning look. "'Cause, you know, the line is moving."

Customs and immigration went surprisingly quickly. Their bags passed through the scanner without a hitch, and an efficient official dressed in blue took their retina prints, fingerprints, and an oral DNA sample, all of which were entered into the Luna City identification database. Noah answered a few questions about the reason for his visit ("student"), his birthplace ("Wisconsin, United States"), his place of residency ("same"), how long he planned to stay on Luna ("between two and four years"), and his source of income ("grant, scholarships, and work-study"). He wondered if Ilene would answer the last question with, "You're kidding, right?"

"What's your preferred input?" the customs official asked.

Noah extended his hand, showing his wristwatch. "Verbal."

"Customs official Regina Peters, registration number 34906A hereby grants Noah Skyler of the United States entry to Luna City with a student visa," she told it mechanically. "Run your watch over the scanner for confirmation and check your output."

Noah touched his watch to the square plate set into the official's waist-high desk, then reached up to his left temple and slid a small square of Plexiglas around so it covered his left eye like a square monocle. Text scrolled across it, confirming his visa. That done, put on his backpack and hoisted his duffel. Both still seemed unnaturally light. Noah left the monocle in place and found Ilene waiting for him just beyond the customs desks.

"Housing's about three kilometers away," she said. "We can take the train."

Noah gave her a tentative grin. "Actually, between the tether and the shuttle, I've spent ten hours sitting down or standing in line. Can we walk part of it? You can show me stuff along the way."

Ilene was amenable. They threaded their way through the crowd and out the port's doors into Luna City proper. Noah tightened his grip on his luggage as he looked around at his new home.

The main thoroughfare was underground, wide, and beautiful. Most of the rounded walls were covered in carefully tended, lush vegetation that thrived in Luna's microgravitic environment. This section had a semi-tropical feel to it. Jungle vines and shrubs flourished in a riot of colors. Birds and small animals chirped in the trees or rustled through the leaves. The air was warm and slightly humid but not uncomfortable, like a mild spring day.

"The University is this way," Ilene said, taking Noah's elbow. "Come on."

She led him down a series of pathways planted with climbable trees and camouflaging bushes. Every so often, the path opened into a beautiful grove redolent with the perfume of flowers. The multiple paths, Ilene explained, allowed people to vary their routes and routines, and teams of students from the University's botany department changed the scenery at irregular intervals to further relieve monotony.

"If you get lost, just ask your onboard for directions," she said. "It happens all the time."

The path Ilene had chosen was wide and flat, but still quite crowded. People walked, jogged, and ran along it in the broad, loopy pace indigenous to the low gravity of Luna City. A few rode bicycles or zipped along on silent electric carts. Noah inhaled the clean air gratefully and moved briskly alongside Ilene, who was still holding his elbow. Her touch was light yet insistent, and a faint, sweet smell followed her.

After a few minutes, Noah stopped. The crowd had thinned a little. Ilene looked at him blankly.

"What's wrong?" she asked, removing her arm from his elbow.

"I want to try something," he said, glancing upward.

Ilene followed his gaze, then gave him a knowing nod. "Go ahead. Everyone does it when they first arrive."

Noah set his backpack and duffel bag on the ground and looked up at the ceiling. It was six or seven meters above his head. He crouched nearly to the floor . . . and *leaped*.

The ground fell away, and the vine-covered ceiling zoomed toward him. Air rushed past his ears. His body felt weightless, like he was flying. Noah didn't even try to suppress a boyish whoop. He slowed just as he reached the ceiling. Red flowers sprinkled the vines up there, and he just managed to snatch one before drifting back down to the floor like a soap bubble. He landed lightly amid a scattering of applause from the people on the thoroughfare. Noah laughed and handed the flower to Ilene.

"There you are," he said. "For putting up with me."

She gave the blossom a deep sniff, then gracefully tucked it into her hair. Several people in the crowd made

"Awwww" noises, which she ignored. "Let's take the train the rest of the way," she said. Noah couldn't help but wonder if Ilene had ever taken public transportation back on earth. Daddy probably had a fleet of limos at her disposal.

The train platform was devoid of vegetation but decorated in mosaics created, Ilene said, from materials found on the Moon itself. This one showed a map of the solar system in bright colors. Several dozen people were already waiting for the train, all of them in their twenties. As Noah and Ilene waited, more and more people came down the stairs, and eventually the train arrived like a silver snake on silent magnetic runners. Noah and Ilene boarded with the crowd and were unable to find seats. They grabbed handholds instead as the train slid smoothly forward. His body pressed unavoidably against Ilene's. She felt soft. People stood or sat crammed around them, their eyes flicking back and forth as they read output from their onboards or listened to music.

"Is it rush hour or something?" Noah asked.

Ilene shook her head. "It's always this crowded. The University's accepting more students than ever, but housing isn't able to keep up. They can't build fast enough."

"Why do they keep accepting people if there isn't room to house them?"

"Money," Ilene said. "More students means more revenue. And Luna City has debts to pay."

Noah nodded. Luna City had been flirting with financial disaster since various governments withdrew funding from the original Lunar base that stood on this site. Now it was just a low-gravity, high-priced college town that supported itself the way every other college town did. It was all about location. Location, location . . . tuition.

After elbowing their way off the train, they climbed a wide staircase and emerged into an enormous open space. Noah stopped to stare. Spread out before him lay what looked like an enormous park. Green lawns carpeted the ground beneath tall trees. Hedges and flower gardens wound along an actual stream. Two- and three-story buildings poked up like alphabet blocks dropped on a rug. Students, professors, and researchers thronged walkways between them or studied on the grass. An enormous geodesic dome arced overhead, showing a night sky broken into triangles.

"Welcome to Luna University," Ilene said.

"It's like being outside," Noah said, awed.

"Wait until you've been here a few months," Ilene said. "Come on—housing's over this way."

She led him toward one of the buildings, stopping along the way to point things out like a tour guide—the creek which kept the air humid, the trees which grew amazingly fast in low gravity, the plants which maximized oxygen replenishment.

"The dome itself is pretty new," Ilene said. "They had only just completed it when I first arrived. Before that, everything was encased in smaller domes or dug underground. A lot of the town still is. You're seeing the showpiece."

Inside the building, they found a line snaking down the corridor just outside the housing department. Noah recognized several of his fellow passengers. He and Ilene exchanged sighs and joined the line.

"So what are your jobs?" Ilene asked.

"I'm not completely sure yet," Noah said. "I know I'll be a deputy under the Chief of Security—obvious, since I'm technically a cop. The other—"

"What do you mean 'technically'? Aren't you a real policeman?"

"I carried a badge and a gun, but I didn't chase down bad guys or shout, 'Halt in the name of the law.' My main job was working crime scenes. You know—gathering evidence, running it through the lab, that sort of thing." He smiled. "I'm the one who gets to say things like, 'The fibers on the suspect's shoes matches the fibers in the victim's carpet.' "

"And you don't do that anymore?"

"I'm on extended leave," Noah explained. "Technically I'm still a police officer, but I won't have any jurisdiction here until the Chief of Security deputizes me."

Noah noticed the people ahead and behind him edging away. He gave an internal sigh. Earth or Luna, it didn't matter—tell people you were a cop, and they got nervous. Like he was going to whip out a pair of handcuffs and haul someone away for jaywalking or having bad breath. If that were the case, the woman behind them would have been incarcerated long ago—the pungent scent of garlic and onions hovered around her in a dreadful miasma.

The line moved forward a few steps. "What's your secondary job going to be?" Ilene said.

"That's what I'm not so sure about," Noah admitted "I sent a list of my skills, but never heard back about it. Probably means I'll be washing dishes in the cafeteria."

"Someone has to do it," Ilene said.

"Someone like you?" Noah asked.

"No," she said, adjusting the bright flower in her hair. "I shovel fish poop."

"Uh huh."

"No really—I do. The ponds at the fish farms are filtered, and someone has to clean out the shit."

"Geez. Who did you piss off?"

She laughed. "It's what I got for having an idle youth—no other skills. My primary job is working the chem labs, of course, and I'm teaching a couple undergrad classes. They keep us busy around here. Less time to be bored."

They finally got to the front of the line. It occurred to Noah that his feet should probably start feeling tired after all this standing and walking, but they felt fine. Another benefit of low gravity. There were actually quite a few advantages to life in low gravity once the bone density loss had been eliminated. A bored-looking older woman perched on a tall chair behind a tall counter. A holographic computer display flickered next to her, showing text that

17

looked backward from Noah's perspective. "Can I help you?" the woman muttered.

"I'm Noah Skyler," he said. "This is Ilene Hatt. We met only an hour ago and we're already living together."

"Congratulations," the woman said. "The justice of the peace is up the hall. Next!"

"We're not *supposed* to be living together," Noah said. "Someone got the data wrong."

The woman tapped a key. "Say your name for the computer."

Noah did. The text—black on a yellow background—blinked and changed. "Says here you're a female."

"I can prove he's not," Ilene said wickedly, glancing at his fly."

"Some other time," the woman said without looking up.

She tapped hidden keys. "Fixed," she said. "Wave your input over the scanner for your new housing assignment. Next!"

Noah and Ilene both obeyed, and a moment later they were back in the park. Noah suddenly felt very tired.

"I'm wiped," he said. "What time is it, anyway?"

A digital readout flashed across his monocle just as Ilene said, "Luna City's on Greenwich Mean Time, so locally it's about two-thirty."

"We boarded the tether shuttle at nine last night for me," Noah said. "So that means it's actually screwed-up-o'clock. I can never sleep on shuttles."

"Don't go to bed now," Ilene warned. "You'll adjust faster. Eat foods with lots of protein and avoid simple carbohydrates."

"I know, I know." Noah rubbed his eyes. They felt sandy. "Right now I just want to find my new place and try to settle in."

"Me, too. Maybe I'll see you around?"

Noah looked at her. Were there hints in those brown eyes? Noah was suddenly too tired to play games.

"I liked meeting you, Ilene, and I'd like to see you again," he said. "I'm not rich, and I don't know one end of a toast point from the other, but maybe we can do something together once the shuttle lag wears off and the rocks drop out of my head. If you're interested."

A moment of silence fell over them. Ilene stared at Noah for a long moment, and his face flushed a little in embarrassment. Well, he had blown it. Again. No biggie—he hadn't known her for more than an hour anyway. So why did he always get flustered in these situations? He could be so damned stupid sometimes. Then a warm smile spread over Ilene's face.

"Now why don't more guys take the sweet, straightforward route?" she said, and leaned forward to peck him on the cheek in a way he liked very much. "I will call you, Noah. Welcome to Luna City."

And she left.

Noah stared after her for a second, then half grinned and shouldered his too-light bags.

Noah's street was underground and made him think of J.R.R. Tolkien's Hobbiton. The corridor was lined with round doors set into the walls. The residents had planted trees and flowers and planter gardens on minuscule front porches, and windows framed by ivy looked out onto these "yards." The plants had happily spread everywhere in their new environment. The ivy in particular was lusher and greener than anything Noah had seen before. Far overhead, the corridor ceiling was painted sky blue, and an artificial sun shuttled slowly back and forth, never actually setting, but lengthening shadows and randomly altering the temperature a few degrees up or down. More birds sang in the trees, and a cat vanished into the bushes at Noah's approach.

According to Noah's onboard, the door to his apartment was a bright red circle several yards off the main path. He placed his hand on it, and it rolled smoothly open.

"Hello?" he called. "Anyone home?"

"In here!" replied another male voice, and Noah stepped inside.

The apartment consisted of a single small room furnished with a plain sofa, an easy chair, and brown carpeting. A coffee table made from a packing crate took up most of the floor space. Two windows on either side of the front door gave a view of the main corridor, and a viewscreen on the living room wall pretended to look out on a sun-drenched beach with a blue ocean stretching to the horizon. Dirty dishes and empty beer bottles made an untidy pile on the crate cum coffee table, and Noah smelled fried food. A minuscule kitchenette lined one wall. There was no table. A door led into a tiny bedroom and another into an equally tiny bathroom. On the floor around the crate sat two young men about Noah's age. The first had short blond hair, blue eyes, and a lean swimmer's build. The other had curling black hair and brown eyes. He was only a little taller than Noah. Both young men were white.

"Hi," the dark-haired one said, reaching up to shake Noah's hand. "I'm Jake Jaymes. This is Wade Koenig. Computer said you're the new roommate."

"Yeah. Nice to meet you." Noah set his backpack and duffel on the couch and glanced around the tiny space. "Um . . . do you both live here?"

"Yeah," Wade said shortly. "It's a two-person apartment with three people assigned to it. You, JJ, and me."

"Don't call me JJ," Jake said.

Noah sighed. "Shit. That's the second time housing has screwed up on me today."

"Screwed up?" Jake echoed.

Noah gave a brief explanation of what happened with Ilene. "So now I have to go back down to housing and—"

"It's not a mistake," Jake said. "It's overcrowding. Most of these apartments have three people in them. The undergrad dorms are even worse."

"You should have stayed with the chick."

Noah's practiced eye noted that all the beer bottles sat on Wade's side of the crate. Jake had a paper napkin on his lap, but Wade didn't, and the thighs of his jeans bore telltale streaks of dark grease. Great. He had stumbled into the odd couple.

"I'll just put my stuff in the bedroom, then," he said.

"There's only one dresser," Jake called after him. "And two beds."

Jake was right. The bedroom was barely larger than a closet, with a narrow aisle between two twin beds. One was neatly made, the other was mess. A single built-in dresser was the only other piece of furniture, unless he counted the tiny vid-screen above it. He also found a clothes closet the size of half a coffin. Noah set his bags on the floor in one corner with a grimace and stepped back into the living room.

"How are we going to sleep?" he asked.

"Couple ways to handle it," Wade said off-handedly. "Last semester when Ned—the guy you're replacing—lived here, whoever went to bed last got the couch. Some people do rotations. I like the last-one-in rule."

Noah thought about sharing sheets with guys he barely knew. Five years of finding blood and semen in bedclothes made him shudder at the idea. Maybe he'd get a sleeping bag.

"Sure, we can do that," Noah said. "What about—"

A chime sounded in his ear and text spilled across his monocle. INCOMING CALL FROM LINUS PAVLIK, CHIEF OF SECURITY. He blinked at the message.

"Got a phone call," he said. "I should probably take it."

Without waiting for a response, he went into the bedroom and shut the door. "Route call to bedroom vid-screen," he said.

A man appeared on the screen. He had fair skin, dark hair salted with a little silver, broad shoulders, and thick hands with square fingernails. His pale gray eyes and serious expression put Noah on quiet alert. Everything about him said, "Boss," and "In charge."

"Noah Skyler?" the man said. *"I'm Linus Pavlik, Chief of Security here at Luna City. Glad to see you arrived safely."* They

exchanged a few pleasantries about Noah's trip while Noah waited for him to get to the point. *"I'm sorry to call you before you've had a chance to settle in, but I've hit an unexpectedly . . . unusual situation, and I need another crime scene guy. Meet me down at the Diamond Street airlock in ten minutes. I'll bring a kit for you."*

"But—"

The screen went blank.

CHAPTER THREE

Linus Pavlik sat impatiently on the bench at the end of the Diamond Street corridor. On the floor at his feet sat a pair of crime scene kits. On a branch over his head slithered a yellow-brown boa constrictor. Linus shot it a quick glance. The animal no doubt made a fine living on escaped pets and experimental animals gone feral—hamsters, mice, even the occasional cat. South American rainforest trees made a pleasant green canopy for plenty of critters, including parrots, insects, and students. Packs of the latter moved up and down the corridor, entering and leaving apartments, finding places outside to study, or just going for a brisk afternoon bound. The Diamond Street corridor was never empty for a moment. Linus sighed. Easier to find oxygen in a vacuum than privacy on Luna City. That worried him more than the dead body lying some distance outside the airlock behind him. Shove five thousand people into space for three, take away some privacy, bake in a vacuum for a few weeks, and ding! You had a perfect recipe for increased violent crime.

Linus checked the back of his hand. The time—2:47 P.M.—appeared for a moment, then vanished like a temporary tattoo. He wondered what working with the kid would be like. Linus had sat on the committee for the Aidan Cosgrove Memorial Grant, a new award that paid all expenses for and a small stipend to law enforcement officers looking to further their education. The committee had received over a hundred applications, which they had whittled down to five finalists. Linus had lobbied hard for Noah Skyler, and had eventually had his way. He didn't give a damn why the kid wanted to live here; the point was that he was an experienced scene investigator with fine references. Linus had liked him on paper—or on screen, anyway—because, credentials aside, he had the humility to admit he still had a lot to learn.

Another glance at the time told Linus two more minutes had passed. Maybe the kid had gotten lost. Linus grinned. Kid. Noah Skyler was twenty-seven, barely thirteen years Linus's junior. He suspected Noah wouldn't much like being called "kid," and Linus resolved not to let himself think of the ki—of Noah that way.

But when Noah finally strode into view, Linus wasn't so sure he could keep his resolution, out of petty revenge, if for no other reason. Life wasn't fair but did it have to be so *blatantly* unfair? The brief glimpse Linus had gotten on the viewscreen hadn't done Noah justice—the kid was movie-star handsome. No two ways about it.

Linus had a private theory about the way men noticed the looks of other men. Women could notice and comment on the beauty of another woman and no one thought twice about it. If a man, however, commented on the looks of another man, people thought there must be a sexual attraction. So men acted as if they had no idea if another guy was handsome or not. It was all bullshit. Men, Linus knew, were just as adept as women at spotting good looks in their own sex—they just viewed them in competitive terms.

Noah easily fell into Linus's better-looking category, and he was handsome enough to make Linus nervous. Handsome men tended to spark jealousy among their lovers, which meant potential violent crime, and the guys themselves often had egos the size of their—

Noah tripped and fell. The kid hadn't adjusted to the low gravity yet, and he overcompensated when he tried to regain his balance. His arms flew forward to catch himself, but he had only fallen half a meter, so instead of hitting the floor, his hands hit empty air. The momentum of his outflung hands and arms pulled him forward a little faster, bringing him even further off balance. A nearby frat boy easily dodged out of the way and turned, grinning, to watch the fun. He had plenty of time. Noah fell and fell, and finally landed in a tangle of arms and legs. He lay still for a moment, face flushed with embarrassment. Then he made the mistake of trying to get back to his feet without moderating his strength. When he pushed off, his entire body leaped into the air like a startled salmon. The look on his face— wide eyes, open mouth—made Linus laugh, even though he remembered going through the same involuntary slapstick routine when he first arrived on Luna five years ago.

By now a small crowd had gathered. Noah drifted down to the floor to land on hands and knees amid enthusiastic applause. Linus supposed he'd have to have a word with the kid about getting his Luna legs quickly. It was hard to command the respect of suspects and witnesses when they remembered seeing you stumble like Charlie Chaplin on crank-ups.

The crowd was drifting away as Linus rose from the bench to greet Noah and offer him a hand up. The kid's face reddened even further when he realized the person standing over him was his boss, but there wasn't anything Linus could do about that. Noah took Linus's hand, and the chief pulled with exactly the right amount of force. It wasn't much. The kid couldn't have weighed more than one-fifty back on Earth. Linus suppressed another surge of jealousy.

Even after swearing off fried food and exercising like a fiend five days a week, he wasn't able to rid himself of a small roll of fat around his midsection.

"Nice to meet you in person, Noah," he said, pronouncing the name carefully. "Chief Inspector Linus Pavlik. Call me Linus, unless I'm pissed at you. Then you should call me 'Right away, sir.' "

"Hi," Noah said. "Uh . . . great way to impress the boss, hey?"

"You'll get used to the gravity," Linus said. "Some people wear weights and gradually taper them off, you know."

Noah shook his head. "I want to adjust as fast as I can. I'll stumble, but no one ever died of embarrassment."

"Then let me give you a piece of advice I wish someone had given me," Linus said, and paused. Noah leaned in closer to listen. "Until you're fully adjusted," Linus whispered solemnly, "sit down when you go the bathroom."

Noah blinked at him. "Sit down?"

"Low-gravity urinals take practice. Not for the faint of heart."

"Ah. I'll take your word for it." Noah looked around. Overhead, the artificial sun shone like warm, liquid gold through jungle leaves. The boa had moved on. "So where's the crime scene?"

Linus cocked a thumb at the heavy metal door behind him. "Out there."

"Outside?" Noah's voice rose a little. "You mean—in vacuum?"

"You're certified for outdoor activity, aren't you?"

Noah nodded. Although many Luna City residents never set foot outside an airlock, familiarity with a vacuum suit was a requirement of residence.

"Then let's go."

Near the entrance to the airlock was a series of orange lockers. Linus set his palm against one, and it clicked open, revealing a pair of silver vacuum suits. He handed one to Noah, who took it wordlessly.

"I almost forgot," Linus said. "By the authority granted me by the Luna City government, I hereby deputize Noah Skyler into the Division of Security."

"Acknowledged," said Linus's onboard, with Noah's echoing a split-second later.

They donned the self-adjusting suits and double-checked each other's seals. Once Linus's helmet was in place, his onboard automatically connected with it and projected a three-sixty view on the sides and back of the helmet's interior. The projection fuzzed a little if Linus moved quickly, but he preferred that over having to turn his entire body to look left or right. This way he could just turn his head. Linus set his gloved palm against the airlock door, and it rolled aside. The square chamber beyond could accept perhaps a dozen people comfortably. The two men entered, and the door shut behind them. Air hissed out of the airlock, and a red flag appeared in Linus's display, warning him that he was standing in vacuum and it would be foolish to remove his helmet. His suit puffed up a little, and it felt like he was covered in marshmallows. Still, these suits were much sleeker than the burly, clunky ones worn by the first inhabitants of Luna City. The air in his suit was dry and smelled metallic. Linus could already feel his lips and eyes drying out.

The outer door rolled open, revealing Luna's dirty-beach landscape. In the distance, domes rose like clear blisters against the absolute black sky and hard, unwinking stars. Near the airlock sat a vehicle the size of a giant go-cart with fat, dune buggy wheels—a police rover summoned by remote control. Linus headed for the driver's side, his boots crunching on the gritty lunar sand.

"You get the passenger side," Linus said into the comm. "I'm driving."

It took him a moment to realize that he was alone. Linus turned. Noah was still standing inside the airlock. He looked like a silvery statue in his suit. The faceplate of his helmet had gone black, so Linus couldn't see his expression. He could, however, guess at it.

"You coming?" he asked.

Another pause. Then, *"Yeah. Sorry. Just not . . . I mean, I'm coming."*

Linus watched warily as the kid made his way to the rover. The suit still hid Noah's face, though it didn't take a detective to see that Noah was nervous. The ex-Marine inside Linus wanted to bark at him to deal with it and get a move on, but this wasn't the Marines. In any case, Linus knew it wouldn't help.

"First time in outdoor vacuum?" he asked instead.

Noah clambered carefully into the passenger seat. *"Yeah."*

"I can't tell you not to be nervous," Linus said. "But I can tell you it'll get better. Let's get over to the scene and maybe the investigation'll take your mind off it."

Noah didn't comment. Once their safety harnesses were fastened, Linus switched on the power and drove smoothly away. The domes of the city receded behind them as they headed into what Linus thought of as Luna's wilderness—an endless series of craters, rocks, and deserts. The sun shone hot and deadly overhead, but Linus felt perfectly comfortable in the suit. His breathing echoed regularly in his ears.

"You get a lot of murder victims out here?" came Noah's voice over the comm. *"Out in vacuum, I mean?"*

Linus paused before answering. "How do you know it's a murder?"

"If you thought it was an accidental death, you wouldn't have called me."

"True." Linus started to scratch his nose, then remembered he couldn't. "Truth is, is, we don't get many victims at all. We get occasional accidents, usually from someone who panics or does something stupid. Some people get claustrophobic in these suits and they freak. Luna isn't very forgiving when that happens."

"Right." Noah's voice was flat and carefully even. *"How far out is it?"*

"Not far," Linus said. "Karen's already on the scene, and we should see her rover just about . . . now."

The rover in question hove into view at the lip of a wide crater. Security beacons made a ring all the way around the depression, shouting a recorded radio message that this was a crime scene and entering it without permission was a felony. Linus parked beside the other rover and made his way down the crater wall with Noah close behind him. Another suited figure was kneeling on the ground behind a fair-sized boulder. Linus skirted the rock and came to a halt. He was in a permanent section of shadow created by the boulder and the wall of the crater. An indicator in the lower right section of his helmet display told him the outside temperature had just plunged from 247°C to –213°C, a difference of four hundred sixty degrees. The interior of his suit felt slightly cooler, though he couldn't tell if it really was, or if it just seemed that way.

In front of the kneeling figure lay the body. It looked like a collection of freeze-dried jerky topped by a mummified head. The skin was mottled and dark, the hair brittle and broken. Its clothes looked too big for it. Linus noticed automatically that one foot was clad in a black sock. The other foot was encased in an ordinary-looking brown loafer. Exposed skin and flesh had shrunk away from the fingernails, turning them into blackened claws.

The figure kneeling near the body was running the wand to a holographic scanner over the corpse. The figure paused when Linus approached, then went back to work.

"This is a bad neighborhood, Karen," Linus said. "You never know what kind of reprobate will find you out here."

"Hoy, Linus," Karen said without turning around. Her voice came crisp and clear over the com-link. *"Are you going to wrap this up for me nice and easy? I'm a doctor, not a medical examiner."*

Linus blinked. "What? Yes, you are."

"That was a joke, son. You missed it."

"Oh. Right." He changed the subject. "Karen, this is Noah Skyler, just arrived from Earth. Noah, this is Karen Fang. She's Luna City's doctor. And medical examiner."

Karen clipped the wand to her belt and rose. Noah waved. *"Dr. Fang?"* he said.

"Actually, my name should be pronounced fong," she said dryly. *"But that's not near as much fun, is it?"*

"Uh . . ."

"Don't let her fool you," Linus said. "She *loves* being Dr. Fang, and you get brownie points for telling her a new vampire joke."

"Why do vampires drink blood?" Karen said promptly. Her voice was low and rich, and had a strange accent—Australian mixed with a pinch of something Asian.

"I don't know," Noah said, and Linus thought he detected a hint of Groucho Marx. *"Why* do *vampires drink blood?"*

"Because coffee keeps them awake all day."

There was a pause. "You don't have to laugh when they're not funny," Linus said.

"That's a relief," Noah said.

"Hey!"

"So anyway, Kid," Linus said, gesturing at the crime scene. "Tell me what you see."

Noah's helmet bent as he scanned the ground. Linus waited patiently. It was a test, of course. Noah knew it was a test, and Linus knew Noah knew it was a test. And the kid took his time.

"Probably a white male, but hard to tell," Noah finally said. *"About one and three-quarters of a meter tall, weight uncertain, since the body fluids have all boiled away. The victim's clothes are those of someone of a proportional weight to his height, however. Average-quality red shirt and brown trousers. One shoe missing, probably a brown loafer to match the one currently worn by the victim."*

He knelt near the corpse as Karen had done, removed a flashlight from his kit, and shined it over the body. *"Bruising and lividity are impossible to check under these conditions. Time and cause of death aren't immediately obvious. It could be the result of exposure to . . . to vacuum, but the victim could have been already dead upon such exposure. I see two post-mortem puncture wounds, one to the upper left shoulder, the other to the upper left thigh."*

Pretty good. Linus felt a little finger of relief. No matter how good someone looks in their application, you never knew if they were *really* any good until they hit the field. Still, it wouldn't be a good idea to let the kid think he had everything completely nailed.

"How do you know the punctures are post-mortem?" Linus asked, a little sharply.

Noah pointed his flashlight at the corpse's shoulder. *"The fibers of the victim's shirt didn't adhere to the area around either wound, indicating that the flesh was punctured after the bodily fluids had boiled away. I'm guessing meteors."*

"All right," Linus conceded. "What else?"

"Pockets are empty. No identification, communication equipment, or other helpful clues there. The victim's onboard might tell us who he is, but we'd be better off checking that during the autopsy."

"Why not right now?" Karen demanded before Linus could say anything. He automatically shot her a hard look, but her helmet hid her expression.

"No urgency in the case," Noah said. *"It's not as if the killer might still be in the area, and examining the onboard out here might damage it. We'd lose evidence."*

Linus folded his arms, growing impressed but still reserving judgment. "Go on, then."

"Several sets of footprints around the body and what looks like a drag mark trailing after the feet. The drag mark has been partially obscured by footprints, either those of the person who brought him here or of the person who found him."

"People, actually," Karen said. *"Two of them."*

"The drag mark indicates the body was brought here post-mortem, so this isn't the site of the actual murder. We need to find the primary crime scene." Noah stood up and shined the flashlight around the body in concentric circles. *"No vehicle tracks in the immediate area, though that's hardly surprising—the crater*

walls are pretty steep. That's all I can tell you without moving the body." He paused. *"So do I pass?"*

"What would you do once the body was moved?" Linus asked.

"Assuming I wasn't checking the victim's back for wounds or other trace evidence," Noah said, *"I'd make casts of the footprints and of the drag mark. I'd also want to examine the soil in the immediate area for further trace."*

"Even though it's unlikely you'd find any?" Linus said. "A vacuum suit doesn't leave fibers, and it would prevent the killer's fingerprints and DNA from being left at the site."

"Still have to check," Noah said. *"Unless there's some rule about Luna City investigations I don't know about."*

"No, you're right," Linus said. "And you pass. So far."

"I love it when you get all hard-assy," Karen said. She leaned over the body again. *"I don't envy you blokes doing the grunt work on this one."*

"Why do the weird cases always come to me?" Linus sighed.

"You get all the cases, love," Karen replied. *"And you aren't fooling anyone—you like the weird cases. So which one of you strapping young gents wants to help me get this poor bloke on a board? I can't just toss him in a body-bag—he might break into bits."*

Linus retrieved a stiff piece of plastic the size and shape of a surfboard from Karen's rover and carried it down to the body. Even after living on Luna for five years and spending countless hours in vacuum, he never got past the feeling that there should be air around him. The board, for example, should have met air resistance when Linus turned, like a sail would. But Linus felt nothing. The board itself weighed next to nothing, though it could support six or seven bodies in the local gravity.

Back at the scene, Linus found Noah and Karen carefully turning the victim to examine its—his?—back.

"Exit wounds from the meteors," Karen said. *"Back of the skull seems to be intact, though that doesn't rule out a head wound. Oh good—bring that over here, Linus."*

Linus set the board to one side and the trio positioned themselves around the body with Linus at the head, Karen holding the middle, and Noah getting the feet.

"Careful you don't lift too hard, Kid," Linus warned. "You don't want—"

Linus felt rather than heard something snap. Stupidly, he looked at Karen, then at Noah. The kid was holding an odd black object in his hand. It was the victim's right foot, the one without a shoe. Noah was staring down at it, his blank faceplate revealing no expression. Karen remained silent. A lick of anger flashed through him. The idiot had compromised evidence at a crime scene. He had—

Linus forced himself to take a deep breath. Shouting wouldn't change anything. Shouting wouldn't help. The kid knew he had made a mistake. Now wasn't the time to deal with it.

"All right," Linus said at last. "Freeze-dried and brittle as an Egyptian mummy. Let's do the rest more carefully."

Using exquisite care, the three of them lifted the body onto the board. It was feather light, maybe seven or eight kilograms. Karen wordlessly strapped it down, putting the broken foot into a strap of its own. Her movements were quick and tight, and Linus knew she was angry. Noah backed up a pace, remaining out of the way. Still without speaking, Karen drew what looked like a shiny sleeping bag over body and board, sealed the end, and picked up the entire assemblage by herself. Linus had to restrain an impulse to offer his help.

"*I'll meet you lads back in the lab,*" she said, and then she was gone.

Linus turned back to Noah, who had his kit open and was going over the place where the body had lain with the wand of a small scanner. A bar of blue light inched slowly over the gray sand where the head had lain.

"What do you have it set for?" Linus asked.

"*I'm doing an exclusion search,*" Noah replied. His voice was flat. "*It'll catch anything that isn't silicon, iron, titanium, or magnesium.*"

"Good," Linus said, pulling out his own scanner. "I'll start at the feet."

They spent an hour going over the area. Noah's scanner picked up traces of DNA and Linus found several red fibers. Although he was fairly certain both belonged to the victim, he and Noah packaged both finds up for the lab. When they were finished, they rose. Linus half expected his joints to complain, but they didn't—kneeling on Luna didn't hurt like it would on Earth. Still, he was a bit tired. Wouldn't hurt to take a break.

"I'll get the casting materials," Noah said, heading immediately for the crater wall. Linus halted him with a hand on the shoulder. Even through two insulating suits, Linus could feel the tension in Noah's muscles. Clearly, he was feeling sorry for having screwed up. Good. He should feel bad.

Linus hadn't decided whether it was worth it to actively bawl the kid out later but one thing was for sure: He wasn't going to throw Junior a pity party now.

After Karen *specifically* mentioned how delicate the body was, he still broke it. He made her job more difficult, and it might even have complicated court testimony, since they'd now have to admit to a mistake in gathering evidence. So little Noah was stewing in his own guilt. Fine. Let him.

"Let's get this stuff back to the lab and take a break. We can do the casts later," Linus said."

"Shouldn't we do them now? Before the scene degrades?"

Linus made a wide gesture. "You're expecting wind and rain?"

"Oh. Right." Noah winced. *"Old habits. Lieutenant Meeks would have skinned me alive for leaving an unfinished scene like this back in Madison."*

"We're a little more laid-back up here," Linus replied. "Let's go."

Some time later, they were back at the airlock listening to air hiss back into the chamber. Linus felt his suit sag a little around his body. He pulled off his helmet and ran a hand through silvering dark hair. It felt good to touch his own skin again. Noah, apparently feeling the same way, scratched his arms vigorously. Linus also gratefully inhaled the more humid, flower-scented air of the corridor. How the old explorers survived days and days of breathing canned air, he didn't know. They were stowing the suits back in the lockers when Noah turned to Linus.

"Could I ask you to do something?" he said cautiously.

"What's that?" Linus set the helmet on its shelf and shut the locker door.

"I'm twenty-seven. Could you not call me *kid?*"

A laugh bubbled up, and Linus firmly swallowed it. Sure, he thought, why, I can think of a dozen other things to call you, but my mama raised me not to cuss in front of the young'uns. *Your* mama, on the other hand— Linus bit his lip.

"I won't call you *kid,*" he said. Then added, "On purpose."

"Attention! Attention!" said Linus's onboard in his ear. *"Incoming call from Dr. Karen Fang."*

"Take it now," Linus said. "Put on three-way with Noah Skyler."

"Hoy, Linus," came Karen's voice.

"What have you got for me, K?" Linus said. "The ki— Noah's listening in."

"I ran a DNA sample from our victim through the identification database."

"And?"

"I came up with nothing. Zip. Naught."

"What?" Linus was shocked. "That's not possible, K. No one's ever avoided giving their DNA to immigration. Security down there's as tight as a gnat's ass."

"I know that. Maybe he never went through immigration."

"Everybody goes through——Oh, you mean he landed here but didn't stay?"

"Exactly. That happens. Shuttle crews sometimes just turn right around and go back to Earth."

"Immigration policy covers that sort of thing. Everyone who lands on Luna, even for 30 seconds, is registered with the ID database. No exceptions. Ever. So the victim has to be in there somewhere."

"*Apparently not,*" Karen said. "*The victim is registered nowhere in Luna City.*"

"Which means he can't exist," Linus said slowly.

"*Tell* him *that.*"

CHAPTER FOUR

The Luna City Medical Center was, like most important buildings in Luna City, located near the University, and in accordance with the unspoken rule of hospitals everywhere, the designers had put its morgue in the basement. Noah trailed Linus down the white-tiled corridor, tension stiffening his muscles until each one ached. He had screwed up, and royally. Of course, it wasn't as if he really had to prove anything to himself. Proving himself to Linus, however, was another matter. If he wanted to study here he had to hold on to his grant, and if he wanted to hold on to his grant he had to impress Linus. Four years of police work had taught Noah that no matter how pleasantly the boss might react, a major mistake meant the screwee—Noah, in this case—would be watched like an ant beneath a magnifying glass for weeks, or even months, to come.

How could he have been so *stupid?* Rule number one of moving bodies: exercise extreme caution. Sure, this corpse had been brittle and fragile, but that should have made Noah even more cautious. He remembered the sickening sensation of the foot snapping off in his hand, and he surreptitiously wiped his palm on his trousers as he followed Linus through the sliding double doors into the morgue.

The place was small, barely big enough to grant space to two autopsy tables and the associated equipment. Sinks lined one wall, and a bank of nine people-sized refrigerators lined the other. Noah guessed they didn't get many deaths in Luna City. The room was a little chilly, but the lighting was bright and harsh, and the air carried the familiar strong smell of antiseptic and chemical preservatives.

One table was occupied. The twisted brown body of the John Doe lay on it inside a sealed, transparent case that reminded Noah of a rounded coffin. The victim's right foot lay like an accusation beyond the ragged edge of the ankle. Even as Noah watched, bits of dry tissue flaked off and fluttered down from the body like brown snowflakes.

Behind the table stood Dr. Karen Fang. Noah hadn't seen her out of a vacuum suit yet and he tried to look at her without appearing to stare. She was quite a lot shorter than Noah and Linus, and pretty, with a definite Asian cast to her features. Her eyes were brown, almost black, and she wore her black hair in a loose ponytail. Lithe build, wiry hands, competent air.

The autopsy table looked just like the ones Noah knew back on Earth. A pair of holographic projectors were mounted on the short ends of the table like two snakes looking down on a bird's next. A small computer console jutted out for the examiner to use.

"I'm keeping him in vacuum for now," Dr. Fang said. "Abrupt exposure to a full atmosphere of pressure might crush him to dust."

"Why?" Linus asked.

"The reason you and I aren't smashed flat by the atmosphere is because our tissues are filled with air and liquid that push back with equal force. It causes the explosive part of explosive decompression if you go for a walk in vacuum. This bloke has neither water nor air in him, so he'd probably *implode*." She scratched her nose. "Once I've done everything I can, I'll gradually introduce atmosphere and humidity for final tests. Come over and I'll show you what I've got so far."

Her voice was neutral, but she wasn't looking at Noah. The withered brown body continued to stare up at nothing. Noah chewed the inside of his cheek. Although he had sat through dozens of autopsies and they no longer made him queasy, this one was different. The wreck in front of him hadn't been destroyed by a bomb or a car accident or a sledgehammer or any of the thousand other things that could mangle human flesh. The very life had been sucked out of this man by a force so terrible that nothing could survive it. It couldn't be ducked, dodged, or antidoted, and it took maybe ninety seconds to kill you. Then it pulled all the fluids from your body and left you desiccated. Noah thought about the silky-thin silver fabric that had stood between him and the deadly vacuum and shuddered involuntarily.

"Do you get many people who die this way up here?"

"You already asked that," Linus said.

"Don't worry yourself on that one, mate," Dr. Fang said. "We haven't had a vacuum death in almost two years. Stupid frat accident, that one was."

"What happened?" Noah asked despite himself.

"Got drunk and went outside. A few minutes later, he vomited into his helmet and took it off. His frat brothers found him half an hour later."

"Nice," Noah said faintly.

"That prompted us to install Breathalyzer programs in the suits," Linus said. "The airlocks won't open for you if your BAC is over point-oh-two." He gestured at the encased body. "Anyway, what've you got for us, K?"

Dr. Fang tapped the computer control and the holographic projectors flickered to life. The clear coffin and the brown body vanished, replaced by a skeleton. Although it looked real enough to touch, it was nothing more than a three-dimensional overlay created by the projectors, which were in turn slaved to an imaging scanner built into the table. The setup allowed Dr. Fang to examine a body inside and out without having cut unless she wanted to. Noah's eye was irrevocably drawn to the right tibia, which ended in a jagged break. He tried not to wince.

"Working from the inside out," Dr. Fang said, gesturing, "you can see that several bones are broken. Three ribs on the right side, right clavicle, left radius, and a cracked pelvis. Right tibia. Except for that last one, I can't tell if these breaks were pre- or post-mortem."

"Why not?" Linus asked.

"Lack of body fluids. Living bones leak blood and marrow when they break. Dead ones remain dry, but the great outdoors vacuum-dried these bones long before I could examine them." She fiddled with the console and the skeleton rotated silently onto its front. "The skull is remarkably intact except for a crack on the occipital bone. If the blow was pre-mortem, I doubt it was the cause of death, though it would almost certainly have knocked him out. In short, our victim was either the victim of a severe pre-mortem beating or of some severe post-mortem trauma."

"Do you have a cause of death?" Linus asked.

"Not yet, but taking a stroll without a suit would be a good bet. I'll try to confirm." Her fingers moved across the console, and the body reappeared, though the coffin remained invisible. "Take a look at this, though. The computer can lighten his skin a little . . . there. Look at his hands."

The image's skin was still taut and brittle-looking, but the coloring on the hands had lightened until they were almost a normal tan. Dark shadows remained around the knuckles.

"Most of the desiccated blood cells are scattered fairly evenly around the corpse," Dr. Fang said. "This argues for death by decompression, actually, since explosive decompression in a micro-gravitic environment precludes lividity."

"The blood won't settle because the fluids get sucked through the tissues into space," Linus translated.

"You're a bright one," Dr. Fang said. "But look here—these dried-up blood cells have clumped in one place under the skin. They were already there at the time of exposure to vacuum."

"Bruises," Noah said.

"Right. This poor lad punched someone—or some*thing*—before he died. I'm betting on the something."

"Explain," Linus said.

Dr. Fang worked the controls again. The holographic view zoomed in and down, creating the unnerving image of a giant mummified hand occupying the entire table. The hand rotated and flipped over so it was palm-side up. The claw-like nails were cracked and splintered. Two had peeled back.

"He was clawing at something," she said. "And I found traces of paint under the nails. It's a common type, often used on ceramic walls—and airlocks."

Noah's stomach churned. "Jesus," he said.

"What are you thinking?" Linus said.

"Someone tapped this guy on the back of the head and shoved him into an airlock," Noah said, "but the victim woke up before the killer could hit the button. He punched and clawed at the door, but the killer ran the cycle anyway. The blast of escaping air tossed him out of the lock. Maybe that's how the bones were broken."

"Airlocks generally don't blast open, except in an emergency," Linus pointed out. "The air gets evacuated first."

"Well, maybe the bones were broken when the killer hauled the body out to the crater. In any case, it wasn't a pleasant way to go."

"Sounds reasonable," Dr. Fang said. Was that a hint of forgiveness in her voice? Noah couldn't tell. "I have more tests to run, of course."

"What worries me," Linus said, "is the lack of ID. The DNA of every single person who enters Luna City is registered. So how did this guy avoid that? Does it have to do with the reason he's dead?"

"Maybe he's a Morlock," Dr. Fang said.

"Don't go there," Linus sighed.

"Morlock?" Noah asked.

"There are stories—urban legends—that the maintenance tunnels under the University are inhabited by groups of homeless people," Linus said. "They supposedly live off scavenged food and escaped lab animals."

"I hear one of them has a hook for a hand," Dr. Fang said with a straight face. "One time he followed this young couple who had found a place for a bit of pashing in one of the side corridors, and he—"

"All right, all right," Linus said, holding up a hand. "Can we concentrate on reality for a while? We still need to figure out who this guy is."

"An illegal clone?" Noah hazarded. "One whose DNA was altered enough to make him look like an entirely different person?"

"The first part would be possible, but not the second," Dr. Fang said. "Changing DNA like that would make rather a mess of your genetic structure—and you. In any case, you couldn't clone someone and raise him from childhood on Luna without *someone* noticing. Maybe it's a computer problem. The victim's file was erased to make it more difficult to identify him."

"I'll get the IT people to check that angle," Linus said. "But it seems unlikely. There are maybe five thousand people in Luna City, and a missing person gets noticed quick. They don't show up for their job or for class for a few days, and people start to wonder. We have no outstanding missing persons claims right now."

"Did you check against people who *used* to be here?" Noah asked. "Maybe someone was scheduled to leave but didn't actually go."

A moment of silence. "No," Dr. Fang admitted finally. "I didn't do that."

Linus's eyes lit up. "Do you have the DNA sample stored, K?"

"I started an investigation file," she said. "John Doe three."

Noah wondered briefly who the other two John Does had been, but the thought was quickly lost in a wash of hope that his idea was right. It might make up for his earlier mistake. Linus stepped over to a counter that sported a full computer workstation, complete with keyboard. His fingers danced across it, and the floating holographic display showed a rotating view of a DNA helix in one column. The column next to it flashed dozens of other DNA helixes. The words CHECKING DATABASE appeared below it. Noah held his breath.

NO MATCH, the computer reported. Noah felt hope rush out of him like water from a sieve.

"Worth a shot," Linus muttered. "So what now?"

"We need to find the primary crime scene," Noah put in almost timidly. "I'm thinking we should check the airlock closest to the dump site, then check the ones further and further away."

Linus nodded and waved his hand through the DNA display. It vanished, and he called up a three-dimensional map of Luna City. The place looked surprisingly small when viewed this way. A large central dome sat surrounded by perhaps a dozen smaller ones. Tunnels snaked in a thousand directions like tentacles connecting a clump of jellyfish.

"Highlight all airlocks," Linus ordered, and almost a hundred tiny lights popped up all over the map in red, yellow, and green. "The green ones are general use," Linus explained. "Anyone can go out at any time. The yellow ones are restricted—you need special access. They're for University personnel or maintenance staff or whatever. The red ones are emergency only. Anyone can use them, but each one sets off a general alarm. You probably already know that anyone can *enter* any airlock at any time—we don't want to strand someone who's about to run out of air—but you'd better have a good reason if you come in through a yellow or red one."

"The computer keeps track of each use, right?" Noah said.

"Of course." Linus shot a glance at the body. Dr. Fang had shut off the holographic projector, and the body once again lay in the vacuum chamber, like a magician's assistant appearing in a sealed box. "Though it'll only tell us who actually opened the door, not who went through it."

"Surveillance cameras?" Noah asked.

"No," Linus said. "Privacy laws on Luna don't allow surveillance on public streets. We were founded by a mess of liberals, you know. In any case, we've never needed that kind of security, so why spend the money?"

"Is that the proper term?" Dr. Fang said from the autopsy table. "A mess of liberals? You know—like a pack of wolves or a murder of crows?"

"*Anyway*," Linus said, "the body was found here." He pointed with a stylus, and an orange dot appeared on the display. "The drag mark pointed in this direction." He drew a line. "And as it happens, the mark points toward an emergency airlock about two hundred meters from the dump site. That's also the airlock closest to the body."

"So it's likely that's where the body . . . exited," Noah said.

Linus called up a second display and checked the text. "There's no record of that airlock ever being used. It's been shut since it was built, except for routine testing."

"Two possibilities, then," Noah said. "The killer is a maintenance worker who ejected the body during one of the regular checks, or someone tampered with the alarm and the records."

"I like the maintenance worker idea," Linus said, scrolling through more text. "Let's see. The last time that airlock was tested was twenty-nine days ago. It's due for testing again tomorrow, in fact. I'll tell them to cancel it."

"Who ran the last test?" Dr. Fang asked.

"Charlene Molewski," Linus said. An identification photograph of a dark-skinned woman in her late twenties appeared. "Grad student in the physics department. No police record. We'll have to talk to her."

"I'll get a kit and check the airlock itself," Noah said.

"You should probably go home and rest," Linus said. "It's been a long day, and I'll need you at your best later."

"No, I'll go," Noah interrupted. "I want to. Really."

Linus looked at Noah for a long time, then nodded. "Go ahead, then. Kits are upstairs."

Noah headed for the door, paused, and turned to Dr. Fang. "What type of coffee do vampires prefer?" he asked.

"Decoffinated," she replied promptly.

"Damn," Noah said, and fled before anyone could respond.

Half an hour later, he was standing at emergency airlock 567-B with a crime scene kit the size of a small suitcase. It felt too light in his hand. The airlock was at the end of an undergraduate dormitory hallway, one done up with rather less flora than Noah's apartment hallway. The ever-present plants were scraggly and thin. No flowers scented the air, and no birds sang among the stunted trees, several of which were scarred with carved initials and obscene sayings. The doors and walls desperately needed fresh coats of paint. The high ceiling, however, still shone with a bright artificial sun, which was trying valiantly to disguise the fact that this section lay completely underground.

The round airlock door was painted a bright red, indicating its emergency-only status. A row of lockers sat nearby. In an emergency, they would unlock and the vacuum suits stored within would spill out in a silver pile for anyone to snatch up and use. Otherwise only authorized personnel could use them.

Noah pressed his palm to the airlock door. Immediately his onboard buzzed and a text display flashed across his monocle.

"This is an emergency-only airlock," said the computer, in case Noah couldn't read the text message. "No emergency has been detected. Please state—"

"Open on authority of Noah Skyler, deputy for Luna City Security," Noah interrupted. "No alarm."

"Acknowledged," said the computer, and the door rolled open. Noah took up his kit and stepped inside. The room beyond was the size of an elevator, with enough room for six or seven people, though a dozen would fit in a pinch. A second door, the one that led outside, sat directly across from the first. Control panels were set beside both doors. Noah looked at the open airlock door that led back to the hallway and at the closed one that led into vacuum. Then he opened his kit and extracted a rubber wedge. He shoved it into the track of the open door so it couldn't roll shut even if the computer forced the issue.

"Better," he said aloud, and pulled on a pair of poly-gloves. "Obie, play music. Compose new Irish folk."

Immediately a live-sounding band played a full-stereo Irish slipjig in Noah's ears. Noah listened for a moment to see how it was coming out. Sometimes it was kind of fun to have the computer create new music on the spot, but the process was really hit or miss. Most of the music came out mediocre or downright boring. On the other hand, wasn't that the case with human-composed music?

The slipjig seemed decent enough. Not something he'd want to actually dance to, but good enough to fill the quiet. Noah pulled out a high-intensity flashlight and shined it over the doorjamb. He found no scrapes or scratches. Next he pulled the wedge and allowed the airlock door to rumble almost shut. He felt the vibration in his shoes. At the last moment he stopped the door again with the wedge and ran the flashlight over every centimeter. This took quite some time, and Noah found himself falling into what he privately called the Zen of Investigation. When repeating the same motion over and over, he often dropped into a trancelike state, his body in robotic repetition, his mind alert to any anomaly. The regular rhythm of the music helped. He scanned the top of the door, the middle, and the bottom. Not a single scrape or scratch.

"Obie," he said to get his onboard's attention, "link with the Luna City University maintenance records on my authority as a deputy."

"Working," said the onboard. "Link established."

"When was the last time emergency airlock 567-B was repainted?"

Pause. "There is no record of emergency airlock 567-B being repainted."

Meaning nothing. Someone could have tampered with the records. "How often is the interior of an emergency airlock repainted?"

"The interior of an emergency airlock is not repainted unless specifically ordered by Engineering Services."

"Has engineering services ordered the repainting of emergency airlock 567-B?"

"There is no record of such an order."

So much for that idea. It seemed unlikely the killer would have thought to purge both types of record. Noah stowed the flashlight in his kit with a sigh and switched on the small, blocky scanner that took up most of the bottom of the kit box. Its tiny readout screen glowed a warm green. A wand, linked to the scanner by wireless connection, was clipped to the scanner's right side. It hummed faintly.

"Obie," he said again, "link with the kit scanner and display."

"Working," said his onboard. "Connected."

Noah adjusted his monocle, unclipped the scanner's portable wand, and ran it slowly over the walls and floor. It cast a bar of soft green light. Several times the light bar, filtered through Noah's monocle, turned yellow, indicating it had found DNA. Each time, Noah ran a cotton swab over the spot and ran it through the sampler in his kit. In all, Noah came up with fifteen samples that yielded DNA from four people, all of whom were listed in the ID database as maintenance workers.

Noah sat back on his heels and thought while the computer blithely played a song reminiscent of "Blind Mary."

47

No scratches or other damage to the airlock, and the only DNA in it belonged to people who had every reason to be there. Linus was following the maintenance worker angle, and Noah had exhausted the possibilities of the airlock itself. That left him only one more place to look for evidence.

Dread settled into Noah's stomach. He carefully repacked the kit, left it on the airlock floor, and returned to the locker area, where he pressed his palm to one of them. He felt a brief warmth as the computer scanned and cleared him. The locker clicked open and for the second time that day, Noah stepped into a silver vacuum suit.

The thought of going outside into that deadly nothingness made his hands shake and his chest turn cold. But the thought that he had screwed up on his first day pushed him forward. He might find something that made up for it. He *would* find something that made up for it.

Noah reentered the airlock, removed the wedge, and let the door roll shut behind him. He forced himself to pick up his kit and operate the control on the wall. He forced himself to stay still as the air was evacuated from the airlock. And as the door ahead of him rolled open, he forced himself to step out onto the lunar sands.

CHAPTER FIVE

"**S**o what do you think of him?" Linus asked.

Karen Fang, who was readying a scalpel for some serious cutting, looked up at Linus. It had taken her two hours to gradually repressurize and remove the storage unit, and the body was now exposed to open air for some final testing. Linus suddenly realized he liked Karen's eyes. They were wide and warm and brown. Very pretty. He forced himself to look back down at the dreadfully wizened corpse.

"What do you think I think? He broke my patient," Karen said.

Linus sighed tiredly and massaged the bridge of his nose with his thumb and forefinger.

"Putting that aside for the moment, though, I think he's seriously cute," Karen said, and snapped the wrist of her glove in a way that managed somehow to be salacious. "I could eat him with a spoon. A really *big* spoon."

Linus snorted. "On the hunt again, K? He could be your son."

"Jealous?" she said archly.

"Should I be?" The words popped out before Linus could stop them. Karen blinked at him. The moment stretched out for too long, and Linus realized his face had grown warm. He should say something, anything. Fill the silence. But words wouldn't come. He became aware of the tiny wrinkles around Karen's eyes, the way her chest moved when she breathed, the pulse at her neck. Karen looked back at him, herself motionless. Still Linus couldn't speak. In the end, Karen rescued them both.

"Jealous," she snorted. "Only if you think I'm into fingerlings, love. And just for the record, I could have been his babysitter, not his mum. Since I'm holding the scalpel, you'll do well to remember that."

Linus forced a laugh, and the moment was smoothed over. Karen bent over the victim. Linus moved behind her so he could watch over her shoulder as she made a careful slit in the desiccated tissue just below the victim's collarbone. He tried to avoid breathing, reflexively expecting some kind of eye-watering smell. Corpses always had a smell, depending on how long they'd been dead. But this one had no smell at all. It was unnatural, and it gave Linus the creeps. Not only had the killer taken away this person's life, he had taken away something so fundamental as the right to smell like decayed meat after death. All Linus could smell was morgue antiseptic and Karen's perfume. The latter scent was far more pleasant than the former, a floral smell that made Linus think of lilacs.

When was the last time he had smelled lilacs for real? They appeared in various walkways and gardens in Luna City once a year—even all the way up here they seemed to sense when May had arrived—but to Linus, lilacs were meant to be enjoyed on long early-morning walks in chilly spring air, when the sun was just rising yellow and the day hadn't yet shaken off the mystery of the previous night. You needed a faint breeze to waft the sweet scent to you, and your boots needed to swish through damp grass that hadn't been mown yet this year.

But when you woke up in your room on Luna, the lighting was the same as when you went to bed. The sounds and smells changed little. Oh sure, the Luna City and the University had a calendar—yearly celebrations, parties, little traditions. But the seasons never changed. The temperature in the corridors and domes never varied by more than a few degrees. The artificial sunlight beamed relentlessly down, come May or December. You could change the view of your holographic window, but you couldn't open it and smell the changes of the seasons. Some days it didn't bother Linus. He never had to rake or mow or shovel. Seasonal allergies were a thing of the past. But other days . . .

Linus became aware that he was standing so close behind Karen that his breath was stirring her night-black hair. He could feel the heat from her body. Karen wasn't moving away, either. Her scalpel stood poised over the victim's dry skin, and Linus noticed her perfectly shaped nails, unpainted, and steady, sure hands.

I'm admiring a woman while we're both standing over a corpse, he though. *How sick is that?*

He took a firm step back with a small cough. Karen cleared her throat without turning around, then slid scalpel across skin. The tissue flaked and powdered more than it cut, but after a moment Karen had an opening. She inserted a pair of forceps, came up with a wafer the size of Linus's thumb, and popped it into a small covered dish. It made Linus think of a tiny, obscene potluck.

"There you are, love," Karen said. "John Doe's onboard."

Linus accepted the storage dish, feeling oddly confused. He thanked her to cover his consternation. "I'd better get this down to Hector," he said. "The boys down there will know what to do with—"

"Boys?" Karen interrupted, waving her scalpel.

"Generic term," Linus said, leaning away from the moving instrument. "Just like you use 'blokes.' "

"Right," Karen said. "Though I notice no one ever uses 'girls' as a generic term, even in this day and age." She sighed and turned back to the body. "You go play with your computer toys. I have more tests to run."

"And I definitely don't want to watch," Linus said. He exited quickly, feeling even more uncertain. He'd been working with Karen Fang for years. Why was he only now noticing . . . noticing her? It wasn't as if he could ever act on any kind of attraction. Like most Lunarians, she was only here temporarily. One day she would go back to Earth while he . . .

Linus rubbed his chest, feeling his heart beat slow and steady. Well, he wasn't going back to Earth anytime soon. And there were other complications.

Linus exited the medical center into the Dome. Although there were several domes in Luna City, there was only one Dome, with its high, arching roof and parklike atmosphere. It was getting on to suppertime, and registration offices were closing, which meant the paths and sidewalks were crowded with students heading home or to their secondary jobs.

Because of the labor shortage on Luna City, the government had long ago decreed that each resident had to take on a primary and a secondary job. The primary job was always related to the person's main reason for being on Luna. Chemistry students helped out in the chem labs. Botany students kept up the gardens and parks. But other jobs also needed doing—washing dishes, janitorial work, clerical duties, and maintenance, maintenance, maintenance. Many were the sort of jobs that would garner low or minimum wages back on Earth. Except on Luna, you couldn't pay minimum wage for anything. Just transporting the workers to Luna City would cost a small fortune, let alone housing and feeding them. And so the residents were forced to spread the scut work out among themselves.

Some people had regular secondary jobs based on talents and skills they already possessed. Others simply drew jobs from a weekly pool, like pulling a slip of paper from a household job jar. A few jobs were assigned as punishment for infractions, either civil or criminal. Linus had a jail, but it was small, and he preferred to keep nonviolent offenders busy. Why should they get the chance to lounge around in bed all day when there were air ducts to clean and gardens to fertilize? It wasn't as if prisoners could escape. Where would they go?

A few people were exempted from secondary jobs. Linus, as Chief of Security and a permanent resident of Luna City, was one of them. Karen ran the medical center, and that was deemed sufficient to keep her busy without another job. Mayor-President Ravi Pandey technically had no secondary job, but if you counted being President of the University as one job and Mayor of Luna City as another, she certainly had more than enough on her plate.

Linus crossed the Dome on a winding garden path and entered an alphabet-block building. The interior smelled of rubber flooring, and the halls were crowded with people loping carefully in the low gravity. At one time, it would have been impossible for anyone to stay on the moon for more than a few months without suffering a debilitating loss of muscle tissue and bone density. Stem-cell treatments, however, now took care of that—a simple customized injection once a month allowed students to return to full gravity with few side effects and let people like Linus set up permanent residency on Luna.

Linus bounded up the stairs to the second floor of the building, which was completely occupied by the University's information technology department—computers to everyone else. Tiny offices alternated with giant rooms divided into ever-shifting cubes. An area was set aside for recreation, where two technology students were batting a slow volleyball over a net and using holographic styluses to scribble code in midair between hits. One of the students got so engrossed in his coding that the ball, drifting with low-gravity laziness, tapped the ground before he noticed.

"Out!" called his opponent.

Linus hadn't bothered to call ahead and make sure Hector would still be in his office. Hector was *always* in his office. You couldn't really call it a second home—the man spent more time there than in his apartment. Linus quickly wound his way back to the man's office door, rapped once and entered.

Hector Valdez, head of Luna University's information technology department, was a dapper, tidy man. Every hair on his head was slicked into place, the handlebars on his mustache turned up with exact precision, and every crease on his clothes stood out crisp and sharp. His spacious office was absolutely spotless. Not a datapad or stylus was out of place. Off-white walls stood guard over beige carpet. A neatly made cot waited to one side. Small pieces of abstract sculpture stood guard in the corners, and a holographic window showed blue waves lapping at a Mexican beach. A trio of grad students chattered over a terminal that occupied most of one wall. Code zipped across the display faster than Linus could read.

Hector stepped around his desk with a grin and a hearty handshake. He was three or four years older than Linus and was another of the few people who didn't have to take a secondary job. "What can I do for the Chief of Security?" Hector asked.

"Get what you can off this." Linus handed him the closed container containing the victim's onboard. "It was taken from a murder victim who spent an unknown amount of time outside."

The grad students stopped talking to stare. Hector looked down at the container as if it might explode. "A dead person's obie?"

"Yeah. Don't worry—it's safe. Karen checked it for nasty microbes. Not very many can survive out there, anyway."

Hector regained his composure and shot the grad students a quick glare. They returned to their work, though their chatter was considerably muted. "I don't know how much I can get, but I'll try. Anything in particular you want to know?"

"Who it belonged to," Linus said. "We haven't been able to identify the victim. We're also having a hard time fixing the time of death, so any clues in that arena would be helpful, too."

Hector held the container up to the light. "Obies are partly organic, you know. Exposure to vacuum isn't good for them."

"Whatever you can get will be a help," Linus said. "How long will it take?"

"No idea. At a guess—two days? Three? It'll depend on how much damage was done. Check back with me tomorrow and I can be more specific."

"You're the best, Hector," Linus said, already moving for the door.

"I want dinner when it's over," Hector shot back. "Those home-made crepes you do."

"Done."

Linus was just heading for home when Karen phoned to let him know she had a cause of death. He all but ran back down to the morgue.

"What do you have, K?" he asked a little breathlessly.

"Take a look," she said. The holographic imagers hummed to life, and Karen zoomed in on the lower half of the corpse's face. She magnified several thousand times, but the dry little blobs that appeared on the table in three dimensions meant little to Linus.

"What am I looking at?"

"Pulmonary material," she told him. "One of the worst things you can do when exposed to vacuum is try to hold your breath, though almost everyone does it. The air in your lungs bursts outward in all directions, shredding them inside your chest as effectively as a shrapnel grenade. Pulmonary material bubbles out of the mouth and nose in a terrible mess, but the liquid part of it evaporates, so it's hard to detect without a microscope. These are desiccated pulmonary cells, and their presence tells me the victim was alive and kicking when he was exposed to vacuum."

"Oh?" Linus leaned over the table despite himself.

"When you die, the muscles of your chest settle, forcing most of the air out of your lungs," Karen explained. "Eventually the space inside the thorax equalizes with the outside pressure. As a result, exposure to vacuum doesn't cause dead lungs to rupture. Unconscious or dead people don't try to hold their breath, you see, and the air rushes out the mouth and nose with minimal damage—beyond the eventual effects of vacuum, anyway. So young Noah's theory was correct. Our victim was alive and fighting when he died, and it was definitely exposure to vacuum—explosive decompression—that killed him."

"Great work, K," Linus said.

"Thank you, good sir," she replied cheekily. Was that a hint of blush on her face? Linus wasn't sure. "But we still don't know who he is."

Linus thought a moment, then went to the computer again. "Let me double-check what I remember. I said there were no outstanding missing person cases on Luna, but I've only been here a few years."

"You think perhaps someone's been missing for longer than that?"

"Maybe." Linus tapped keys and the display flashed. "Let me see if . . . aha! Two cases, right here."

Karen came over to look, and Linus smelled lilacs again. "Linus, both of those are from Sueyin Dai's time, when the UN was in charge and this place was just called Luna Base. And both missing people went out with vacuum suits on."

"The killer could have taken the victim out of the vac suit after the murder."

"No, love. Remember the frat boy? The inside of his suit was a block of ice. The water had been sucked from his body, and then it froze around him. The suit kept the water from evaporating right away, just like a block of meat left in a freezer bag for too long. If our lad on the table there had died with his suit on, the killer would have had to chop him out of the ice block to remove him from it, and that would definitely have left traces."

"Traces like broken bones?" Linus asked.

"Traces like severed limbs," Karen said. "And if the killer waited for the ice to sublimate before removing the suit . . . well, that would take a long time. There would have been missing limbs again because the corpse would have been freeze-dried and brittle by then, as Noah showed us. Bits would have broken off during the removal process. Our lad there definitely didn't die inside a vacuum suit. These two—" she gestured at the screen "—definitely did."

Linus sighed. "You're right. I'm just running out of ideas."

"I've sent the DNA sequence to law enforcement agencies in America and the European Union," Karen said. "But I don't have high hopes. Most countries only keep DNA records of criminals. If our lad has a record, we might find him, but otherwise . . ." She shrugged. "We don't even have a good image of him. His face is so dried and twisted that his own mum wouldn't recognize him."

"Yeah," Linus said. He turned back to the corpse and looked down at the taut, dry skin pulled across the nearly bare skull. Who was this man? What hobbies had he had? Who had he loved and who had loved him? And most importantly, what did he really look like?

Karen mimed flipping him a coin. "Penny for those thoughts."

"I just came back from computer programming," Linus said slowly, "but I think it's time to get hold of someone in computer graphics."

CHAPTER SIX

Irish folk music blasted through Noah's helmet as he looked down at the footprints forever frozen on the lunar sand. With the music going, it was easier to forget about the vacuum around him and concentrate on his job. So far he had found and marked footprints from seven different people, not counting him, Linus, and Dr. Fang. All of them were within twenty-five meters of the body. Noah wondered how many people had passed by, not realizing a corpse lay hidden in the icy shade.

He was about to start the casting process when a jaw-cracking yawn split his face. Noah checked the time and was startled to discover it was almost midnight, local time. When had he last slept? The crime scene shouted for him to finish, but suddenly Noah was just too tired and too fed up to continue. Deliberately he turned his back on it and made his way back up to the lip of the crater.

Half an hour later, he was back at the door to his new apartment. He slipped quietly inside, sure that Jake and

Wade would be asleep in the bedroom, leaving Noah the couch for tonight. Noah didn't much care—he was tired enough to sleep on a bag of cement. To his surprise, he found Jake dozing upright on the sofa. A dim line of light limned the bottom of the bedroom door and the place smelled of stale fried food.

"Jake?" Noah murmured. "What's going on?"

Jake roused himself and blinked up at Noah with weary brown eyes. "Hmm? Oh. Hey, Noah."

"What's going on? You look as wiped as I feel."

"Wade's using the bedroom," Jake yawned. "I'm waiting for him to finish. It's been a while, though."

Noah checked his watch. Quarter to one. "What do you mean 'using the bedroom'?"

"You know. He's . . . *entertaining.*"

Noah eyed the door. Faint rhythmic sounds emanated from it. "How long has he been in there?"

"Two hours, give or take."

Two hours? Noah felt his jaw drop in disbelief. "Does he do that a lot?"

"Enough."

"Jesus, it's almost one o'clock. It's not fair for him to tie up the bedroom like that." *Without inviting his roommates,* a treacherous part of his mind added.

"Yeah, well, Wade usually gets what he wants around here."

Noah closed his eyes. He did *not* need this. Right now, he just wanted to lose consciousness on something relatively soft and unmoving. Roommate conflicts he didn't need. And who the hell did *anything* for two hours, anyway?

Options flickered across Noah's fatigued mind. A lifetime of being the middle child among seven had taught him that some people were simply selfish and would take advantage of anyone who let them, and Noah had long ago stopped letting them. So sitting in the living room with Jake wasn't a possibility. On the other hand, it was entirely possible Wade thought no one minded his bedroom monopoly because no one had challenged it. So just barging in wasn't really fair. A glance at Jake, who had clearly sat on the sofa for two hours doing nothing, told Noah not to expect any help there. He finally stepped up to the door and rapped sharply on it. His knuckles stung.

"Hey, Wade," he called. "Ten minutes, and then we're coming in."

No response from the bedroom. The noises continued. Shadows flickered across the line of light. Noah leaned against the wall with his eye on the clock. Jake sat on the couch, watching with a sort of horrified interest. Five minutes passed and Noah rapped on the door again.

"Five minutes, guy."

Still no response. When the allotted time had passed, Noah took a breath and shoved the door open.

The bedroom was atangle with naked arms and legs. Several sets of clothes lay strewn across the floor. It took Noah a moment to sort out that Wade had three guests—two female and one male. All of them were piled on one bed. Wade, his pale, naked torso streaming with sweat, sat up from under a pile of people and swore. The two female guests cried out and dove for the clothing. The male rolled onto the floor with a soft thump. Breasts and buttocks bounced slowly in the low gravity.

"What the fuck are you—?" Wade snarled.

"I gave you two warnings," Noah said. "Find someplace else to party."

The male, who had curly brown hair, a mustache, and small green eyes, sat on the floor with his folded his arms across his chest and said, "You can't just stomp in here, asshole. You can't just—"

Thirty seconds later, he and the two women were standing in a pile of clothes in the sunlit hallway. Noah slammed the door on them and turned to face an outraged Wade, who had yanked on a pair of shorts. The remnants of his erection made a ridiculous-looking tent pole in the loose fabric.

"You fucking asshole!" Wade screamed. He drew back a fist. "I'm gonna—"

Noah didn't even think. He grabbed Wade's wrist, spun him around, and shoved him face-first into the wall with his arms twisted behind him. Wade's skin was hot and sweaty, and Noah's own skin crawled at the contact. He was vaguely aware of Jake staring at him in the background.

"That's assault on an officer," Noah murmured quietly in Wade's ear.

"You ain't a fucking cop," Wade hissed.

"Deputized just this afternoon," Noah said. He tightened his grip. "Let me tell you what's going to happen. I'm going to forget you attacked me and let you go. No charges will be pressed. You're going to take some deep breaths and calm down. If you have a problem with me wanting to get a good eight hours' sleep every night, then you can go down to housing tomorrow morning and ask for a transfer. Clear?"

There was a long pause. Noah waited, his grip on Wade unyielding. Finally Wade growled, "Clear."

Noah instantly let go. Wade stormed back to the bedroom and slammed the door.

"Wow," Jake breathed. "You really pissed him off."

"One of us was going to lose," Noah said. "Better him than me. Would you do me a favor and toss my duffel bag out of the bedroom? I have the feeling I should take the couch tonight."

"Yeah," Jake said with a certain amount of admiration. "Sure."

Noah found a spare blanket and pillow in the hall closet, presumably left behind by the guy who used to live here. What was his name? Fred? Ted? Ned? Ned. The blanket smelled faintly of a stranger's cologne, but Noah was too tired to care if it had been recently washed. Jake had already disappeared into the bedroom. Noah undressed down to his underwear and lay down on the sofa. He had only a few moments to notice that he didn't sink very far into the cushions before black sleep fell upon him.

"Attention! Attention! Urgent call from Linus Pavlik."

Noah rolled over, his mind foggy. This wasn't his apartment. This wasn't his bed. What the hell was going on? Then memory snapped like a rubber band. He sat up and accidentally pushed himself several inches off the sofa before floating back down to the cushions. The living room was empty and looked exactly as it had last night, except the window was showing a rich red sunrise on the tropical ocean. The bedroom door was shut. Noah told the lights to come on and slid the monocle around from its usual place at his temple. The call notice flashed again, and the time readout told him it was barely six o'clock. Noah ran his fingers through tousled chestnut hair.

"Take call," he said. "Audio only."

"*Noah, it's Linus,*" the chief said, as if Noah wouldn't know. "*I need you to finish processing the outdoor crime scene this morning, and then we have a—*"

Uh oh. Noah could see it coming. Linus was one of those bosses who expected his people to be on-call twenty-four hours a day—or whatever the phrase would be up here. Except Noah wasn't on Luna to be a criminologist. He was here to be a grad student. If he didn't set the limits with Linus now, he'd end up in Security full-time and he'd never get his degree.

"Linus," he said, "I can't really work for you today."

"*Excuse me?*" His tone was surprised.

Noah stifled a yawn. He should probably have felt nervous about facing down his boss, but he wasn't completely awake yet and couldn't summon the energy. "I have to meet with my advisor, register for classes, arrange access to the textbook and library databases, go food shopping, and do all the other new student stuff."

"*That's why I called now,*" Linus said. "*It's not even six o'clock, so you'll have time to suit up and—*"

"No," Noah said.

There was a pause.

"I can't go out to the scene this morning," Noah continued, polite but firm. "I'm not going out in a vac suit on five hours' sleep."

"This is a murder case," Linus said very slowly, as though he were speaking to a three-year-old.

Noah winced and played his trump card. "Linus, according to the terms of my grant, I'm a student first and everything else second. If I work for you this morning, I'm violating the terms of my grant. And like I said—I can't go out in vacuum on five hours of sleep." He dug around in his memory, looking for a name. "Call Dr. Mayfield at the University. She's my advisor. If she says I should work this morning, I'll do it."

Noah waited nervously, then silently rebuked himself for his worry. Sure, he needed this job, and up to the boss was no fun, but there was no way Linus was going to call anyone else at six in the morning. Noah knew it, and Linus knew he knew it. There was also the subtle rebuke about safety in a vac suit. It was dangerous to be out in full vacuum when your mind was fogged with fatigue.

At last Linus said, *"Fair enough. You're a student first. But the minute, and I mean the minute you get your errands done, you're calling me. Got it, Kid?"*

He signed off and Noah lay back down. Linus reminded Noah a little of Lieutenant Charlie Meeks, his superior back in Madison. Meeks put his work ahead of everything, which was one reason he was such a great cop, even if he was a pain in the ass as a boss. The only way to handle him was to lean on the rules defining your job and keep the union informed.

By all rights the small confrontation should have wired him up and made him restless, so he completely surprised himself by falling almost instantly back to sleep. When he awoke two hours later, the tropical sunrise had turned to tropical day, though the sound was muted and the ocean remained silent.

The bedroom remained stubbornly shut and as quiet as the holographic ocean. Noah showered quickly, but with difficulty. The water seemed to ooze more than it flowed, and the back spray that bounced off his chest hung in the air and nearly drowned him until he learned the trick of keeping his back to the showerhead at all times. Then he dressed and left the apartment. A check with the computer showed him a cafeteria not far away. The food, while adequate, cost more than Noah was willing to pay except on an occasional basis. He wondered if the grocery stores were just as bad, and then he wondered what Ilene was eating that morning. Toast points and caviar with champagne and orange juice?

After breakfast of toast, coffee, and a gooey pastry, he had a quick meeting with his advisor, a short, grandmotherly woman named Arissen Mayfield. He already had a good idea of what his courses would be, and she agreed with his choices. This semester he would take three classes: low-gravity physical metallurgy, materials fracture and fatigue under radiation, and cell matrix mechanics in microgravity. Next semester, if he felt he could handle the workload, he might take four classes, but for now this seemed plenty. Noah knew he was smart, but he wasn't brilliant, and would need a fair amount of study time.

Arissen walked him through the registration process on her computer, and he received immediate notice about what texts he needed to download—and at what price. Noah whistled when he saw the total for tuition, lab fees, access fees, and books. One semester cost twice his annual salary as a crime scene technician back in Wisconsin.

"A lot of people react that way," Arissen said with a smile. "But every year, we get thousands more applicants than we can accept. People claw and fight to get into Loony U."

"Thank god for my grant," Noah said.

"Oh, that's right," Arissen said. "You're the Aidan Cosgrove recipient. You know, something close to four hundred people applied for that grant. You should feel pretty proud that you got it."

"And grateful," Noah said. "Without it, I wouldn't be here."

A bit later, Noah exited the academic building into the warm, eternal spring of the Dome. He was about to ask his computer for directions to the closest grocery store when a call came in from Roger Davids, a name he didn't recognize. Curious, Noah sat down on a park bench and accepted the call on visual. His monocle showed him the image of a man in his late thirties. Dark brown hair, fair skin, sharply defined features, ice-blue eyes. He had an easygoing smile and a quiet voice.

"I'm the entertainment coordinator for Luna City," he said after introductions. "Sorry I didn't get hold of you earlier. Your secondary job is working for me."

"Really?" Noah said. "Doing what?"

"Your file says you worked your way through college doing vaudeville revival."

"That's right," Noah replied cautiously.

"We want you to do a few shows for us," Roger explained with a quiet grin. "Entertainment's always in short supply up here. It's expensive to upload the new vid-feeds from Earth, and the interactives always suffer from time delay. So we depend on a lot of live stuff and locally recorded broadcasts." He glanced down at something off-screen. "I've got you down for an hour-long show twice a month, if you work out well at your first one. Style and content is up to you. We don't get a lot of kids, but you'll still want to be careful with any blue stuff until you get a feel for how audiences react up here. I should probably warn you that newcomers always play to packed houses. Everyone will be curious to see who you are. Your first show is in two days, but you'll need to get with the theater manager and tell her what you'll need for—"

"Whoa, whoa, whoa." Noah held up his hands. "I haven't done vaudeville in five or six years, Mr. Davids."

"I guess that means you've got some rehearsal ahead of you. I'm sending you contact information for the theater. And call me Roger."

His image vanished. Noah stared through his empty monocle at the green grass beneath his feet. Ilene clearly hadn't been kidding when she said they didn't leave you much down time up here. Maybe he should cut back on a class?

No. He was the sole recipient of the Aiden Cosgrove Memorial Grant. He could handle it. He *would* handle it.

With a sigh, he gently pushed himself to his feet, noticing with a surge of satisfaction that he was getting better at it already. He barely bounced at all. The Dome arced far overhead, and birds twittered in the trees. Noah wondered if they stayed green year-round or if they ever changed colors. He would miss the smell of autumn leaves, though he imagined they'd be a real headache for the groundskeepers. Loose leaves in low-g—what a mess. And then you'd have three or four months of bare branches to stare at. Autumn trees were pretty, but winter trees were depressing, and you wouldn't want anything like that up here if you could avoid it.

Noah checked a computer map of Luna City and found the grocery store closest to his apartment. He hadn't discussed food with Jake and Wade, but he had the feeling that after last night, no one was going to want to set up a household food supply and take turns cooking. Wade didn't look trustworthy in that arena, in any case.

The store, of course, accepted orders electronically and would bag and/or deliver Noah's groceries for small fee. Noah, however, preferred to squeeze the produce and heft the packages himself. His Midwestern upbringing also nagged at him, muttering that it was a waste to spend money on something he could easily do himself. Mom and Dad had never hired anyone to do yard work, shovel driveways, or clean the house. That was what children were for. At the time Noah and his siblings had snarled under their collective breath about "all this work," but in retrospect, Noah was glad he had learned the basics of running a household. It was obviously a lesson no one had taught Wade.

Noah was thankful that Luna U Grocery did *not* use slogans like "Out of this world prices" or "Stellar selection!" The store, located entirely underground, would have been a medium-sized grocery back home—except for the prices. They were more than triple what he was used to. The price of a bottle of juice got a gasp. A can of soup cost enough to make Noah's eyes widen. And the fresh produce made them bug out. The Aidan Cosgrove Memorial Grant paid all University costs and a small stipend for living expenses—emphasis on the word "small." Well, Noah had known he'd have to dig into his savings to survive two or three years of graduate school. He hadn't thought the food bill would bankrupt him, though.

"You're still standing," said a familiar voice. "I'm surprised. A lot of people faint dead away their first time."

A smile crossed Noah's face and he faced Ilene Hatt, who had maneuvered a grocery cart of her own up beside him. "Hi, Ilene. I think you came just in time. I was about to collapse gracefully to the floor."

She laughed. "Let me show you how it's done around here. You *can* eat well without breaking the bank."

"If this place can break *your* bank, I should probably leave while I can still afford the flight home."

"None of that, now," she admonished. "I had a fight with my parents once and had to live like a *real* person for two whole months."

"That makes me feel so much better."

"Come on, smarty. Let me show you how it's done. First, put those apples back. You won't need them."

Noah obeyed. "Why not?"

"Because the botany department raises local apples in the greenhouse and my friend Erik says they're harvesting in a few days. He'll get me my usual two bags, and I'll tell him to set some aside for you. I'll introduce you." She fixed him a hard look. "You aren't gay, are you?"

"What? No," Noah said, a little startled at the change in subject.

"Bi?"

"Not that I've noticed."

"Then it's safe to introduce you to Erik. From my perspective, anyway." They guided their carts down an aisle of prepackaged food and into a chilly refrigerated section. "Anything that's dried will be cheaper, so you'll want to get beans and macaroni and the like here at the store, unless you're a fanatic about home-made pasta. You'll have to do without real milk"—she placed a white container of it in her cart—"unless you're me."

"I'm from Wisconsin," Noah moaned. "We drink milk like fish drink water."

"If you're very nice to me, I'll give you a taste," she said. "And speaking of fish . . ."

Noah, still recovering from the double entendre, followed like a slightly stunned duckling. A fish counter took up most of the store's back wall. Fish of all shapes and sizes were on display, some on ice, some in water, some wrapped up, some precooked. The strong smell of fresh fish permeated the air, and several customers were vying for the attention of the counter workers.

"Fish," Ilene explained, "are easy to raise in low gravity because they already live in it back on Earth. They don't develop the attendant muscle atrophy land animals do. All these little guys were farmed right here, and they'll be your main form of animal protein while you're on Luna. Having said all that, don't buy any."

Noah blinked. "Why not?"

"Because I work the fish farms, remember?" she said. "I can get you a nice fresh batch of trout and tilapia for nothing, assuming you don't mind cleaning and scaling them yourself."

"It's been a while," Noah admitted, "but I think I can remember."

"Smart lad," she said, and moved her cart away.

Noah hurried to catch up. "Does everyone gather food like this? Buy half and scavenge half?"

"All the smart people," Ilene said. "My only regret is that I haven't been able to find a good tofu supplier. But you can't have everything." She gave him a long look up and down. "Unless you try really, really hard."

"Right." Once again, Noah felt a little uncomfortable. "So what *do* I buy here?"

Ilene took him through the rest of the supermarket, efficiently finishing her own shopping and helping with his. They were bagging their goods—the computer had already deducted the shocking total from their accounts—when Ilene leaned close. Her soft hair brushed his cheek.

"I hear you're giving a show in a couple days."

"How did you know that?" Noah asked, surprised. "I only found out about it this afternoon."

"I checked the nets for your name," she said. "It came right up. Said you do vaudeville?"

Noah straightened with four bags of groceries in each hand. His brain told him to brace for pain as the handles cut into his fingers, but the light gravity let him lift them with ease. "Yep. The vaudeville revival hit when I was in high school and I sort of fell into it. By the time I was in college, I had my own site and was doing two shows a week there. I did a theater show a couple times a month. Paid a lot of bills."

"How did you fall into it?" They moved toward the door and onto the main path toward the train station. Gray gravel crunched beneath their feet.

Noah shot her a grin. "I'm the middle child out of seven," he said. "The only way to get attention was to demand it— or earn it. I wasn't much for acting out, so I tried acting. The drama teacher at my high school put together a little vaudeville troupe as an after-school thing, just for fun. We even competed and did pretty well."

"Are you being modest?" Ilene asked.

"Yeah," Noah laughed. "We beat the pants off everyone else. A theater manager approached me one day and said he'd save me a slot in his house. Between that gig and my net downloads, I earned some nice money."

"Is your show archived on the net anywhere?"

Noah shook his head. "Police work kept me too busy to maintain an archive. I'm a little nervous, to tell the truth. I haven't done a show in ages."

"What do you do?"

"Sing a little, play some music, do some stand-up, tell stories. It's half improvisation, really. I do whatever the audience seems to want."

Ilene gave him a long look. "Ever play for an audience of one?"

Noah gave her a long look back. "It's been known to happen."

"Good. So there'll be a front-row ticket waiting for me at your first show?"

"Sure," Noah said without thinking. "You're getting me fish and apples."

"You're learning life on Luna," she said, flinging her hair back with a quick motion of her head. It hung about her head like a golden cloud for a moment before falling into place. "It's all about what you can trade."

Despite what he had said to Linus, the afternoon found Noah back at the crime scene with Irish music—real stuff, this time—blaring through his helmet again. He was truly tired of breathing dry, metallic air. He also wasn't alone. Another vac-suited deputy named Gary Newberg had just arrived at the scene when Noah showed up. Rather than be glad for the extra help, however, Gary had greeted Noah with a surly hello over the com-link, ignored Noah's outstretched hand, and turned to his kit.

Okay, Noah thought. *Well, not everyone is nice.*

The main order of the day was to finish casting the various footprints around the spot where the body had lain. Noah had privately decided the work would yield nothing— whoever had brought the body out here had probably used a public suit, and they all had the same boot treads. They might get shoe size out of it, but not much else. Still, you had to cover all the bases just in case a wild pitch came your way.

Noah got a square frame from his kit and set it down so that it surrounded one of the suspicious footprints. It was odd not hearing the sound of the frame as it crunched into the sand, though he felt the faint vibration. Noah ran the wand of his scanner over the print to take a three-dimensional image of the print in question. Although the scanner would yield a perfect hologram of the print, computer files could be changed, corrupted, or erased, a fact defense lawyers were quick to leap on. It was always best to have a solid cast for backup.

Noah took a small silvery bag of polymerized ceramic from his kit and twisted it hard as his private music swept into "My Fair-Haired Lad." He felt something inside burst, and the sack grew quite a lot softer as the liquid ceramic inside mixed with the reagent and became pliable as caulk. Noah tore the sack open and squeezed the squishy contents into the frame. It oozed slowly downward like lazy toothpaste, unfazed by the cold and lack of atmosphere.

Out of the corner of his eye, he saw Gary kneeling over another footprint. He had set the frame down and was getting ready to squeeze a sack of his own. Noah turned down the music.

"Gary," he said, "did you get the holographic image first? I think Linus wants to be—"

"*Yeah, yeah, I'm getting to it,*" Gary snarled back. "*Just hold your horses.*" But he set aside the sack and reached for the scanner wand clipped to his belt. Noah stared at him for a second, then turned back to his own work with an internal shrug. If Gary wanted to be a jerk, he could be a jerk. Nothing Noah could do about it.

A few minutes later, Noah noticed out of the corner of his eye that Gary was about to walk across the drag mark. "Wait!" he shouted. "Gary, freeze!"

Gary froze, his foot only a few centimeters over the partially obscured drag mark. Noah wanted to snap at him to be more careful, but modulated his tone. No point in getting him even more pissed off.

"Linus wants a cast of the drag mark," Noah said, stretching the truth in order to stay diplomatic. "We can't walk across it yet."

"You don't need to shout," Gary snapped, pulling back his foot. *"I thought you'd done it already."*

"Why don't you take these solid casts back to your rover," Noah said through gritted teeth, "and I'll do the drag mark right now?"

Gary accepted this idea with bad grace, and Noah set about scanning and casting the drag mark. He also amused himself by imagining what Gary looked like outside the anonymous suit. Acne and moles all over his face, small piggy eyes, a snoutlike nose with hair growing out of it. Sausagelike fingers. Greasy hair. A face that made children cry and women flee in horror. Yeah.

Noah ran the scanner over the drag mark and dismantled ten footprint frames to surround it. Eight bags of polymer later, he had it. The cast was the size of a surfboard. Noah gently freed it from the ground and stood upright.

"Gary, can you—?"

There was no sign of him. Noah loped to the edge of the crater and carefully bounded up the side. Noah's rover was still there, but Gary's was gone, along with all the footprint casts and the remains of Noah's equipment.

Noah blinked. What the hell was going on? Maybe Gary was trying to make nice by taking care of the final cleaning up. Or maybe he was still being a jerk. He could have had said something, after all.

At that moment, his onboard told him Linus was trying to contact him. Noah accepted the call on voice.

"The crime scene is finished," Noah told him. "I'm heading back right—"

"Good, good," Linus said. *"Listen, I've got another death."*

Noah felt his eyebrows rise. "Related to this one?"

"*Doubt it. It happened just last night. Can you field this one? I've got something else going.*"

"Sure," Noah said, a little surprised.

"*Great,*" Linus said. "*You'll want to start by interviewing the victim.*"

CHAPTER SEVEN

Linus set the box in the exact center of the white scanning table and stood back with a prim smile. Professor Julia Espinoza looked at the container warily.

"There is a head in that box," she said in her lilting accent. "I can tell. And I am not touching it."

"Technically speaking, it's *part* of the head," Linus said. "The inside, to be specific."

"The inside meaning the brains or the inside meaning the skull?"

"The second." Linus opened the box and took out the skull. It was brown, shiny, and light, even for lunar gravity. It felt like it was made of balsa wood. Once Karen had finished her tests, she had spent considerable time removing the freeze-dried skin and flesh from the underlying bone, then stabilized the skull by coating it with simple varnish. Still, Karen admonished him, it was as fragile as a porcelain teacup, so Linus had better be careful with it.

"It is disgusting," Espinoza said, making no move to take it from him. "Why can't you just re-create this person's features from a DNA profile?"

"That only gives us limited information," Linus said. "Your features are very much affected by your environment and by personal choices. I mean, our guy here might be a weight lifter or a vid-feed addict, and both would affect his features. Eye color can change over time, and so does hair. I was blond when I was a kid, but you wouldn't know it by—"

"Yes, yes, yes." Espinoza cut him off with a wave. "I am too busy to help you right now. I thought I made that clear on the phone, Chief Pavlik."

Linus gave her a quick glance, creating and prioritizing responses. At times like this, he really wished he worked in a real police department with its own computer people, its own lab workers, and its own full-time investigative staff. A place where he could say, "I need you to do this," and the instant response was, "Right away," with maybe a "sir" tacked on the end for good measure. Instead he was stuck on Luna making do with student helpers who wouldn't get up at a decent hour and wheedling help from cantankerous professors. He made a choice and ran with it.

"Look, Dr. Espinoza," he said, settling on flattery, "I wouldn't trust anyone else with this. This kind of re-creation is more art than science. You're the best there is, and I really need your help. So do the victim and his family. They deserve to know who's responsible."

"And when would I fit this in?" she asked, her brown eyes hard as stone. "It is the beginning of the semester and I have a thousand things to do in my studio. Maybe in a few weeks."

So much for flattery, Linus thought. The retired Marine sitting on his right shoulder told him that he could get a judicial order forcing her to help, but the cop sitting on his left shoulder reminded him that you got better results from people who cooperated voluntarily.

"How long do you think it would take to finish this project?" Linus asked.

"Who knows?" she shrugged. "I have never done such a thing in my life."

Linus wrestled with his temper and forced it to stay calm. A nugget of information surfaced in his head, and he seized it like a mouse making off with a bit of cheese. "As you like, Dr. Espinoza. Sorry to have bothered you." He set the skull gently inside the box and closed it. "I'll just take this over to IT and see if Hector can handle it."

Her eyes went flat. "Hector Valdez?"

"He owes me a couple favors," Linus lied. "Maybe one of his grad students could do the job. I hear he trains them pretty well."

"Hector is a code monkey," she spat. "A mechanic. He knows nothing of the real potential, of the *art* of computer graphics."

"He's all I've got," Linus said. "But as I said, sorry to have bothered—"

"Leave it on the table," Espinoza said. "I will find time today."

"Oh, I couldn't," Linus said, wondering how far he should push this. "You're so busy. I'm afraid the job would be rushed, and—"

"Do you think I am unable to do this job?" she said, temper flaring. "That Hector could do it better?"

"No, no," Linus said. He set the box on the scanning table like an offering to an angry god. "If you insist. Let me know when it's done." And he vanished out the door before she could respond.

Computer people shouldn't be allowed to date each other, Linus mused as he exited the building. *Especially the anal-retentive ones. 'Course, if the fallout gives me leverage, who am I to complain?*

Back at his own office in Xiao Yen Hall, Linus set to work on paperwork that in no way involved actual paper. His office was bare and utilitarian, despite the fact that he spent most of his waking hours on the job. A simple desk held nothing but a terminal with both flat-screen and holographic output. The walls were bare except for the usual holographic window. At the moment, it showed a burbling mountain stream with ice rimming the edges. Tiny buds swelled at the ends of bare branches, waved by a chilly-looking breeze. The room itself was never quite warm. Linus liked it that way—bare and cool, as if he might leave at any time. He had once had the departmental budget for carpeting, some plants, and some other basic decorations befitting a Chief of Security, but he'd never gotten around to using the money. Luna City's bureaucracy, like bureaucracies everywhere, had decided that any department that didn't use its full budget every quarter could survive having its budget cut, and Linus had, at the last minute, reapportioned the money to buy lab equipment. It seemed a better buy.

He was nearly finished with the forms when he received notice of an incoming call. His onboard identified Ravi Pandey, and she was asking for visual.

Linus sat up straighter in his chair as a hint of nervousness trilled through him. The normally cool office felt abruptly chilly, its white walls and tile floor like the inside of a refrigerator. Communication etiquette did not require anyone to make or take calls on visual. After all, you might be lounging around the living room in your underwear, scruffy and unshaven. This request for visual, however, was coming from his boss, which carried a little more weight. He accepted the call. The display on his desk switched from a report about his recent meeting with Espinoza to the image of a dark-skinned woman with long black hair and a rounded face. She was just over fifty, and had allowed a few streaks of gray to shoot through her hair. Her loose red blouse was covered with a blue shawl, and she came across as brisk and business-like.

"*Linus,*" she said in a low, rich voice. "*I've heard a report about a second murder?*"

"We have a report of a suspicious *death*," Linus corrected. "Down by one of the fish farms. I have a deputy on it. He's interviewing the victim right now."

"*This makes two deaths in two days*," Mayor-President Pandey said.

"Technically, it's the *discovery* of two deaths in two days," Linus replied. "The first one happened some time ago."

Pandey waved a hand, dismissing the distinction. "*What matters is how it appears on the news services. It's already coming across like we are experiencing a tidal wave of crime on Luna City.*"

Uh oh. Only an idiot would have missed the tension in that last statement. "I haven't checked the services, Madam Mayor-President," Linus said carefully. "We're working hard to resolve both matters."

"*Work harder, Linus*," Pandey responded. "*I want these cases cleared by the end of the week.*"

"Ma'am? You have to know that you can't rush police work. Sometimes a case clears quickly, sometimes it takes weeks. We don't drag our feet on purpose or because we're lazy."

Pandey pursed her lips. "*I'm under a lot of pressure here, Linus. Roger Davids and I are in delicate negotiations with Comvilla and Viamar. They're both interested in opening outlets here in Luna City and greatly expanding Tourist Town. At their own expense.*"

"I see," Linus said slowly. He recognized the names, of course. Comvilla and Viamar were entertainment conglomerates that owned and oversaw dozens of smaller entertainment companies. They produced films (both flat and three-dimensional), virtual-reality games, onboard plug-ins, news services, books, and more. Tourist Town was the local nickname for the entertainment sector of Luna City. It was actually fairly extensive, with a casino, three theaters, a tiny amusement park, and some low-gravity game areas. A handful of well-heeled tourists came and went, spending money Luna City was all too happy to snatch up. Students and University personnel, of course, used the place at reduced rates, though only the fools set foot in the casino.

"This isn't public knowledge yet," Pandey said, leaning forward, *"but Comvilla is negotiating to buy the Loony Casino. Viamar wants to expand the amusement park, and both of them want to set up recording facilities for games and vid-feeds. They've also agreed to pay for more housing. I hardly need to tell you what all this would do for Luna City's debts."*

Linus nodded, beginning to understand. Fifteen years ago, when Luna City had been known merely as Luna Base, primary funding had been provided by the European Union and China. The United States, which was focusing on Mars and unmanned exploration of the outer planets, only got on board when the project was nearly completed.

The research base made two important discoveries. First, a fair amount of ice turned up in the substrata. Second, lots and lots of scientists wanted to study on the moon.

The first discovery was duly relayed back to Terra. Sueyin Dai, the base commander, made note of the second discovery but didn't make waves about it. Instead, she began quietly amassing a long waiting list of people who would climb over their own mothers to spend a month researching on Luna. She also bullied several scientists-in-residence into holding back on patenting and publishing of some of their discoveries, specifically those involving microgravity genetic manipulation and medicine production.

At that time, Luna Base answered to a combined European Union, Chinese, and United States council. Dai petitioned for control of Luna Base to be transferred to the United Nations on the basis that three countries were already trying to govern it and more countries were trying to get involved. Putting it under the control of the UN only made sense.

Fortunately for Dai, the world economy had recently taken a serious downturn. The Luna Base was expensive to maintain, and money was short. It only took two years for Luna Base to be cut loose, on the condition that it pay back its parent countries. This, the parent countries thought, would ensure Luna Base would remain under their control, but without the attendant financial headaches.

That was when the scientists on Luna Base published their findings and filed their patents. A steady stream of money trickled in, enough to keep Luna Base going, but not enough to make the mortgage payments. Dai then revealed the next stage of her plan—establishing Luna University. Instead of accepting only a handful of scientists, Luna Base would now bring up hundreds, even thousands, of researchers and students—*if* they could pay. And people somehow scraped up the cash. Tuition and grant money poured in. Now, fifteen years later, Luna Base, renamed Luna City, was within five years of achieving full independence.

If it paid off its debts. An expanded tourist trade would bring in a great deal of tax and tariff money, making that five-year goal even more realistic.

"*One of the big selling points of our negotiations,*" Mayor-President Pandey said, "*is the low crime rate. But now we have one definite murder and one possible murder in two days. This is not good, Linus. Roger and I need those cases cleared and we need them cleared now.*"

Linus felt his temper rise. "I can clear them now or I can clear them right, ma'am," he said evenly.

"*Do both,*" Pandey replied in a crisp voice. "*I want twice-daily reports on your progress, is that clear?*"

It was on the tip of Linus's tongue to snarl at her, but two things held him in check. The first was Marine discipline— you didn't snap at a superior—and the second was his own vulnerability. Like it or not, his job rested solely in the hands of Mayor-President Pandey. If she didn't like him, she could replace him anytime she liked. It wouldn't be difficult to find a dozen police brass from Earth who would jump at the chance to be Chief of Security for Luna City. And then where would Linus be? He started to rub his chest, then forced his hand back into his lap.

"We'll do our best, Madam Mayor-President," he said instead. "I'll send you my first report within the hour."

Mayor-President Ravi Pandey nodded and terminated the connection.

Linus phoned Noah for an update on the new case.

"I'm just finishing with the victim's interview," the kid said. *"I've processed his body and I'm gathering his clothes now."*

Linus duly dictated this into a report for the computer to transcribe and combined it with what he, Karen, and Noah had uncovered in the first investigation so far. His temper, hot in the cold room, remained in firm check. Pandey was the boss. If she wanted a report every ten minutes, it was her prerogative to demand one. But every moment he spent in this kind of stupidity was a moment spent away from the investigation.

He got up and paced around his office while he talked to the computer. The holographic mountain stream trickled along its icy shore, wending its way among rocks and melting snow.

". . . Fang is still working on fixing a time of death. We're hoping the victim's onboard will provide us with . . ."

Blah blah blah. A sudden longing filled Linus, and he tapped the window twice as he talked. The scene wavered, shifted, and morphed into a small white house set amid a dozen others almost just like it. The image was taken from a high angle, as if the camera were at the top of a building. A young maple tree stood guard in the center of the front yard, and clumps of tired-looking winter snow clung stubbornly to shady areas. A late morning sun shone overhead, and Linus imagined it looked warmer than it felt. Even as he watched, an athletic-looking woman trotted down the sidewalk in front of the house. She had short honey-blond hair, and was jogging behind a large-wheeled stroller. Linus's words trailed off. The woman parked the jogging stroller on the front porch, lifted a baby from the inside, and disappeared into the house.

"Do you wish to save, continue, or delete?" asked the computer.

Linus didn't answer, and the computer repeated the question with perfect patience. "Continue," he said, and tapped the window twice. It morphed back into the mountain stream, and he finished the report in a firm, no-nonsense voice. Then, with firm, no-nonsense steps, he left his office, strode past the two clerks and one deputy in the common area of the security office, and began walking. He was standing outside the studio of Julia Espinoza before he realized exactly where had been walking. Linus knocked on the door as if he had intended to come here from the beginning.

The door jerked open and Dr. Espinoza glared out at him. The smell of coffee wafted through the hall. "Good. You got my message. Come in."

Message? Linus checked his wristwatch display. It was flashing that he had missed a call from Julia Espinoza and that he had a message from her. It had probably come in while Linus was dictating the report. He had been so preoccupied, he hadn't noticed the incoming message alert.

"Yes," he said, easing into the white studio beyond. "Your message. What have you got for me, Dr. Espinoza?"

"A better piece of work than anything Hector Valdez could have done."

The white scanning table sitting in the center of the white room was just as Linus had remembered it, except this time the brown skull of the victim sat in the center. The box was nowhere in sight. Linus continued to smell coffee, but he saw no signs of it anywhere. Espinoza moved to the other side of the table, and Linus was reminded of being in the morgue with Karen. He saw no controls or projectors at all, but Espinoza moved her hands and suddenly a human head replaced the skull on the table. Linus felt there should be some kind of sound effect, a pop or a ping. But there was nothing.

"It was good you brought this to me instead of . . . *him*," Espinoza said. "I have studied anatomy extensively, including bone structure and facial features. I immediately recognized the skull as Caucasoid, of course, but I could not determine everything. Skulls do not indicate hair and eye color, for example. But I called Dr. Fang, and she told me she had found traces of wavy black hair on the victim's head. Most people with black hair have brown eyes, so that it was I gave him. The bones showed attachment of ligaments and gave hints about how deep the tissue that lay on them was. He looked Spanish or Italian to me, so I gave him that coloring. You can, of course, make him paler or darker as you like."

Linus circled the table, studying the head. It was of a man in his mid- to late twenties—grad student age, no surprise. As Espinoza reported, he had black, wavy hair, brown eyes, and skin that was either naturally dark or given to easy tanning. Strong jaw, flat cheekbones. Nose a bit too big to be attractive. An average, see-it-and-forget-it face. To Linus's disappointment, the young man didn't look even vaguely familiar.

"Wonderful, Dr. Espinoza," Linus said. "This is perfect. I can—"

"It is not perfect yet," Espinoza interrupted. "It looks dull and lifeless, which will make him harder to recognize. So I added this."

Her hands moved again, and the head turned. Linus jerked away from the table. The lips parted as if to take a breath, and the eyes blinked. Espinoza gave a small smile, and Linus recovered himself. He studied the head further, trying to keep thoughts of John the Baptist out of his own head. Despite his initial reaction, Linus had to admit the movement added quite a lot. Holographic muscles moved beneath holographic skin and made the victim much more real. The head blinked again and looked up at Linus, who half expected it to speak. He was profusely thankful that it didn't.

"Very lifelike," he said faintly. "You're clearly an artist."

"Thank you." Espinoza pulled a button out of the table and handed it to Linus. The head vanished, replaced by the skull. "Now you can take the image and this skull out of my studio."

Linus left quickly, the boxed skull under his arm and the image button in his wristwatch. Outside the transparent Dome, the warm sun shone high overhead. The newsfeeds would spread the image around, and maybe someone would recognize him, though it would mean putting someone in charge of fielding all the calls. It was also possible Hector Valdez had information about the victim's onboard by now as well. He was about to call the man and see when his stomach growled and he realized it was close to lunchtime. All of sudden, Linus didn't want to be alone, and he placed a call to look for company.

Noah rode the elevator to the fourth floor of the medical center, carrying a by-now familiar crime scene kit. A quick check with Dr. Fang had given him the name and location of last night's victim—Viktor Riza. The next several steps were routine whether Noah was on Earth or Luna, though Noah still found the process interesting. Mysteries were a jumble of evidence waiting to be sorted. It was as if Noah's baby brother Ken had scattered a jigsaw puzzle around their shared bedroom when they were kids, and Noah had to reassemble all the pieces. Except in this case, Noah didn't mind.

The top floor of the med center was given over to in-patient care. The med center itself was fairly small. Dr. Fang was the only full-time doctor for Luna City's five-thousand-odd residents, though she wasn't the only person who dispensed medical care. All homes were equipped with an autodoc that could handle many injuries and most illnesses. Nurses, medical technicians, and physicians' assistants handled most of what was left, leaving Dr. Fang surprisingly free to conduct research as well as oversee Luna City's medical community.

At the entrance to the patient ward, Noah showed his identification to the nurse on duty, and she led him toward Viktor Riza's room. The corridor, like all hospitals, smelled of cleaner and disinfectant.

"What kind of shape is he in?" Noah asked.

"Pretty good, considering," she said. "Official cause of death was drowning. He lost oxygen long enough to kill more than seven percent of his brain tissue. We regrew it, of course, but he still qualified as dead. He's retained most of his physical functions, but his speech is a little odd. He can't say the letter 'p,' for some reason. We'll be starting physical therapy with him as soon as he's recovered enough."

"How was he found?"

"A maintenance worker discovered him lying face-down in one of the fish ponds, half in and half out. No one else was around. The worker pulled the patient out and called for an emergency crew. The paramedics rushed him here on life support until the med techs could replace the damaged neural tissue with new stuff."

"What about his blood work?"

The nurse checked a monocle similar to Noah's. "He came back positive for tetrahydralocyathine," she said. "Blue. We're seeing a lot of that lately. Levels didn't seem to indicate he's an addict, but it was definitely enough to knock him out. It may have sped up his death, but we don't know for sure."

"You're getting a lot of Blue up here?" Noah said, surprised.

"Unfortunately," the nurse sighed. "It's easy enough to make, if you have a well-stocked chem lab, and lord knows we have plenty of those around."

Noah wondered how Linus would take this news, then decided the Chief probably knew already. He thanked the nurse and entered the hospital room. It looked the same as hospital rooms the world—galaxy?—over. Tiled floor, bits of machinery, window that looked out over the Dome. Viktor Riza occupied the bed in the room's center. He turned his head on his pillow when Noah entered, and Noah almost dropped his kit. The man's face was pale, and his dark brown hair was mussed and flattened against his head. His brown eyes were bloodshot, and his freckles stood out above his mustache like grains of sand on white paper, but Noah recognized him. Noah called Linus to recuse himself, but the chief wouldn't have any of it.

"I don't care how you know him. He could be your long-lost father, and I still wouldn't let you out of this case. Look, kid, I understand your position, but we simply don't have the staff up here to let people pick and choose like that." Before Noah could reply, the murder victim spoke.

"I . . . know you," Viktor said, voice hoarse. "You threw us . . . threw us out of Wade's . . . a'artment . . . last night. I thought you . . . were bluffing when . . . you said . . . said you were . . . a co'.'"

"I'm Deputy Noah Skyler," Noah said, setting his kit on the tiny bedside table and setting his onboard to transcribe the conversation. Text scrolled across the bottom of Noah's monocle. "Why don't you tell me what happened last night? Everything you remember."

"I remember . . . you threw us out," Viktor said. His left hand was twisting under the covers like a snake. "Me, Crysta, and Bredda."

"Do Crysta and Bredda have last names?" Noah asked, making a mental note to corroborate the information with Wade later, and wouldn't *that* be fun?

Viktor thought a moment. "Crysta . . . Nell and . . . Bredda Meese. We were 'artying with . . . Wade and you . . . came in and threw us out."

"You were using Blue?" Noah asked. "It was in your blood screen."

Viktor remained silent for a long time. His left hand continued to twist, and Noah wondered if it was a nervous habit or an aftereffect of the brain damage. Finally Viktor said, "Blue is . . . illegal."

"Officially you died," Noah said gently. "You've lost enough memory and brain function to qualify yourself as a different person after the medical center brought you back. Any crimes Viktor Riza committed can't be pinned on you. You'll have the option of naming yourself Viktor Riza again, if you want, and any possessions you had will come back to you unless you made a will specifying otherwise, but legally you're someone else. So you can tell me anything you want without worrying about reprisal. I just want to know what happened."

A tear leaked out of Viktor's eye and trailed down his cheek. He made no effort to wipe it away. "You know . . . what? My earliest . . . memory is driving to the . . . tether 'ort to board the shuttle . . . for Luna. I don't . . . remember my family or . . . my friends. I don't remember anything . . . from when I . . . was little. But I . . . do remember two girls . . . and a guy . . . I fucked after talking to them . . . at a bar for . . . half an hour." Another tear followed the first. "They . . . should have let . . . me die."

Noah kept his face impassive, though his insides were twisting up. Would Viktor be lying on this bed right now if Noah hadn't tossed him out the door last night?

"How much Blue did you take in the apartment?" Noah forced himself to say.

"Not . . . much. Just enough to get . . . us a little high and . . . kee' me and Wade from coming . . . too fast. It's the way . . . you're su—su—su'osed to . . . use the stuff. Lets us . . . kee' it u' . . . all night, if we . . . want, without blasting."

Hence the name "Blue," Noah thought. The trouble was, Blue was also addictive. The first symptoms of dependence included an inability for males to function sexually without it. "Tell me what happened after you left the apartment," he said.

"I hadn't . . . finished, right? And . . . Crysta and Nell were . . . willing to kee' 'artying. One of the . . . girls said she knew . . . a s'ot down by . . . the fish'onds . . . where . . . we could find . . . some 'rivacy, so . . . we headed down there." Viktor's hand twisted some more.

"Did you talk to anyone along the way?"

Viktor started to shake his head, then stopped. "Wait. Yeah. One of the girls . . . talked to some . . . guy in the 'ark on . . . the way over. They walked . . . off a ways for it. I . . .

think they were . . . arguing. I don't . . . remember very . . . well. That's the last . . . thing I remember."

"Did you talk to the man?"

"I don't . . . remember."

"Do you remember whether it was Bredda or Crysta who argued with him?"

Viktor thought. "No."

Noah asked several more questions, but learned nothing more. "I need to check your body for evidence," he said at last, opening his kit. "You have the right to have a witness in the room, of course, and if anything I do makes you feel uncomfortable, you can say so and I'll stop."

"Just . . . do it," Viktor said. "I don't have . . . anything else to lose."

Noah nodded, pulled on a set of gloves, and set to work. He started with Viktor's hands, checking for defense wounds and finding none. The man's fingers were cool, almost cold. The fingernails showed flecks of green and gray, and Noah took careful scrapings of the material. Checking Viktor's right hand was difficult—Viktor couldn't stop it from twisting. Noah managed with some effort. That done, Noah helped Viktor out of his hospital gown, leaving the man naked under the white sheet. Viktor lay there with his eyes screwed shut, unmoving except for his breathing and the ceaselessly twisting hand. Noah worked his way up Viktor's arms to his shoulders, checking for wounds, bruises, or residue by eye. Then he did the same with a scanner and an imager. Viktor remained absolutely silent and kept his eyes screwed shut. Noah understood the silence and the closed eyes—he'd seen it many times in murder and rape victims, and he suspected he'd react the same way to a stranger going over every inch of his naked body in a hospital room.

Noah went over Viktor's head and ran a fine comb through his coarse hair, shaking the bits of debris into a polymer envelope. He found more greenish material inside Viktor's ear canals and took samples. Then he worked his way down Viktor's neck, chest, and stomach. Viktor was well-muscled, but not overly so. His genitals lay flat amid a nest of dark, curling hair. Noah gently ran swabs over penis and testicles to gather samples of any vaginal secretions left behind. Viktor accepted this treatment without comment. When he finished, Noah twitched a corner of the sheet over Viktor's waist and continued down to his thighs, shins, and feet. He photographed and scanned carefully, leaving nothing unchecked. Once that was finished, he opened the small wardrobe and found Viktor's clothes in a clear sack on the floor. Noah opened the sack and smelled fishy dampness. He would have to take these back to—

"Attention! Attention!" A call was coming in from Linus. Noah took it.

"How's it going down there?" Linus asked in Noah's ear.

Couldn't be better, he thought. *I'm partially responsible for our victim's death, that's all.*

"I'm just finishing with the victim's interview," he said quietly. "I've processed his body and I'm gathering his clothes now."

"Great," Linus said. His voice sounded tight with tension. *"Keep me posted."* And he signed off. Noah turned to Viktor.

"Thank you," he said. "I think I have everything I need. We may have more questions for you later, though."

"Sure," Viktor said in a dull, lifeless voice. "I'll be . . . here."

Noah took up his kit and the clothes and left. In the echoing corridor he nodded to the nurse at her station and headed for the elevator, feeling wretched. If he hadn't tossed Viktor out last night, he would never have stumbled down to the fishponds high on Blue and he wouldn't have drowned. He'd probably be perfectly fine, none the worse for wear. So Noah would have been a little tired today—big deal. A man's life was worth more than a night's sleep.

Unless Viktor's death was murder. In that case, it would be the killer's fault, not Noah's. And there was definitely something odd about all this. Who had the girls talked to? Where had the extra-large dose of Blue come from? And who had drowned him? It wouldn't take much pressure to keep a man high on Blue from struggling. Noah grimaced. A quick drowning that left a wreck in a hospital bed.

Noah left the medical center, determined to find the answers.

Before he came to Luna City, Linus had visited Las Vegas any number of times to attend law enforcement seminars and forensics conferences. His friends always snorted at this, as if attending a conference in Las Vegas was nothing more than an excuse to gamble and take in shows on department time. Major conventions, however, were always held in someplace like Las Vegas or New Orleans or London. After all, Linus had pointed out, who would attend a conference in Mud Hole, Arkansas?

Tourist Town reminded Linus of Las Vegas with a dash of Valium. It had its own little dome with a little amusement park, complete with a little roller coaster. After graduation, it was traditional for new grads to ride it facing backward, something which took a fair amount of flexibility. It was also supposed to be a prime place for losing one's virginity, but Linus had his doubts about that. If you weren't firmly strapped in, the roller coaster dropped out from under you in the low gravity, leaving coupling couples hanging in midair like cartoon characters.

Underground, beneath the amusement park, was a wide avenue with a tasteful little casino, three hotels, half a dozen theaters, and a sprinkling of restaurants. Luna City University didn't have a sports arena—yet. Linus strolled down the avenue and wondered if Mayor-President Pandey's negotiations with the entertainment companies would include building one. The cynical Marine whispered it probably did—you could probably make some good money making vid-feeds of college students playing low-gravity volleyball in bikinis. Bounce bounce bounce.

Tourist Town was actually fairly busy, and the avenue was crowded with people, many of them clumsy in the low gravity. New students who came from wealthy families often came to Luna with their parents in tow, and they filled the little hotels to capacity for a month or so. Lights, holograms, and music vied for Linus's attention, but he tuned them out. Instead, he followed his nose to a pair of red double doors inset with gold filigree. A silver fountain surrounded by exotic plants tossed slow-motion water high into the air, where it glittered like molten glass before pouring slowly back down. The bottom of the fountain was littered with small coins. A tastefully lit sign told him he was standing in front of the Moon Dragon Restaurant.

Linus touched the doors, and they opened silently inward. The heady smell of frying fish and spicy rice flowed over him. The interior was surprisingly small, with red walls and thick carpet. Lunch rush had ended, leaving the place half deserted. The remaining diners talked in hushed tones, their voices punctuated by the wooden clatter of chopsticks on china. Karen Fang, seated in a back booth, waved her menu at him, and Linus slid in across from her.

"Posh place for a lunch invite," she said. "What's the occasion?"

"I . . . didn't want to eat alone," Linus replied, feeling suddenly embarrassed. "I eat in the cafeterias a lot, but you can only handle so much student food, you know?"

"I do know." Karen ran an expert eye over the selection as a waiter deposited a teapot and small round cups on the table. "Looks like fish is in season. And oh my—the tofu harvest must have been a bumper!"

"No crispy duck?"

"They can't fly this far. And don't torture me." She closed the menu and sighed. "Sometimes I want to shove all this fish through a sphincter and enjoy a good Australian fry for breakfast."

"Isn't that an Irish fry?"

"Don't quibble with the coroner." She poured a cup of tea and said, "You want to go home. To Earth."

The abrupt statement hung in the air for a moment. How long had he known Karen—two years? Three? Did that much time give her the right to say such things? Suddenly Linus didn't care if it did or not.

"Yeah," he said. "It's rough knowing I'll never get down there again. Not in this lifetime, anyway."

"That's overly pessimistic," Karen replied. "You're on the transplant lists. A compatible heart donor might—"

"Not gonna happen, and we both know it," Linus interrupted with a wave of his hand. "My life isn't in danger up here, which automatically bumps me to the bottom. The transplant registry knows I'm fine as long as I stay away from full gravity." His throat became unexpectedly thick and he took a sip of hot tea to cover his consternation. It was so stupid. *He* was so stupid. Four years ago, only a few months after his arrival on Luna, he'd started feeling a little sick. Nothing major—he just seemed to tire easily. Linus had put it down to overwork. After all, he was taking classes as a masters candidate, working for Security as a deputy, and washing dishes in one of the cafeterias. He had taken an entire day off—and slept through most of it. The end of the next day found him as exhausted as ever.

He should have had the autodoc in the medicine cabinet check him out. He should have gone straight to the medical center. Should have, should have, should have. Instead, he had slogged on for another week.

And then had collapsed.

Linus awoke in the medical center, bleary and confused, with no idea how he had gotten there. Dr. Gertrude Piltdown, the gray-blond and soft-spoken woman who had preceded Karen Fang as head of the medical center, explained to him in her gentle voice that a virus had infected his heart, with devastating consequences. Dr. Piltdown had managed to repair the damage. Or most of it. The virus had badly weakened his mitral and pulmonary valves.

Dr. Piltdown had tried to grow new heart valves for Linus using his own stem cells. That was when he had gotten the second bit of bad news.

Stem cells, Linus learned, were basic, unformed cells. When they divided, they could become any other type of cell, from brain to skin to bone. Once a stem cell differentiated into, say, a skin cell, there was no going back. Stem cells could also divide any number of times—as long as they remained stem cells. Differentiated cells could only divide about fifty times before deteriorating. Occasionally, differentiated cells ignored this limitation and divided uncontrollably, causing cancer.

Ninety-six percent of the population could safely receive stem cell treatment to regrow lost or damaged organs. These days, even neural tissue could be replaced.

As a matter of course, Dr. Piltdown had stimulated some of Linus's stem cells into becoming cardiac tissue. And there she ran into a problem. It turned out that Linus was one of the remaining four percent. His stem cells, when stimulated artificially, were overly prone to cancer. And a cancerous heart valve was worse than a weak one.

Cancer, of course, was treatable and could be sent into permanent remission, but not without side effects. The treatments were guaranteed to weaken Linus's valves, sending him right back to his starting point.

Dr. Piltdown also explained that Linus was lucky, in a way. If this had happened on Earth, his valves would have collapsed under the heavier gravity. Here on Luna, the pressure on his valves remained lighter, allowing him to survive. The stress of traveling to and living on Earth, however, would kill him.

Linus had shut down, then fallen into a depression, and then thrown himself into his work. He earned his masters degree in record time and had gone on to work full-time in Security. The high turnover rate on Luna had put him on the promotional fast track—his immediate superiors kept finishing their studies and going back to Earth, leaving him to step into their shoes. Within two years, Chief Inspector Linus Pavlik had full charge of Security.

It was poor compensation for being a castaway.

When Linus put his cup down, Karen put her hand on top of his.

"You have friends up here, love," she said quietly. "People who care about you."

"All transitory," Linus said, suddenly not wanting to be comforted. "Everyone finishes their project and moves on. Except me."

"And me."

Linus blinked. "You?"

"I've decided I like it up here," Karen said. "Back home, the best I can hope for is to be a single researcher or a specialist among dozens on a team, lost in the bureaucracy of a hospital. Up here, I get to do it all. I'm doctor, researcher, lab lady, administrator, and—oh yes—medical examiner, all rolled into one. I'm finding I like it. I'm thinking of applying for full citizenship and staying on permanently."

"Really?" The thought made Linus much happier than he thought it should have, and he found he was grinning. "K, that's wonderful! I mean—look, I'll write a recommendation for you, talk to the Mayor-President. I'm sure she'll want you to stay."

"You have enormous eyes, Linus," she replied. "Has anyone told you that?"

The remark caught him off-balance. "Once or twice," he said. "Why?"

"They're even bigger right now," she said. "They make you look like a little boy. Or a puppy."

He noticed her hand was still warm on top of his, and Linus felt uncertain again. Was the gesture meant to be more than friendship? He didn't know how to respond. Karen often did that to him—threw off his equilibrium. Oddly, he found it endearing. She could always surprise him, but unlike the surprises brought to him by police work, Karen's little jolts weren't disturbing.

Though they *could* be unsettling.

The waiter saved him from further comment by arriving and asking for their orders. The Moon Dragon still depended on human waiters and physical menus. The place was priced accordingly, but Linus had already decided he needed a treat. Karen pulled her hand away as she ordered unicorn mandarin fish while Linus chose fresh scallops and fried fish balls, with an admonishment to Karen that she didn't need to make any obvious comments. She sniffed in disdain at such an easy target.

They passed a convivial, delicious meal, after which Karen insisted on picking up the tab. "I make more than you do, love," she said with a light grin, and slapped her thumbprint on the check before Linus could react.

As they were exiting the restaurant, Linus received a call from Hector Valdez.

"We're done with the murder victim's onboard," he said. *"Are you free to come down and have a look?"*

"I recognize that expression," Karen said. "Security business. I'll catch you later." She pecked him on the cheek and vanished into the tourists crowding the avenue. Linus watched her walk away for a long moment, then told Hector he was on his way.

Hector's office was empty except for a single graduate student who Hector introduced as Wesley Yard. Wesley, a tall, thin young man, pushed one hand through dark brown hair and nodded at Linus. For a moment Linus considered telling Hector that Julia Espinoza sent fond greetings. Karen must be rubbing off on him. He set the thought aside.

"The obie was severely damaged," Hector said, "which surprised me. I was expecting to lose the organic components, but I wasn't expecting destruction quite this severe. I brought in Wesley here to help me. No one knows computer destruction better than he does."

Wesley gave Linus a weak smile and a shake of the head. "I'm not bad."

"Not bad." Hector clapped Wesley on the shoulder with thunderous force. "Such modesty."

"So did you find anything?" Linus asked, feeling impatient and trying not to show it.

"Nothing helpful," Wesley said. "Nothing worth—"

"Don't be ridiculous!" Hector said. "We found a few file fragments. Music and graphics files. The information itself was scrambled beyond recognition, but we found a time stamp. It was dated December sixteenth, last year—almost exactly six months ago."

Linus grew excited. "So our victim was alive six months ago."

"So it would seem," Hector said. "But there's more, and it's the reason I called Wesley in here."

"Go on."

"As I said, vacuum shouldn't have destroyed the obie so thoroughly. Most of it should have been readable even by an amateur like you."

"Right," Linus said dryly. "So?"

"So someone deliberately destroyed the obie," Hector said. "This isn't easy to do. They're built to take quite a lot of punishment. I had a suspicion and I called in Wesley to confirm it. Wes, why don't you tell him what you found?"

Wesley had pressed himself against the wall as if he were hoping it would eat him. He was looking at the floor. Cop jitters, Linus wondered, or just shy?

"I . . . Dr. Valdez said . . ."

"I said nothing," Valdez said with a hint of steel. "I wanted to see if you would come independently to the same conclusion. And it was . . . ?"

"That someone used an EMP on the obie," Wesley said.

"Okay," Linus said. "Why is that such a major revelation?"

"An electromagnetic pulse is hard to control," Hector said. He stroked the end-curls of his mustache. "We techies use them in emergencies, to disable a robot miner, for example, or shut down a system in an emergency. The problem is that the pulse usually takes out not only the target, but every other computer within a certain radius. If the killer used an EMP to wipe out the victim's onboard, he would have taken out every other computer in the immediate area, and someone would definitely have noticed. I checked—there have been no unexplained computer outages since last December."

"Meaning what?" Linus asked.

"Wes?" Hector prompted.

Wesley Yard looked shyly at the floor. "It means the killer used an imp gun."

"An imp gun," Linus repeated.

"It's a specialized tool that squirts a focused electromagnetic pulse in a small cone," Hector said gleefully. "It only works at close range and it takes a fair amount of skill to use one. They're also very expensive and rarely found in a layman's hands."

"Who uses imp guns, then?" Linus asked, though he had a feeling he knew the answer.

Hector thumped himself on the chest. "People like me. Most IT departments keep several on hand."

"I don't suppose," Linus said, "that you would happen to know who on Luna would be qualified to use an imp gun like this?"

"Every student in the information tech department is trained on them," Wesley said quietly. "And of course the professors know how to use them. It amounts to about two hundred people."

"I can get you a complete list, if you like." Hector rubbed his hands together with glee. "Does that mean I'm a suspect?"

"I'll let you know," Linus said sourly.

On his way back to Security, notice of yet another incoming call trilled in his ear like an annoying little bird. He sighed. During quiet times, he could go days without a notification. Now it seemed like half of Luna City was trying to get hold of him. He accepted the call, and Gary Newburg's voice popped into his ear.

"*Chief,*" Gary said, "*we have a big problem.*"

"What else is new?" Linus growled. "Let's hear it."

"*I need to report we've got bad trouble with the new guy.*"

CHAPTER EIGHT

Water splished and sloshed as Noah surveyed the scene of Viktor's death. A strong fishy smell hung on the damp air. Waist-high concrete tanks filled with greenish water and separated by meter-wide pathways stretched in all directions like a giant checkerboard beneath harsh fluorescent lights. A square green hedge made a border all the way around the underground farm. The place was weirdly regular after the carefully planned chaos of the domes.

Viktor had died near a corner of the fish farm, on a path lined by hedges on one side and a tank on the other. The holographic stripe surrounding the area marked it as a crime scene. Noah had already taken several images with a long-distance lens, but there wasn't much else he could do right now. Several small puddles blobbed the floor in the crime scene, and Noah knew they were probably footprints, or even evidence of a scuffle. He itched to examine them close up, but he had to wait for the water to dry up first. Otherwise his own feet would mix the puddles around and ruin the evidence. It would be easier to analyze the debris left behind once the liquid evaporated, though that could take days down here in this damp, fishy basement.

He leaned over a tank and peered into the water. Fish—trout, if he was any judge—swam among algae leaves and water plants, their mouths opening and shutting like busy gossips. He stood up and put his hand in the chilly water. Eight or nine centimeters down—more than enough water to drown in—a screen stopped his hand. Two trout, expecting to be fed, rushed up and bopped their noses against the barrier. The screen was there, Noah had learned, to keep the fish from jumping out. In the moon's microgravity, the average trout could leap three or four meters, and a serious jumper like a salmon could easily brain itself on the ceiling.

In the background, he was aware of workers moving about. They lifted screens, hauled out nets full of struggling fish, changed tank filters, and performed numerous other tasks Noah couldn't identify. All of them avoided the cordoned-off area, and none of them was Ilene.

Noah took the imager and forced himself to turn his back on the crime scene. He couldn't guard it twenty-four hours a day, or even one hour a day, and he couldn't process the place yet. Nothing for it except to wait.

Well, wait and check out other possibilities.

Upstairs, he checked the time. Later today he had a tech rehearsal for his show. This, he knew, would involve a great deal of boredom. He would stand on the stage while the technicians checked light and sound and asked him what cues he wanted. Since Noah did a one-man show, all these would be minimal, but it was dull work nonetheless. He hoped it would go quickly.

A short, crowded train ride took him back to the Dome station. The air in the car was stuffy. A man trod on Noah's foot as they exited the train and Noah winced in anticipation, but felt no pain. Oh yeah—light gravity. The man apologized and moved on, and Noah climbed the steps up into the Dome carrying his crime scene kit. The crowded, alien park spread out before him, and Noah was abruptly seized with the desire to run all the way back to the familiar sights of Wisconsin, of Madison's brick downtown and the rolling hills farther upstate. Homesick already. That was pretty pathetic.

"Obie," he said, "upload directions to the office of Melissa Rose."

Obediently, a small red arrow popped into being across his monocle. It was pointing left. Yellow text told him he was two hundred meters away from his goal. Noah turned left, and the arrow straightened out. He followed its directions, weaving through the lush greenery of the park, sometimes crunching on gravel pathways, other times passing down silent concrete. Other students swarmed around him, alone and in groups. Someone had chalked FREE THE SUB-STRATA SEVEN!, whatever that meant, on one of the sidewalks.

The arrow directed Noah to a building, up two flights of stairs, and down a corridor faced with doors. He knocked at the one labeled DR. MELISSA ROSE, and received a cheery call to enter.

The large room beyond was crammed with greenery. Small trees stood in pots on the floor. Plants spread from baskets hanging below the ceiling. Ivy covered one entire wall and was making a run for it across the ceiling. A wide window looked out over the Dome, but Noah would need a machete and a native guide to make it across the sill. He didn't see anyone actually present.

"Hello?" he said. "Anyone home?"

One of the potted trees shuddered and tilted sideways. A woman's face peered out from behind it. "Hey," she grinned. "Just checking my sugar maple for pear thrips. You can't use pesticides on them unless you want nasty chemicals in your maple syrup, but I've genetically modified a hatching of painter beetles, and they seem to find the thrips pretty tasty now." She stuck a hand through the foliage. "You must be Noah Skyler."

He shook it. "That's me. Can you spare some time?"

"Just let me disentangle myself." More rustling, and Dr. Rose stepped from around the tree. Her hair, Noah noticed, was the color of oak bark, and she wore it in a straight pony-tail down her back. Her green-brown eyes sparkled with controlled energy, and she moved with the confidence of a woman who knew exactly where she was and what she was doing. A data pad peeked out of the pocket of her white lab coat. Noah's first thought was that she was near his own age, but her University bio put her in her late thirties.

"What can I do for you?" she asked.

"I'm hoping you can identify some organic material for me," he said.

"From a crime scene?"

"Yeah. Chief Pavlik said that's how it mostly works around here." Noah gave her what he hoped was his most earnest smile. "We don't have the facilities to process every-thing ourselves, so we depend on you professor types."

She gestured at him to follow her to the back of the room, where a cluttered table sat pushed against the wall. Plants grew in ice-cube trays, each neatly labeled with a small stake. Small bags of earth and plant fertilizer lay scattered everywhere, along with an assortment of gardening tools. Scanning and computer equipment took up one corner, and a bonsai tree sat dead center, like a miniature king on a tiny throne. Smells of peat moss mingled with the harsh scent of chemical fertilizer.

"Let's see what you have," Melissa said, drawing on a pair of gloves.

Noah handed her the clear envelopes with the scrapings he had taken from Viktor's fingernails. She carefully dabbed them onto a slide, dropped a cover on it, and pushed it into a scanner. It activated automatically, and an image bloomed just above the tabletop. It was a gray-green jumble to Noah, but Melissa gave it a quick, expert glance.

"Benthic algae here," she said, pointing, "and these are fish scales. Trout. So I'm guessing this sample came from one of the fish farms."

Noah waited for more, then realized that was all she was going to say. Disappointment washed over him. "Nothing else?"

"That's it. What were you hoping for?"

Human DNA, he thought. *Evidence that Viktor fought his attacker.* But he kept this to himself. "Nothing in particular," he said aloud. "Just making sure."

"Well, if you need anything else . . ." She made to turn back to her maple tree.

"Uh, thanks. Right." Noah scooped up the sample envelopes and headed out the door. Melissa Rose watched him go with a thoughtful expression.

"A really *big* spoon," she muttered, and went back to her thrips.

Noah's next stop was the medical center. An idea popped into his head along the way, and told his obie to run a quick search. As a result, he was able to enter the office of Dr. Karen Fang and ask, "Where does a vampire eat lunch?"

"At the casketeria," Dr. Fang replied without a moment's hesitation. "Nice try. What do you need?"

Noah sighed and held up more clear envelopes with swabs in them. "Viktor Riza had sex with two women not long before he died. I need to know who they are."

"Vaginal contributions?" Karen asked, taking the envelopes.

"Yeah." He left out the fact that he'd been hoping Melissa would have given him the attacker's DNA. "How long will it take you?"

"Less time than it'll take you to learn how to walk on Luna."

He felt the hot blush climb his face. "Linus told you about that?"

"No, it was just a guess. Everyone stumbles, love." Dr. Fang dropped the swabs into a tiny drawer set into the front of a scanner. The drawer slid shut, and the display flickered like a dancing flame over the word WORKING. Dr. Fang didn't speak further, and Noah felt abruptly uncomfortable. He wondered if Dr. Fang was using the silence to entice him into talking—an ancient cop's trick—and he found it was working. He couldn't keep his mouth shut.

"How long have you been on Luna?" he asked inanely.

"Two and half years," she said, hands plunged into the pockets of her lab coat. "I'm thinking of staying on permanently, actually. I like it. What about you?"

He smiled self-consciously. "I've only been here a day. Hard to tell yet. My family's a long ways away."

"Married?"

"Yikes," Noah said. "And, no. You?"

"Touché," Dr. Fang replied. "Three times, actually. Twice on Earth and once on Luna. I'm always looking for ex-husband number four."

For some reason, that remark made Noah uneasy. Rather than let the silence fall again, he asked, "Where did you grow up? I can't place your accent."

"*I* don't have an accent, Yank," she growled. "*You* do."

"Australian," Noah said, as if thinking aloud, "and something else. Beijing? Or is that too obvious a guess?"

Dr. Fang seemed to give up. "I was born in Australia, but my parents got divorced when I was little and my father moved back to Hong Kong. I had dual citizenship, and I shuttled back and forth between both places most of my life. I'm here because I couldn't get into vet school."

"Allergic to cats?"

"I wasn't smart enough," Dr. Fang corrected. "You want to learn to carve up the family pet, it's bloody hard to qualify. You want to carve up the family, though, it's not that bad."

The DNA scanner pinged. Both Noah and Dr. Fang leaned in for a look, and the images of three people popped up. One was Viktor. The other two Noah recognized as the women he had thrown out the apartment with him. The first had a round face surrounded by curly brown hair. The other's features were more pointed and her hair fell somewhere between brown and black. Both of them had blue eyes.

"Crysta Nell and Bredda Meese," Dr. Fang said. "You want to download their files to your obie?"

Noah did so, pulling their addresses and pictures from the computer. "They're both less than ten minutes away," he said. "Man. This is so different from Madison. Just getting out of the parking lot takes ten minutes down there. Up here, you get around in seconds."

"Good," Dr. Fang said. "Linus is getting some pressure from the higher-ups to clear these cases, you know."

"No," Noah replied slowly. "I didn't know."

"Not to put pressure on you or anything."

"Right."

"Because I wouldn't dream of doing such a thing."

"I see." Not sure how serious she was, Noah decided to sidestep the issue. He turned to go.

"And by the way—it wasn't your fault you broke that bloke's foot off."

Noah swung around to stare at her. An odd tension—hope?—gathered in his stomach. "What do you mean?"

"I ran the final tests today," she said. "The bone was already cracked when you picked him up, practically broken already. That foot would have come off no matter who was lifting him."

A weight Noah hadn't realized he was carrying suddenly vanished. "Really? You're not just saying that?"

"Vampire's honor," she said, holding up her right hand. "Now out! You have interviews to conduct."

Noah left the building feeling lighter than even the lunar gravity could account for. The air in the Dome smelled sweet and clear instead of alien, and the plants looked fresh and natural beneath the hard sun overhead. He checked his watch again. Plenty of time before his tech rehearsal for an interview or two. Noah bounded off with barely suppressed glee.

Ten minutes later, he was ringing the doorbell of the apartment Crysta Nell shared with a roommate. She opened the door herself. Her curly brown hair was mussed and dark circles lined her eyes. She was chewing something, and Noah caught the minty scent of caffeinated gum. He introduced himself. She didn't even blink when he introduced himself as a deputy.

"I remember you," she said in a nasal voice. "You threw us out. Naked."

"That was me," he said. "Can I come in? I need to ask you a few questions about Viktor Riza."

Chew chew chew. "Who?"

"Viktor Riza. The guy you and Bredda were sharing with my roommate."

"Oh. Him. What about him?"

Noah shot a glance up and down the corridor. Other people passed in a continual stream. "This might be better discussed in private. May I come in?"

She wordlessly stepped aside and Noah entered.

The tiny apartment smelled of coffee. Clothes were strewn over a second-hand couch and over a tiny table that took up most of the floor space. The holographic window showed a blank gray slate. Crysta made no apologies for the state of the apartment, nor did she try to shove the clothes out of sight. Instead she leaned against the table, making it clear this had better be short and sweet.

"Is your roommate here?" Noah asked. He set his obie to transcribe.

"Nope. You really pissed *your* roommate off. He still mad?"

"I haven't talked to him. Are *you* still mad?"

She shrugged. "I've been through worse. What's going on? I'm busy."

"When was the last time you saw Viktor?"

"Last night." Crysta rummaged around in the mess on the table and came up with a packet of caffeine gum. She unwrapped a piece and folded it into her mouth, adding it to the wad she was already working on. "Why?"

"Where did you see him?"

"We were crossing the Dome. Bredda said she knew a place where we might find some privacy. What's this about?"

"Viktor drowned last night in one of the fish ponds," Noah said.

Crysta gasped. "He *died*?"

"The medical center resuscitated him, but he's legally dead. I'm trying to find out what happened."

"Oh geez." Her face looked distracted, but her jaws never stopped chewing. It was as if they were hooked to a separate machine. "Poor guy."

"What can you tell me about that night after you left our apartment?" Noah asked.

" 'Left'? That's a cute way of putting it." But it was clear the barb was reflexive. Crysta's face remained distracted as she thought a moment. "Like I said, we went down to the Dome. From there we were supposed to go to some place Bredda knew. I didn't go, though."

"What happened?" Noah prodded.

She hesitated, though her jaws continued to move. "Bredda and Viktor . . . they took more . . . they were . . ."

"Were they taking drugs?"

"Look, I don't want to get anyone into trouble," Crysta said.

"I'm investigating a death," Noah said. "I'm not really concerned with who was taking what. Were they on something?"

Crysta hesitated again before responding. "Yeah. It was Blue. Viktor . . . Viktor had already taken some. I'm not really into that scene, especially not that heavy, you know?" Chew, chew, chew.

"Where did he get it? The Blue, I mean."

"I don't know. But there was this guy in the Dome."

"A guy?"

"Bredda saw him and made us stop so she could talk to him. Viktor talked to him, too. I kind of stood back because he made me nervous, you know? I didn't *want* to get close. There are some real weirdos up here."

So Viktor *had* talked to the guy in the Dome. He had said he couldn't remember. Was that a lie or the truth?

"Can you describe the man?" Noah asked.

Crysta shook her head. "They were standing in shadows, and I was looking around in case someone else came by. I was getting nervous. I don't know why. Something felt off, you know?" Chew chew chew. "Anyway, when they finished talking to that guy, both Bredda and Viktor took more hits of Blue. Viktor was pitching a tent in his pants and he kept grabbing at Bredda. She was pushing him away, but not trying very hard, you know? They were both staggering and kind of giggly. He started grabbing for me, but I'd had enough. I told them to fuck off and I came home."

"Did Viktor argue with anyone? The guy in the park, maybe?"

"Not that I saw. They talked real quiet."

"What time did you get home?"

Shrug. "I don't know. Two o'clock?"

"Did you wake your roommate up?"

"Wendy? She sleeps like the dead."

"Did anyone see you in the Dome?"

Crysta folded yet another piece of gum into her mouth. "I don't know. It was pretty deserted at that time of night."

"How did you hook up with Bredda and Wade and Viktor?"

"We were all in the bar, having a few drinks, feeling good. Wade and Viktor were pretty cute, and I was feeling horny, so I was up for whatever. Wade said his roommates didn't care if he partied in his room, so we all four went back there. I thought about asking the other roommate—you know, to be polite—but Wade didn't want to. More men than women always makes it more difficult, he said, unless the guys are into each other. We partied around for a while. Then you showed up and tossed us out."

Noah switched off his obie. "Okay, thanks. I may have follow-up questions."

"So Viktor's not Viktor anymore?" Crysta said. "I mean, he died and everything."

"That'll be up to him," Noah replied.

"So even if you got him on drug charges, it wouldn't matter because he's a different person now, right?"

Noah switched his obie back on. "What kind of drug charges do you think Viktor might come up on?"

"Well, he used all that Blue. That's a crime, right?"

"Did he sell Blue to anyone that you know of?"

"Not that I saw."

Noah thanked her again and left. He felt like he had a few more pieces to his puzzle, but it was obvious several more were still missing. Who had Viktor talked to in the park? It might be worth it to stop by the medical center and ask, see if Viktor had regained any memories or if he'd "accidentally" left out any parts of his story. Victims were often reluctant to come forward about every single thing they had done prior to a crime, either because they feared reprisal or they were embarrassed. A Blue dealer was one of those things that often got left out. First, though, he had to interview Bredda Meese.

Following his obie's directions, Noah walked a few underground blocks to her apartment. Plants lined every tunnel, and vines covered the walls. Parts were so narrow that the bushes brushed against Noah as he walked, and the ceiling came down to just above his head. There was barely enough room to let people pass in the other direction. Feeling vaguely claustrophobic, he called up Bredda's picture on his monocle. Bredda Meese was all lines and angles, sharp of profile, sharp of gaze. Her eyes were gray flint, her hair done in dark spikes. Her chin came to a point. Noah kept one eye on the picture and one eye on where he was going. It was late afternoon now, and the plant-lined corridors were crowded with people who had finished classes for the day. They paid no attention to Noah. Already he was learning the loose, careful stride adopted by humans on Luna. It was simply a matter of paying attention, of learning how much strength to use. He still couldn't get over feeling like a barely tethered balloon, though.

The person who answered the door at Bredda's apartment clearly wasn't Bredda. This woman was rounder and plumper, with buzz-cut blond hair, and she gave Noah a predatory look up and down when he asked for Bredda. Her gaze made Noah felt like a piece of beef hanging on a hook and he forced himself not to shift his feet.

"Bredda hasn't been here in weeks," the woman said. "It's great, actually—I have a whole apartment to myself." She opened to door wider, and her low-cut blouse exposed some bosom. "Want to come in and look?"

"When was the last time you saw her?" Noah asked instead.

"Not since the middle of last term. She must be paying her rent, but I never see her, and her stuff's gone." A look of concern crossed her face. "You aren't going to report this to housing, are you? They might try to put someone else in here, and—"

"If you see her," Noah interrupted, "would you get hold of me through Security?"

"Anytime you like, sugar."

He left before she could respond further. He stuffed his hands into his pockets, then removed them when he discovered it threw off his newfound balance. Okay. Crysta, Bredda, Wade, and Viktor had all hooked up at a bar and come over to use Wade's apartment for an orgy. Viktor had taken a couple hits of Blue. Then Noah had come home and thrown them all out, except for Wade. They were all still horny. Bredda claimed to know a place where they could do a three-way, and what guy with a hard-on would refuse that? Presumably, Bredda was thinking of the corner of the fish farm. On the way there, the trio had gone through the Dome and talked to a mysterious stranger, possibly a Blue dealer. Crysta had gotten nervous and bailed, nullifying Viktor's chances for a threesome. Down at the fish farm, or maybe en route, Viktor had taken a whole lot more Blue. Then someone had held his head underwater in a water tank and killed seven percent of his brain. All this Noah knew. The problem was, it didn't really take him anywhere.

So now what? A moment ago he'd had a lead. Now he'd hit a dead end. Still, Bredda might have more information, and she had to live *somewhere.* Unless the Morlock rumors were true—something Noah doubted—Bredda had to be holed up someplace besides her apartment. The most likely connection was the guy in the park, whoever *he* was.

Noah's obie buzzed, and a small message window popped up on his monocle. The message reminded him that the tech rehearsal was set to begin in fifteen minutes, and he was ten minutes away from the theater in Tourist Town. Noah loped toward the train, then forced himself back into a walk as his body threatened to bound toward the ceiling again. Maybe he could work some low-gravity urinal jokes into his act?

As Noah boarded the crowded, stuffy train, it occurred to him that he still hadn't really thought about what he was going to do on stage. On the other hand, the lack didn't bother him. Back in college, when a sizable portion of his income had depended on his ability to please an audience, he had spent hours researching, writing, and developing his material. Up here, though, he had just been too busy to think about it. In any case, he was a captive performer and they were a captive audience. Besides, he had a dozen stock songs, stories, and jokes that he could sew into an hour's worth of entertainment at a moment's notice. If he sucked, the worst that would happen was that he might get reassigned to shoveling fish poop.

And speaking of Ilene—or something related to her— maybe he should hold off on the urinal jokes if she was going to be in the audience. Although she seemed to have a straightforward sense of humor, it was too early to tell how much was real and how much was impress-the-other-person bravado.

The train halted, and Noah disembarked with a small knot of people. It occurred to Noah that their footsteps sounded . . . different. Lighter gravity combined with tile made on Luna of lunar materials made for odd-sounding footfalls. A blond woman gave him a brief glance, and he thought of Ilene again. Did she want to impress him? It seemed more likely she was used to everyone trying to impress *her*. Well, Noah wasn't going to worry about it. Ilene probably wasn't anyone he would end up with on a long-term basis.

Still . . . what would it be like to marry into the Hatt family? Would he continue working at the crime lab or get involved in Hatt Testing Laboratories in some way? Maybe he'd just live a life of leisure, a trophy husband to a rich and beautiful woman worming his way into the horseback and canapé crowd. He could winter in the Bahamas and summer in Switzerland, with the occasional jump over to Hong Kong for variety. With his staff, of course. Someone would have to arrive ahead of him to ensure the meals were ready and the mints were on the pillows.

These pleasant thoughts kept him occupied as he made his way through Tourist Town to the Sueyin Dai Memorial Theater. Because the entire theater and the corridor it occupied was underground, only a large pair of double doors and a lighted marquee indicated its presence. Noah looked up and was both surprised and pleased to see his name there. NOAH SKYLER: NEW VAUDEVILLE REVUE, it read, and listed the performance as starting tomorrow at eight o'clock.

Noah grinned. He hadn't seen his name in lights since college.

Maybe it would impress Ilene.

He reached for the front door, then stopped. It was bad luck for actors to enter through the main entrance. He glanced around and found a side corridor that took him around back to the stage entrance. Much better. The rear alley was surprisingly clean, with none of the usual garbage smells. Almost everything on Luna was recycled, so there wasn't much garbage to throw away. Even table scraps could be made into fish food. The back door was unlocked. Noah stepped inside and climbed a short flight of steps into a dark, echoing space that smelled of wood, old ropes, and makeup. A sense of home swept over him—he was backstage again. Before his eyes had even finished adjusting, a woman with her hair pulled back in a severe, no-nonsense bun swooped down on him like a phantom from the curtains.

"Can I help you?" she asked frostily.

"I'm Noah Skyler," he said. "I've got a tech rehearsal?"

She thawed, but only a little, and checked her watch with obvious care. "You were almost late. I'm Judy Roberts, the stage manager. Follow me. Please."

Almost late? Noah resisted the urge to make faces at her back and followed her onto the stage instead. The floor, curtains, and walls were matte black. An apron spread toward the audience, and his footsteps echoed in the tremendously open space. Lighting was dim. Judy planted Noah in the center of the apron.

"Do you need any props or costuming?" she asked crisply.

Noah shook his head. "I just need to link my obie to the theater. I handle my own sound and music cues. I can't handle lights, though. No good at it."

"Very well," Judy said. She raised her voice. "Yard!"

In response, Wesley Yard scurried onto the stage. He had a keyboard slung around his neck like a food seller's tray at a ball game, and he gave Noah a quick glance. "Hi," he said. "You're the deputy who does vaudeville?"

"That's me."

Wesley looked at the floor and muttered something that sounded like, "Lot of cops around."

"I'm not your first cop of the day?" Noah asked lightly, feeling an odd need to put Wesley at ease.

Wesley seemed surprised, either that Noah had heard him or that he had taken an interest. "Hector Valdez and I helped Chief Pavlik with an investigation. We dissected the obie of a murder victim."

"I helped process—examine—the crime scene," Noah said, feeling a stab of excitement. "What did you find?"

"He was alive six months ago and someone used an imp gun to destroy the obie."

"Interesting," Noah said, making a mental note to ask Linus for more detail later. "So if you're in the computer department, this must be your secondary job?"

"Yeah. Weird, huh?"

"No weirder than me doing vaudeville."

"Noah needs to work out light cues," Judy put in. "Get it right, Yard, and let's try to be quick, okay?"

"Before we get started," Noah said, "can I have a front-row ticket set aside for a friend?"

"What's the friend's name?" Judy asked.

"Ilene Hatt. Two t's."

"Anyone else?"

"No, just her."

Judy put a finger to her ear and spoke in an undertone to her onboard. "All set. The ticket will be waiting for her at the box office. Let's get started, then."

She bounded from the stage into the center of the audience, or house, in a single, precise leap that Noah could only admire, even as he wondered at her brusqueness. Wesley looked nervously after her, then at Noah.

"I'll try to be quick," he said. "What parts of the stage will you be using?"

Noah scanned the area around him. "The apron, I think. I won't back up past the proscenium."

Wesley nodded and followed Judy down into the house, though with rather less grace. He planted himself in the middle of the house and tapped his board. Immediately a series of bright lights slammed Noah's eyes backward into his skull. He yelped and threw up a hand to shade them.

"Sorry!" Wesley said, and the lights faded. "I was going for general lighting."

"Scale it back," Judy said. "And add some amber. What do you want for your set, Noah?"

"Plain wooden floor and walls," Noah said. "And a plain stool center stage."

"We'll have one for you. Water glass?"

"Yeah."

"Let me get the setting," Wesley said. The matte black floor and walls swirled into sickening yellow fractals, then oozed into a yellow florid pattern. Judy clicked her tongue in irritation. Wesley flushed and worked his keyboard faster. After two more tries, the stage settled into the warm wood pattern Noah preferred.

"Is someone going to introduce me?" Noah asked.

"We'll get a computer recording for that," Judy said. "How do you want to come out?"

"From stage left onto a generally lit stage with a spotlight on me. Dim, not harsh."

"On it," Wesley said. The lighting phased into a warm yellow tone nearly like sunlight. Then a spotlight stabbed down like a blinding laser and Noah again flung up a hand against it.

"Dammit!" Judy said. "Yard, check your boards. Soft lights are second and fourth circuits."

"Right, right." Noah heard the clicking of keys, and the spotlight softened.

"Move around, Noah," Judy said. "See if the spotlight follows you."

Noah stepped sideways into near darkness. The spotlight didn't budge, pouring its light onto an empty section of floor.

"Yard!" Judy said through clenched teeth.

"Sorry," he said. More key clicks, and the spotlight swung around to shine on Noah. He moved downstage, and this time the light stayed with him. Noah began to understand Judy's attitude. This was taking three times as long as it should have.

It took, in fact, over two hours. Lights flashed awkwardly. A strobe light bobbled and gave Noah a throbbing headache.

Twice Wesley hit the wrong commands and erased the entire program, forcing them to start from scratch. Judy became more and more impatient, which only seemed to make Wesley more nervous. Noah sympathized entirely with Judy and began to understand her attitude. He'd be short-tempered if he had to work with Wesley Yard, too. At long last everything was set. Judy double-checked that Wesley had saved the cues correctly and told Noah he could leave. He did so, feeling wrung out and close to exhaustion. Tech rehearsals were a pain in the ass, but this one . . . Noah couldn't ever remember one going so poorly. His feelings toward Wesley had quickly gone from pity to an intense need to smack him with a golf club. Incompetent idiot.

Noah sighed and trudged back to his apartment, the one he had barely spent any time in. Only his second day, and he was ready for a vacation. Maybe he'd fork out the cash to call his brother Darren. The two of them had always gotten along well, and Noah needed to hear a familiar voice. Sure, it'd be expensive, but—

He stared down at the area in front of his apartment door. The contents of his duffel bag—all his belongings—were strewn across the floor.

Chapter Nine

"**T**rouble with the new guy," Linus repeated. "What do you mean, Gary?"

"*Well . . .*" Gary began, the hesitation in his voice clear. "*I hate to bear tales, but I figured it's better for you to know.*"

"Know what?" Linus allowed an edge of impatience to creep into his voice. He did *not* need this. The Mayor-President breathing down his back was bad enough. He glanced around the room, as if the bare white walls and dull floor might hold some sort of solution. Maybe it was time to spruce the place up a little.

"*I'm almost at your office,*" Gary told him. "*It might be better to tell you in person.*"

Linus took advantage of the wait to upload the computer image of the victim's head to a couple contacts among the newsfeeds. With any luck, someone in the general public would recognize John Doe. The process only took a moment, however, and Linus was drumming his fingers impatiently on his desk when Gary entered a few moments later.

"What's going on, then?" Linus demanded.

Gary, a big, square-built man with a blond crew cut, looked uncomfortable. He was about Noah's age and, like Noah, was working on a masters degree in criminal science, though he was in his second semester. Linus also knew Gary spent a lot of time in Tourist Town—not a good idea for someone on a student budget. The man also wore too much aftershave, and the sickly-sweet smell hung around him in a heavy cloud.

"I hate to bear tales," Gary repeated.

"You said that," Linus said. "Bear the bearing and I'll decide what to do, if anything."

"Yes, sir." Gary cleared his throat like a dog preparing to bark. "It was when Noah and I were outside doing the casts. A couple of times, I noticed him about to make . . . make mistakes. He started to make one cast before taking a hologram, and he almost walked across the drag mark before either of us had processed it. Both times when I stopped him to make corrections, he . . . well, he snarled at me, sir. I don't want to sound petty," he hastened to add. "A little snarling is really nothing. But he almost ruined evidence. In a big case like this one . . ." He trailed off.

"I see." Linus kept his face police-level impassive, but inside, his mind raced. He had been greatly impressed by Noah's credentials and apparent desire to learn, and had pushed the committee hard to ensure Noah would get the Aidan Cosgrove grant. Linus also had to admit that Noah reminded Linus of himself at a younger age—eager to travel, sniff around, pick up whatever he could. The four other finalists had been highly qualified, but for whatever reason, they just hadn't grabbed Linus's interest. Had he been blinded by this and made a mistake in pushing for Noah?

All this flashed through Linus's head in an instant. He looked across his desk at Gary. "Do you want to file a complaint?"

"No," Gary said quickly. "I just thought you should know."

Linus nodded a dismissal and Gary quickly withdrew. His forehead puckered in a frown, Linus called up Noah's application to reread it. A copy of his work record with the Madison police was included. No citations for poor performance, no reprimands, no filed complaints. And his references had all given him excellent reports. That didn't mean anything, though—who would list a reference that might give you an iffy response?

Linus sighed and leaned back in his chair. It creaked, even beneath his slight lunar weight. He had several choices here. He could open a formal investigation. He could add a private, informal note to the confidential files Linus kept on all the deputies. He could ignore the entire situation. But before he did any of those things, he supposed he should talk to Noah about it, get his side. Linus had no doubt it would be unpleasant.

He was just opening his mouth to order up the call when his desk chimed, alerting him to an incoming call. It was Noah. Linus blinked. Had the kid gotten wind of Gary's complaint? He accepted the call, which was on audio only.

"Linus, I have a crime to report," the kid said. Anger, perhaps even fury, shook in his voice.

The greeting caught Linus off-guard. "A crime? What do you mean? Who committed a crime?"

"My roommate Wade Koenig. I want him locked up. I want him on fish shit patrol. I want him on fucking bread and water."

"Whoa, whoa," Linus said, putting his hands up even though Noah couldn't see him. "Slow down. What happened?"

A furious, rambling tirade followed. Linus recognized the symptoms—an angry victim venting in the direction of the closest police officer. Funny how even cops, who should know better, could get caught up in it. But the longer Linus listened, the more he began to wonder about Noah. It sounded like a simple roommate spat. Wade Koenig—Linus recognized the name from Noah's initial report on the death of Viktor Riza—had apparently scattered Noah's possessions up and down the hallway in front of their apartment. Linus couldn't count the number of roommate conflicts he had been dragged into over the years, some of which had even become violent. This one sounded fairly minor. Was Noah unstable? Linus shook his head.

"All right, all right," he finally interrupted. "Listen to what you're saying. Do you *really* want to charge your roommate with theft and have the area processed as a crime scene?"

"It would teach him a lesson," Noah snapped.

"And it would mean all your stuff would be impounded into the evidence room," Linus said. "That what you want?"

Pause. A deep breath came over the link. *"No."*

"Listen, ki—Noah, the University has a counseling department, and they have people who help mediate roommate conflicts all the time. Give them a call, see if they can help."

"Yeah. Okay." The voice was calmer, more subdued now.

Linus hesitated. He was about to bring up Gary's complaint but then suddenly he just couldn't do it. Yeah, the kid needed to know, and sure, eventually Linus would probably have to have it out with him, but the confrontation could wait a day, couldn't it? Right now Linus just had too damned much on his plate to mediate a spat between deputies.

"Anything new on the Viktor Riza case?" he said instead.

"Melissa Rose in the biology department told me he had fish scales and algae under his fingernails—no human DNA. So he didn't fight his attacker. On the other hand, we know he was doped out on Blue, and he may not have had the chance." Noah coughed. *"I also tracked down the women Riza was with. One of them said she saw Riza and the other woman talk to an unknown male in the Dome. She suspects they bought Blue from him, and I'm thinking it's where Viktor's near-overdose came from. The dealer—if that's what he was—creeped her out, so she went home. I tried to talk to the other woman, but her roommate said she*

hadn't occupied their apartment in months. Possessions gone, everything. I checked with the databases, and she's still listed as a student, though she hasn't registered for classes yet."

"Really? Interesting. Where do you think she went?"

"Unless she's gone Morlock , she's probably living with some-one else and not registered the fact with housing. I'm guessing a lover, one who somehow got a private apartment or who has a re-ally laid-back roommate. Maybe even the dealer from the Dome."

"Sounds worth following up on," Linus said. "Any leads on the dealer?"

"Not yet. I don't suppose there's any surveillance in the Dome?"

"Nope. Privacy issues, you know."

Noah sighed. *"I'll keep digging and keep you posted."* He signed off.

Linus drummed his fingers some more. Noah's investigative instincts were sharp, no doubt there. Maybe it would be best to wait a bit longer before acting on Gary's complaint. Or should he? Linus grimaced. He *hated* being in doubt, hated having half the evidence. His detective instincts told him to haul the kid into the office, sit him down, and get his side of the story. His managerial instincts told him to lay off for a while. Why did the two sides never match?

The door opened, and Karen Fang walked in without knocking, her shiny dark hair bouncing slowly, in contrast to her quick stride. "Hoy, love. How's things down here in the refrigerator?"

Linus looked up, and was surprised at how glad he was to see her. Karen held a competent, no-bullshit air, but she also retained a doctor's practiced bedside manner. And she was damned fine to look at.

Now where the hell had *that* come from?

"Refrigerator?" he said to cover his consternation.

"You always keep it so cold in here." She hugged herself for warmth. "Makes us delicate tropical flowers want to close up for the winter."

"Oh. Sorry."

"So getting back to my original question," she said, "how are things?"

"Messy," Linus replied. "I've just had a . . . I guess you'd call it a run-in with Noah."

Karen raised her eyebrows and lowered herself into the only other chair in the room. "What's that, then?"

Linus told her. She listened without interruption. "So you think there's a problem with Noah, then?"

"I don't know," Linus said. "That's the damned problem. I still have to talk to him."

"Give the lad a break," Karen said. "He hasn't been here three days and already he's up to his eyebrows in two murder investigations. His classes haven't even started yet, and Roger Davids bullied him into giving a vaudeville show tomorrow night. Anyone might crack under all that." She paused. "And besides—it wasn't his fault that the bone broke."

Linus sat up straighter. "Oh?"

"I examined the break in greater detail. The bone was already cracked at the time we picked the body up." She drew a data button from her pocket and flicked it toward Linus, who had plenty of time to catch it as it sailed slowly toward him. "I took images. When Noah broke the bone, a fair amount of powdery calcified material sifted into the surrounding desiccated tissues, but it wasn't enough to account for the entire break."

"So something cracked or broke the bone before the body was fully dried out," Linus said.

"Exactly. Might have been the same trauma that broke the victim's other bones. In any case, that foot would have come off no matter how carefully someone lifted the victim."

"Have you told Noah?"

"Of course. He was relieved, I can tell you." Karen got up and leaned across the desk. Her blouse was professionally high-necked and showed no cleavage, but Linus found himself checking for it anyway. He was also seized with an odd desire to touch her face, let her warm skin heat up his chilly office. "And I've got tickets."

"Tickets?" Linus repeated, caught off-guard again.

"Tickets to Noah's show. Tomorrow evening at eight. Want to go? I hate sitting alone in a theater."

"Uh . . . all right," Linus said. "Sure. It'll be fun."

"I'll pick you up, love," Karen said, and turned to leave. Linus, still feeling off-balance, failed to notice the happy smile on his own face.

Noah set his duffel bag on the living room carpet, still fuming. At least everything appeared to be there. Either Luna City's crime rate really *was* as low as advertised or Noah had gotten home before anyone else had come across the mess. He stood next to the packing crate coffee table, taking deep breaths and trying to get his temper under control, but it was difficult. He wanted to wrap his fingers around Wade's neck and rap his head smartly against a nice, hard object. One with corners. Or maybe spikes. Calling Linus had probably been a mistake, he could see that now. Still, that didn't mean he couldn't be . . . creative.

Besides, Noah was still investigating a crime, one that Wade had a connection to, however tenuous.

He sat down on the sofa, his carefully packed duffel at his feet, and told his obie to hook into the Security database. Text and images scrolled across his monocle as he searched for the name Wade Koenig. In seconds, he had full information. Wade Koenig. Citizen of Miami, Florida. Student visa. Graduate student in biology. Did Melissa Rose know him? Something to pursue, perhaps.

Busted twice for drug possession. Blue.

"Well, well, well," Noah said aloud. "You've been a bad boy, Wade."

A few more commands conjured up Luna City law regarding illegal substances. As Noah suspected, Luna City and Loony U had a three-strikes law. One more drug bust, and Wade would take the long fall back to Miami.

Whistling a little Irish tune, Noah pulled on a pair of gloves, stepped into the bedroom, and pawed expertly through Wade's dresser drawers. Nothing interesting. He checked the clothes hanging in the tiny closet. Nothing there, either. Then he stood in the doorway of the minuscule closet and ran his fingers carefully around the inside lintel. His questing hand found a smooth lump. Noah pulled, and it came off. It was an ampoule, half-full of clear blue liquid.

"Busted," he murmured.

Noah tilted the ampoule, and the Blue inside flowed sluggishly from side to side. A thought occurred to him. Had *Wade* administered Viktor's overdose? He could have slipped out of the apartment, found Viktor with Bredda, given the drug to him—either accidentally or on purpose— and then drowned him in the fishpond. Motive? Lover's quarrel. And Wade clearly had a temper.

The main door to the apartment opened. Noah pulled off the glove that held the ampoule, folding it inside out around the little vial to create an impromptu evidence beg. Then he stripped off the other glove, stuffed it into his pocket, and poked his head into the living room. Jake was setting his backpack on the couch.

"Hi," Noah said. "Been a while."

Jake turned with a grin. "Yeah. You're turning into the ideal roommate—never around. How've you been adjusting?"

"Decently. I haven't really had time to think about it." Noah paused. "Jake, does Wade use Blue a lot?"

Jake looked at him for a long moment, and Noah let the silence hang. "Are you talking as a cop or as a roommate?"

"Look," Noah sighed, "I know he uses the stuff. He's been busted for it twice, and I found an ampoule of it in the bedroom just now. Unless it's yours."

"Nuh uh." Jake held up his hands in a defensive posture. "No way. It's like tying your dick in a knot. I don't know how Wade stands it."

"So how often does he use?" Noah pressed. "Is he an addict?"

Jake dropped onto the couch, a languid gesture on Luna. "I don't think so. Give him another couple of months and maybe. Look, I don't want to get caught in a fight between you two. I hate that shit."

"One phone call and Wade's history." Noah waved the glove with the ampoule in it. "Third strike. Hard to have conflicts with a guy who's Earth-side."

"Don't," Jake said. His large brown eyes turned pleading. "I know Wade can be a jerk, but he can be a nice guy, too. He's fun to hang out with, and he helps me study for English."

Noah perched on the coffee table. The rough boards pressed uncomfortably into his backside. "Maybe, but the guy who was killed yesterday had enough Blue in his system to keep a prize stallion from launching his rocket. Maybe Wade gave him the overdose."

"How?" Jake countered. "I slept in the bed next to his all night, and you were sleeping out here on the couch. He couldn't have snuck out without waking at least one of us. Hell, I wake up if someone gets up to take a leak, let alone rummages around in the room to find drugs."

"Did you wake up last night?"

"Nope. Not once. You?"

"No," Noah admitted. "Okay, so he didn't administer Viktor's overdose. He still dumped all my stuff out in the hallway."

"Oh." Jake paused. "Well, I said he can be a jerk. Look, why don't you talk to him first?"

"I will," Noah said. "I have to. Any idea when he'll be back?"

"Well . . ."

"Oh god—now what?"

"Sometimes Wade's the ideal roommate, too," Jake said. "He disappears for two or three days at a shot. It's why I haven't tried to move out. Even I can only take so much Wade jerky."

"Wade jerky?"

Jake blushed. "Oops. My term for Wade being a jerk. Don't tell him, okay? Please?"

"I won't. I have to keep *some* friends around here." Noah got up and checked the refrigerator. Green Luna-grown vegetables and pale tofu cheese looked back at him. His groceries were still there. Apparently Wade's rampage hadn't extended to innocent foodstuffs. "You think he's avoiding me?"

"Probably. And in a total change of subject," Jake added, "I hear you're doing a show tomorrow night?"

Noah groaned. "Yeah. I just had the tech rehearsal, and I'm wiped. I don't need this right now. Why'd they hand this to me fresh off the shuttle, anyway?"

"I'm sure they thought it'd be easier on you," Jake told him. He crossed his ankle over his knee. "You know—get it out of the way before classes start and everything gets hectic."

"If this is *before* hectic, I think I'll take a stroll in vacuum now and get it over with."

Linus Pavlik's com-link chimed. He reached automatically across his desk, then saw the call was originating from the Mayor-President's office. His hand froze. Not now. Maybe he could pretend his link was off, let the computer take a message.

And have the call hang over him until he returned it. The link chimed again. Linus abruptly remembered a chilly spring day when he was maybe seven or eight years old. Spring in the Near North Side of the St. Louis projects meant people on the upper floors—the floors that didn't worry about gulp-heads breaking in to steal food or pets to eat—were opening windows and hanging threadbare rugs out to air like strange flowers draped over the rails. It meant traffic noises in the house and damp air wafting in from the river. It meant roasting in his winter coat because he didn't own a jacket and squishing in damp shoes because he didn't own boots. Mom had started spring cleaning, and Linus had been assigned the task of airing out their own rugs.

"Don't you let any drop," Mom had said. "You stay on the balcony to make sure they stay."

Linus took the heavy throw rugs to the balcony, already plotting how long it would be before he could beg off to play at Tim Napoli's apartment. Tim's dad drank and hit a lot, but felt guilty about it afterward. The latest slap-fest had resulted in a new sim-game suite. Tim had said Linus could try it out, and Linus was dying to see how many zombies he could kill in Death Spree IV. Outside, gray clouds hung low in the March sky, and the air carried a snip of winter yet. Linus lugged the heavy rugs out to the small wrought-iron balcony and carefully draped them over the rail, taking care to ensure more rug hung over the near side so it wouldn't slip over the far side. The tiny apartment Linus shared with his parents and sister was on the tenth floor, halfway up the building. He was long accustomed to the dizzying drop and scarcely gave it a glance.

A noise caught his attention and he glanced up. On the balcony above, Gina Belle, two years older than Linus, was setting out rugs of her own. He waved to her, but she didn't pay attention. She flung her rugs carelessly across the railing and vanished back inside.

Linus's last rug was scarcely in place when a shadow dropped down from above with a faint rushing sound. One of Gina's rugs had fallen. It rushed past Linus's carefully positioned rugs and swept one off the rail. Linus lunged, but he wasn't quick enough. Both rugs dropped away and fluttered to the concrete far below like a pair of wounded kites. They landed in a puddle of slush. Even as Linus watched, someone dashed over, snatched them up, and ran off. They hadn't been on the ground for more than a few seconds.

Dread clutched Linus's stomach. The rugs were all handmade, woven from old towels and old clothes. Mom had spent hours on each one. Now he had to go tell her what had happened. He knew it wouldn't matter that Gina had been the careless one, that it was her fault. Mom would tell him he should have been paying closer attention, that it didn't matter what other people did. He could only control himself. Tears welled in eyes. He might be able to duck out and run up the hall to Tim's apartment. But what good would that do? Mom would find him soon enough, and he wouldn't be able to enjoy killing zombies with her hanging over his head like a hawk ready to dive on a field mouse. Swallowing hard, he trudged back inside to face the music.

The link chimed a third time. Linus forced himself to tap his desk and accept the call. Face the music. Mayor-President Ravi Pandey appeared on the display.

"I was preparing an update for you, Ms. Pandey," he said. "Though I'm afraid it doesn't say much more. I've sent copies of the victim's likeness to the vid-feeds, and we're hoping someone will call with an identification, but not much else has happened."

"So you haven't found either killer yet," Pandey said. She paused, clearly waiting for a response to her rhetorical statement. Linus gritted his teeth and gave it.

"We're still investigating."

"Tomorrow morning the next shuttle lands," Pandey said. *"On it will be the representatives of both entertainment companies. The ones we are desperately trying to court, Chief Pavlik. Talks and negotiations are scheduled to begin two days after that—plenty of time for them to learn that Luna City's famous low crime rate has climbed sharply."*

"With all due respect, Mayor-President," Linus said, "it's only been a few hours since we last talked. It's unreasonable to expect results so—"

"It's unreasonable to expect China and the European Union to forgive us our debts," Pandey interrupted. *"It's unreasonable to expect our genetics people to modify fruit trees so they grow Euros instead of oranges. It's quite reasonable for me to expect my Security people to solve a crime once in a while. Or am I wrong?"*

"We're still gathering evidence, madam," Linus said, masking his rising temper behind icy civility. "And the more time I spend at my desk, the less time I have to analyze it."

Pandey closed her eyes and took a deep breath, apparently trying to contain her own temper. "*We need those contract talks to go smoothly, Chief. We need that money, we need that housing, we need those facilities. If these companies back out, Luna City may well go bankrupt, and we'll all be Earthside. And I do mean* all *of us.*"

The veiled threat was not lost on Linus. He realized he was rubbing his chest, and he forced himself to stop. "We're doing everything possible. Is there anything else, Mayor-President?"

It was as close to dismissing a superior as Linus dared come. Pandey accepted the remark with a simple shake of her head and terminated the connection.

Linus sat back in his squeaky chair and realized he was suddenly exhausted. He checked the time and was startled to realize it was well after eleven o'clock. He had thought about going down to the lab and going over the vacuum victim's clothes, but now . . . exhaustion and stubborn pride decided it was time to go home.

He was halfway there before he remembered he hadn't yet talked to Noah Skyler.

CHAPTER TEN

It was next morning. Linus set his face into a neutral expression before telling Noah to come in. The kid entered the office, carrying a lidded coffee mug and looking vaguely distracted. He sat down at Linus's invitation and put the mug on the floor. Coffee-scented steam wafted from under the lid of the mug.

"What's up, Chief?" Noah asked. "I barely had time to finish breakfast."

Linus gave a mental sigh. Times like this he really hated his job. His hands were even sweating, and he was forced to fold them carefully in his lap. The cold mountain stream continued its holographic burble on his office wall.

"A potential problem has come to my attention," he said, deciding to plunge right in. "It involves you, and I need to investigate."

Noah's face went rigid. "Okay. Should I have some kind of advocate here?"

"That's your right," Linus said. "Why don't I tell you what's going on and you can decide if you need someone here?"

"Fine." The kid's tone was flat, completely without inflection. Quickly and crisply, he told Noah what Gary Newburg had said about the footprint casting and Noah's attitude. Noah sat without movement or expression, and Linus found himself looking for a clue to his mood. He got nothing. Noah didn't blink, didn't twitch, didn't flush. Linus could have been talking to a rock.

"Do you have a response?" he asked when the story was over.

"Do I need one?" Noah said.

"You have three choices. You can either refuse to respond, wait until you have an advocate who can respond for you, or you can respond."

"And what will happen in each case?"

"If you respond or have an advocate respond for you," Linus said, "I'll weigh your word against Gary's. At worst, you would be given a verbal reprimand and I would put a note in your file."

"A verbal reprimand that got written down, in other words," Noah said. The sarcasm was the first hint of emotion Linus had seen in him.

"Yes. If you don't respond, or if your advocate tells you not to respond, then I will have to act on what Gary tells me and nothing else. I'll try to find out more from other sources as well, if I can find any." Linus paused. "What do you want to do?"

"I need to respond to tell you if I'm not responding," Noah said, the sarcasm rising again.

"Is that where you want to take this?" Linus asked.

"Not necessarily. I just thought I'd point that out, along with the verbal reprimand that gets written down."

"I should probably tell you," Linus said slowly, "that your tone lends credence to Gary's version of events."

"How can it when I haven't told you what happened?"

"Do you want to tell me?"

"I want to tell you," Noah said, "but there's no way to do it without making me look bad."

Linus tried to inject a fatherly tone into his voice. It was a trick he'd often used with youthful offenders, and it worked surprisingly often. "What do you mean, son?"

"I mean that if I tell you what happened out there, it'll look like I'm covering my own ass instead of telling the truth." Noah continued to sit rigid in his chair, ignoring the coffee mug at his feet.

"Try me," Linus said. "Look, Noah, we aren't so formal up here. True, we have two advocates for situations like this, but most of the time we're able to clear this kind of stuff up without resorting to legal maneuvering. If you have something to say, just say it."

Noah paused for a long moment. Linus tried to read his expression, see if he was using the time to fabricate a lie or simply word the truth.

"Gary told the truth," Noah said at last, "except he traded around what happened. *I* noticed that *he* didn't get a holographic image of the footprint he was about to cast, and *I* stopped *him* from walking across the drag mark. I was perfectly polite to him about it—like you said, we all make mistakes—but he just snarled at me. Then he left the scene, and I had to take everything in."

"I don't suppose you recorded the conversation," Linus said slowly.

"Why should I have? Gary was a jerk to me, but he didn't threaten or anything."

Linus scratched his head. Mirror-image stories, and no way to tell which was the real one. Great. He-said, he-said.

He decided to try a shot in the dark, try to catch Noah off-guard. "So how'd that roommate problem go down yesterday?"

Noah waved a hand dismissively. "I cleaned up and talked to my other roommate about it. I decided it was no big deal after all, just like you said."

A carefully concocted response, or the simple truth? Linus found he still couldn't read Noah's expression or tone. If the kid was lying, he was a natural.

He was also a performer—an actor. Was all this an act? Linus found his mind running in circles and gave himself a mental shake. He was reading too much into the situation.

"All right," Linus said. "There isn't really enough information here for me to act on, so I think we'll just let this one drop unless more evidence comes up. Good?"

A flicker of relief spread over Noah's handsome features. "Good."

Linus got up. "Well, then—how about a nice, brisk bit of investigation to get the morning going?"

Noah bounded out of his chair and almost clocked his head on the ceiling. Linus guided him back to the ground, just missing the mug on the floor. The coffee smell continued to percolate through the room.

"Still getting the hang of this gravity," Noah said, flushing now.

"You'll still stumble," Linus said. "I gave myself a concussion once, even though I'd been here for almost three years at the time."

"Did Dr. Fang treat you?" Noah asked.

"It was how I met her." Linus grinned.

Noah bent to retrieve the coffee mug. He took a sip. "So how long have you two been seeing each other?"

Silence slammed through the chilly room. Linus stared at the kid, and Noah, no dummy, realized he had made a mistake.

"Sorry," he said. "Geez, I—sorry. I really thought you two were—I mean—"

Linus realized his fists were clenched. He relaxed his hands and forced a laugh. "We're good friends, Kid," he said, deliberately using the nickname this time, "and I suppose to a newcomer we might sound like an old married couple, but we aren't seeing each other. Feel free, if you want to make a move."

"Not me." Noah backed away in mock horror. "She cleared me of the bone-breaking thing, but she could be my mother."

"More like your baby-sitter," he corrected just as the door opened and Karen Fang walked in. Linus froze and felt his face flush. Had she heard—?

"Why did the vampire give his girlfriend a blood test?" Noah asked without missing a beat.

"So he could see if she was his type," Karen replied instantly. "That's an *old* one, lad."

"Which is why you've heard of it?" Noah said, wide-eyed.

"Uh oh," Linus said, relieved at the distraction. "I think I'll just duck behind my desk here. Much safer."

"If that's the best material you can come up with, mate, your show is in deep kimchee," Karen shot back.

"I don't need material," Noah said. "I just read the news-feeds before I go on. Gives me everything I need." He paused. "There *is* freedom of speech up here, right? I don't want the Mayor-President cutting off my head or anything."

"Founded by a mess of liberals," Linus repeated. "Speech is all free."

"Oh yeah." Noah scratched his nose. "Gotta love those liberals, then."

"So what's on the schedule today, Karen?" Linus asked.

"Very little. All those autodocs in the medicine chests make my job so easy, I barely have to come in most days. I checked on Viktor Riza—he's still on the mend, but feeling understandably depressed—and then I thought I'd come down and look at crime scene bits with you."

"Oh," Linus said, nonplussed. Karen had never asked for this before. Was she . . . was this an excuse to get closer to him? He gave himself a mental shake. Silly thoughts. They were *friends*, and she had come down because she was bored. Linus turned to Noah. "You up for it, Kid?"

"Nope," Noah replied. "Not only do I not want to be called *kid* all day—"

"I didn't call you—"

"Yes, you did," Karen and Noah said together.

Linus folded his arms and pouted. "It's a conspiracy."

"As you like," Karen said with an impish grin. It made her even more attractive, and Linus tried very hard to think of dead puppies and cold showers. He didn't need this right now, not with two murder cases and the Mayor-President breathing down his neck.

"—*and* I have to work on the Viktor Riza case," Noah finished. "The floor at the fish hatchery should be dry by tomorrow morning. I can examine for trace and footprints."

"See you, then," Karen said with a little wave. "And break a leg at your show tonight. We've got tickets."

"Oh great," Noah groaned. "I don't want to know what kind of stuff a medical examiner might throw at the stage." And he left.

"Nice to see you two are getting along," Linus observed.

"How could we not?" Karen said. "I used to baby-sit him."

"Uh, right." Linus got to his feet. "And now that my morning meeting is over, there's evidence to examine with my favorite Luna City doctor."

Two doors down from Linus's office was an evidence examination room. A large light table took up most of the center, and debris from the crime scene lay spread out across the surface—boot castings, the drag mark, sample envelopes, the red shirt, the brown trousers, a single brown loafer. White light shone up from the table and down from the ceiling, sweeping all shadows from the room and making it harder for clues to remain hidden. Linus and Karen pulled on gloves and got out a set of scanners. The room was considerably warmer than Linus's office.

"These clothes look like they've been dry-cleaned," Karen commented.

"They have, really," Linus said. He bent over the red shirt. "That's part of the problem—any liquid-based trace evidence is long gone. Still, we might find a stray hair or flake of paint or something similar."

Karen had already picked up a scanner and was running the light bar over the trousers. "Cotton-poly fabric," she reported, now all business. "Synthetic thread, plastic button on the fly. I'll run an exclusion scan for anything not matching any of those substances."

"Take a scan of the weave, too," Linus said. "Just in case it's unique. We might be able to learn where the clothes were made or sold."

"Grasping at straws already?" Karen asked. "Clothes made in Mexico are routinely sold to the European Union."

"Yeah, but there's no point in ignoring the possibility of a clue when it only takes a second to check."

They worked in silence for a while. Linus ran his own scanner over the shirt, looking for anything that wasn't a cotton-poly blend. Nothing. He took a scan of the weave and ran it through the database. Half a dozen clothing manufacturers in various countries used it in clothes made for export. Dead end there.

After half an hour of tedious work, Linus's frustration level began to rise. He was no closer to identifying the victim than he had been yesterday, and the Mayor-President was breathing down his neck. Usually Linus loved teasing at a case, pulling at this thread or that until something came unraveled. But this was an exercise in pure bafflement. He set the shirt back down and turned to the casts. Footprints and the partially obscured drag mark made a neat row on the table. Linus picked up the first footprint and examined it, then examined the second, third, and fourth ones.

"Treads look like a public-issue vac suit," he said.

"So do these," said Karen, who was working toward him from the other end of the line. "And even if we *did* know who made them, it wouldn't prove much. The footprints could have already been out there when the killer dumped the body. No wind or rain to change them. They could have been out there for years before our poor lad showed up."

"Yeah." Linus shook his head. "So why do I keep thinking I'm missing something here?"

"You are," Karen said. "You're missing a shoe. Or the victim is."

"Uh huh." Linus picked up the victim's sole remaining brown loafer and scanned it. Nothing of interest. "Why is he missing a shoe?"

"Maybe the killer knew there was trace evidence on it, so he removed it and destroyed it?"

"You're very helpful."

"Aiming to please, love."

"In most cases, the simplest answer is the correct one," Linus mused aloud. "And the simplest explanation is that the shoe fell off while the killer was transporting the corpse and the killer didn't notice."

"So it's still out there somewhere?"

"Most likely." Linus set the shoe back down and turned for the door "Come on."

Karen folded her arms. "Come on where?"

"We need to go outside and look for it."

"Why?"

"It might have trace on it," Linus replied impatiently. "And its location might give us a clue about which airlock the killer used. *That* might lead us to something else. Coming?"

Karen sighed. "All right. But only because it's you asking, love. I don't put on silvery vac-suits for just anybody, you know."

A few minutes later, they were suited up and bouncing across the lunar landscape in a rover. The pitiless sun poured harsh light over them. The lunar day lasted about twenty-nine and a half Earth days, meaning it took the sun about two weeks to cross from horizon to horizon. Earth itself just seemed to sit there in the sky, going through phases just like the moon as seen from Earth. Linus, however, kept his eyes on where he was going. Rover accidents were rare—between the driver and the computer, very little could happen—but he didn't see that as a reason to tempt fate. It also gave him an excuse to keep the conversation to a minimum. Linus was very aware of Karen's silver-clad form in the seat next to him. It felt nice not to be alone, and nice to be alone with Karen. She was funny, she was pretty, she was intelligent, she was—

Linus set his mouth. There was no way he was going to entertain this sort of thing.

And why not? whispered a treacherous little voice. *You're almost fifty thousand miles away from Earth. Do whatever you want.*

He told the voice to shut up so he could drive.

They arrived at the crater lip without incident. The two of them clambered out of the rover, and Karen put her hands on her hips. Linus took a few breaths of metallic air and wished he could get a few lungfuls of *real* outdoor atmosphere, feel a real breeze against his face, maybe even run naked through a field of grass and flowers. Homesickness washed over him, and he suddenly understood the drunken frat boy who had taken off his helmet. Sometimes you just had to *try*, even when you knew it would end badly.

"*Where do we start looking?*" Karen asked, breaking into his reverie.

Linus gave himself a mental shake. "We know the shoe isn't in or around the crater," he said, "because we already looked there. But the drag mark pointed that way—" he gestured "—so let's try that way."

"*Just bring the rover,*" Karen said. "*I don't fancy walking all the way back.*"

With a few quick commands, Linus connected his obie with the rover's onboard computer and told the vehicle to stay a few meters behind him. Then he took a few experimental steps forward. The rover followed like an obedient dog.

"Forward!" he said. "The game is—"

"*I am not Dr. Watson,*" Karen growled. "*And I am* definitely *not a sidekick.*"

"Too bad," Linus said. "I've always wanted one."

"I'll kick your side, though, if you want."

Linus called up a navigational display to keep them going in a straight line. He and Karen took up positions four or five meters apart and moved forward, visually scanning the ground ahead of them. Smooth gray dust and misshapen rocks filled Linus's field of vision, and the steady hiss of air in his helmet made a comforting noise in the background. The rover followed behind them, silent as Eurydice on the heels of Orpheus. The blank faceplate on Karen's helmet only added to the eeriness of the situation.

"So what did you do last night?" Karen asked out of nowhere.

"Me?" Linus said.

"I don't see anyone else around, love."

"Nothing much. Ate a late supper, read for a while, went to bed."

"What did you read?"

"A romance novel. *Winds of Passion.*"

Karen laughed. *"No, really. What'd you read? I'm curious."*

"Psych book," Linus said. "Chapter on human behavior in dense populations."

"What's wrong? Have trouble sleeping?"

"It's practical application," Linus protested. He skirted a large rock, and the computer beeped a warning that he was straying from his course. "We're getting more people than we have room for up here, and it worries me."

"Me, too," Karen admitted. *"I've been able to keep up with being the only doctor so far, but I've seen the projections. By the end of next semester, I'll be overwhelmed if they don't bring in someone to help."*

"I had to fight hard for another deputy," Linus said. "The Mayor-President's gung-ho to get Luna City out of debt, but she doesn't have to directly deal with rising crime and violence. You might want to start demanding another doctor now."

"Already started that battle," Karen replied. *"I just hope I can win it."*

They continued forward. Twice Linus thought he saw something, only to realize it was a shoe-shaped rock. Karen halted, raising Linus's hopes, but she only squirmed inside her suit for a moment before resuming the search. After an hour of slow, careful walking, they found themselves within a few meters of an airlock. It was the one Noah had investigated as the murderer's most likely exit point. No shoe.

"You game to keep going?" Linus said. "There's another airlock up ahead. The killer may have used that one."

"Anything for a handsome cop who reads romances," Karen sighed. *"I'm batting my eyes, in case you were wondering."*

"I wasn't, but thanks for sharing that," Linus laughed, though he wondered if Karen was halfway serious. It was getting damned hard to read the situation. He'd have to sit down with her eventually and flat-out ask if she'd been flirting with any serious intent. It was the only way to know for sure.

Of course, if he were wrong, it'd be embarrassing all around and make their working relationship awkward. On the other hand, it was already growing more and more awkward by the moment.

They loped onward, past little domes and occasional vac-suited people wandering about on errands of their own. Linus wondered if they'd missed the shoe because someone had already picked it up without realizing it was the clue in a murder case. It might be worth his while to publicize what he was looking for, see if anyone came forward with the lost footwear like Cinderella's prince. Ahead, the antenna of Luna City's spaceport crept over the horizon, followed by the spaceport itself. A flare of white light caught Linus's attention, and he stopped to look up. A miniature tongue of flame rose up to the velvet sky bearing the rounded shape of the weekly shuttle to Tether Station. In a few hours it would dock with the station, take on passengers and cargo, then return to Luna City. Among those passengers would be the entertainment representatives who worried Mayor-President Pandey so much. Something itched at the back of Linus's mind, like an imp tickling his brain with a feather. He knew the sensation well—it meant he was missing something, and it was usually something obvious.

"*Listen, love,*" Karen said, "*much as I love being your sidekick, I have patients to see this afternoon and it's getting on toward lunch.*"

"Take the rover, then," Linus said absently. "I'm going to keep going. The next airlock's not that far ahead."

"*Just don't forget that you're taking me to Noah's show tonight,*" Karen reminded him. "*Are we having dinner first?*"

"Dinner?" Linus shook his head, not sure what she was talking about. "Dinner."

"*You know—that meal you eat between lunch and bedtime. Dinner.*"

"Oh. No. I'll be working. Dinner at my desk. You know how it goes." He couldn't take his eyes off the shuttle. It rushed across the sky like a demon fleeing an angel. "I'll meet you at the theater."

"*Fine, then.*" Karen jumped into the rover, wrenched it around, and drove away. Linus tore his eyes away from the sky and watched her go. Had he pissed her off? He couldn't think of what he might have said.

Itch itch itch. The imp at the back of his brain waved the feather some more. What was he missing? A shoe. Airlock. Drag mark. Close proximity to the site where the body had been dumped. No DNA entry in the immigration or security databases. He stood there, letting his mind wander a bit to see if it would connect with something. Metallic air hissed through his suit. Nothing.

Linus started walking again. He passed the airlock second closest to the dump site without seeing anything unusual. This part of the lunar surface received more traffic, and he kept finding more footprints and rover tracks, but no shoe. His stomach rumbled, reminding him it was now well past lunchtime.

And then he found it. A single brown loafer lying on the gray dust as if it were a completely normal, everyday object. Linus removed a holographic imager from his belt and made a scan of the immediate area, then gingerly picked up the shoe. It was dry and cracked, of course, and he quickly popped it into a sealed evidence bag. Linus looked at the bagged shoe, then at the airlock behind him. Why was the shoe *here* instead of between the first airlock and the body site? Had the killer used the airlock, taken the body in this direction, and changed his mind? But why? Transporting a body was risky enough without going in half a dozen different directions while you did it. Panic might have been involved, but it didn't seem likely. The killer would have had plenty of time to calm down while putting on the vac suit and cycling the airlock.

Linus looked down at the shoe again, then looked up into the impossibly black sky. The fiery streak of the shuttle was just barely visible in the distance.

And then he knew.

CHAPTER ELEVEN

Noah exited Xiao Yen Hall and the security offices therein with quick, firm steps that bounded only slightly in the lunar gravity. The Dome was as crowded as ever, with students clogging the paths like salmon in a river. Conversation mixed with shouts and laughter. Noah made a smart left turn outside, marched down a little path that ran alongside a bicycle rack, and stepped into a copse of trees. He looked around to make sure he was alone—or at least not visible—then buried his mouth in the crook of his elbow and yelled.

It was a trick he had picked up growing up in a crowded household where he shared a bedroom with two brothers, and where a cathartic yell would bring instant, unwanted attention. On this occasion, Noah had intended for the shout to be short and sharp, but once he got going, he couldn't seem to stop. Noah yelled and screamed and hollered and shouted into the soft fabric of his shirt until his vocal cords protested under the strain. He hadn't been on the moon for two days and already he'd been yanked into two murder investigations, gotten into a major fight with his roommate, messed up a corpse, been ordered onstage to do a show he'd barely had time to prepare for, and been falsely accused of carelessly processing a murder scene. What next? Maybe he should just get on the next shuttle and head for home. All of a sudden he wanted to hear his mother's voice, calm and soothing. The voice that made sickness feel better and childhood fear recede. It was stupid to stay in such a cold, hostile place when he could be with warm friends and loving family.

Noah slowly realized he was on his knees and his throat hurt. He stopped screaming and just knelt there on the ground, the dirt and wood mulch pressing lightly through the thin fabric of his trousers. Then he got up, dusted his knees, and made his way back to the path. He felt a little better. Time to get a little perspective. He was *used* to investigating murders. The show would be easy. Linus had made it clear that he didn't necessarily believe Gary's version of events.

Noah's hands knotted into fists. Gary Newburg. What the hell was up with him? The bastard had out-and-out *lied* about the investigation, blamed Noah for his own screw-ups. Noah tried to think of a reason for it and came up empty. He hadn't even *met* Gary until yesterday at the crater crime scene.

Well, he told himself, *you're an investigator. You'll just have to find out.*

Other priorities came first, though. Linus seemed to be handling the John Doe in the crater, and that left Noah free to devote his full energies to the murder of Viktor Riza. Noah checked the time. Ten o'clock. On a hunch, Noah loped to the train station and caught a tram back home to his apartment. He palmed the door open and strode into the living room.

Wade was sitting on the couch watching a vid-feed on the window screen. He shot Noah a startled glance and tensed visibly. Noah allowed himself a small, triumphant smile. Wade had been avoiding Noah, but he obviously figured

Noah was out for the day and had come back to the apartment. The idiot hadn't counted on Noah popping in unexpectedly.

"Hi," Noah said.

"Hey." Wade turned his gaze pointedly back to the vid-feed. Two robots were zapping at each other with laser weapons. Noah wondered what it would be like to have one of those puppies for real, then grabbed a hard ladderback chair from the kitchen area and faced Wade over the back of it.

"Got some questions to ask you," he said.

Wade didn't respond. He kept his eyes on the vid-feed, but Noah easily spotted the rigid jaw, the tense fingers.

"You tossed my stuff," Noah went on. "Not a great thing for a roommate to do."

"You mean like throwing my friends out in mid-fuck?"

Noah sighed. "We can go on about this all day if we want. I probably won't convince you that I was right for wanting to sleep in my own apartment and you probably won't convince me that you were right for heaving my stuff into the hallway. But you know that Viktor Riza was murdered, right?"

Zap! Pow! One of the robots exploded in a shower of sparks.

"Yeah," Wade muttered. "I heard about it on the newsfeeds. You must feel great about tossing him out like that. He'd probably still be alive if it weren't for you."

A stab of guilt knifed Noah's stomach, but he refused to rise to the bait. "I blame his killer. The one who gave him the overdose of Blue and held him underwater at the fish ponds." Noah paused. "Where'd he get the Blue overdose, Wade? From you?"

Now Wade turned away from the vid-feed. His face was pale. "What the hell are you talking about?"

"Two convictions for possession of Blue, Wade," Noah said. "And oh yeah—a little stash hidden the closet." He cocked his fingers like a laser pistol. "Zap! Three strikes and you're out."

"You went through my closet?" Wade said in outrage.

"*Our* closet, roomie. So I don't even need a warrant."

"You can't prove that ampoule was mine. It could be Jake's."

"I found your fingerprints all over it," Noah lied. He hadn't processed the ampoule yet—the meeting with Linus had blasted all thoughts of evidence work out of his head. The ampoule was, in fact, still nestled in Noah's pocket, protected by an evidence bag. It made a hard lump in his pocket. "I didn't find Jake's prints. Once I make an official report, Wade, you're history. Hell, you'll be so far gone, you'll be *mythology*."

And Wade's bravado evaporated. He collapsed backward onto the couch and his lower lip trembled. Noah wondered if he'd burst into tears. It happened with macho guys more often than most people thought.

"Please," Wade whispered at last. "Please don't."

"Don't what?" Noah asked calmly. "Turn you in? Why wouldn't I, Wade? You're a criminal, and catching criminals is my job. Besides, you threw all my stuff out into the hall. Why should I do something nice for an asshole?"

"It'll ruin me," he said. "And it'll kill my mom. God, I worked so hard to get into Luna U. I've only got one more semester before I graduate." He looked up at Noah, his long face looking fragile as antique china. "Look, I'm sorry about throwing your stuff around. I'll do anything you want. I'll move out. I'll—"

"—tell me who your supplier is?" Noah finished.

That caught Wade off-guard. "What?"

Noah leaned in and down, almost in Wade's face. The chair tipped forward, but the light gravity let Noah keep his balance. "Who's your supplier? Who sells you Blue?"

"How do you know I'm not making it myself?" Wade shot back with some of his old bravado.

Because you asked that question, Noah thought. But he said, "Because dealers don't usually use. Cough up the name, Wade, and I *might* forget I found your stash."

"Shouldn't I have a lawyer or something?" Wade temporized.

"If you want. Though that'll mean I'll have to tell my superior why you want one, and I doubt *he'll* be willing to forget about the Blue."

"Look, I'm just . . . I'm just nervous about telling, okay? I don't want him to come after me."

So the dealer was a man. "I won't mention you to him," Noah said. "No point. Now quit stalling and *tell me*."

Wade pursed his lips and refused to meet Noah's stare. "I don't know his real name, I swear. Everyone calls him Indigo. Probably a color thing—indigo, blue. Ha ha."

"Ha ha. Description?"

"I dunno. A little taller than me. Short brown hair. White guy."

"Age?"

"Late twenties, I think."

"And he's a student."

Wade shrugged. "I suppose. I don't make conversation with him."

"How do you hook up with him?"

"He hangs out in Dai Memorial Park in the Dome. It's not hard to find him out there."

Noah took a shot in the dark. "How well does he know Bredda Meese?"

"I think they fuck around sometimes," Wade said, "but it's not exclusive or anything."

"No kidding," Noah said. "Okay. I won't tell about your stash. But you better quit using, especially if you're going to live with a cop."

"I didn't know you were a cop when you moved in," Wade muttered. "Shit."

The doorbell rang. Wade remained on the couch with his attention on the exploding vid-screen, so Noah opened the door. Ilene was standing in the corridor holding a largish box. Noah blinked, slightly dumbfounded. Her lilac perfume filled the hallway. He didn't remember giving Ilene his address. Maybe she'd seen it at the housing department. Not that it wasn't nice to see her. It just felt out-of-context seeing her just after he'd finished interrogating his roommate.

"Uh, hi," he said.

"Aren't you going to invite me in?" she asked, batting her eyelashes with silly coquettishness. She held up the box. "I brought you a present."

"Oh. Uh, right. Come in."

She did so, and Noah noted with some relief that Wade had vanished into the bedroom and shut the door. No need for introductions, then. Ilene set the cardboard box down on the counter next to the sink.

"So how've you been?" she asked.

"Busy," he said weakly. "Busy beyond belief."

Her forehead furrowed. "Classes don't start until next week. What have—oh! You're probably investigating those murders."

"Yeah. Got sucked right into it. In fact, I should probably—"

"Well, this'll give you a little break," Ilene said as if he hadn't spoken. "Open the box."

Noah looked at her for a moment, then put his hands on the box lid. It was chilly. He opened the flaps and a small cloud of cool mist puffed up. Inside the box was a series of clear polymer bags, each designed to keep the contents cold. He pulled one out and held it up. There was something hard and white inside.

"Most people bring flowers," Ilene said, "but hey—I've always been different."

Light dawned. "Fish!" Noah said. "It's fish."

"Just like I promised. Trout, tilapia, and a couple pieces of salmon. I even had them cleaned and scaled for you."

"This is great, Ilene!" Noah rummaged around in the box. There was enough to feed a dozen people. "Wow. What can I do to repay you?"

"Ticket," she replied promptly. "For your show tonight?"

"Already done. It's waiting for you at the box office."

She leaned forward and kissed him. Her mouth was warm and insistent. Noah hesitated, then put an arm around her. Ilene moved into his embrace and slid a hand through his hair. Noah shivered and brought his own fingers up to touch the smooth skin of her face. Ilene's breasts pressed into Noah's chest. Their lips parted, and Ilene's eyes grew bright with anticipation. She let a hand drift across Noah's shoulders and down the muscles of his arms.

"You're so hard," she whispered, her breath brushing his ear. "So sexy."

"My roommate's in the bedroom," he said, though his groin was tightening. He knew she could feel it—her body was moving against his.

"I don't share," she replied with a small smile. Her right hand slipped lower, plucking at the waistband of his trousers. "Do you think he'll come out soon?"

Noah swallowed, feeling both aroused and uncomfortable. Growing up a large household had made him hypersensitive to privacy issues, and he didn't relish the idea of Wade getting an eyeful. But Ilene's warm hands and soft lips were making him wonder why he cared.

"I don't know," Noah temporized. "He might."

Ilene's fingers dipped lower and found what they were looking for. Noah inhaled sharply as she massaged him with gentle intensity. Almost on their own, his hands slid around the curves of her breasts. She slitted her eyes like a contented cat and kissed him again. Her fingers continued to move. Noah realized he was panting even as the kiss continued. His heart sang in his ears and Ilene's silky, skilled massage increased in speed and intensity. Noah ran his hands over her breasts, through her soft hair, down her back. He felt as if he could pull himself into her, pull *through* her. His body tensed, ready to burst, ready to—

She pulled away so quickly Noah stumbled. He regained his balance, still panting slightly.

"You were right," she said. "Your roommate might come out."

For a moment, Noah considered picking her up and planting her on the coffee table, Wade or no Wade. Then reason returned and he nodded, not quite trusting himself to speak. His groin ached.

"But let me adjust that for you," Ilene said in a low voice. She gently twitched Noah's waistband back into place and, with a quick tug, moved his erection so it wasn't so noticeable. "We can do a better job with that later, big guy. And I do mean *big* guy."

Noah realized he was blushing hotly. "It's not—I'll just— I mean . . ."

"Enjoy the fish. I'll see you after the show." She kissed him lightly on the cheek and vanished out the front door. Noah looked after her, wondering what the hell had just happened. Aching hardness continued to grip his groin, and he glanced at the bathroom. The door had a lock on it, and he could get a few minutes of guaranteed private time in there. Then he shook off the idea. Experience had taught him that it would be better to wait, that finishing by himself what Ilene had started would lessen his desire to see her that night.

But it would be a damned long wait. On the other hand, maybe that was a good thing.

The bedroom door opened. Wade went into the bathroom without looking at Noah and clicked the door shut. Wade. Viktor Riza's death. Noah had people to see, a crime to solve. And after that, he had a show to put on. Thoughts about Ilene would have to wait.

Noah left the apartment, his mind going over what he had learned from Wade. Bredda Meese was Indigo's lover, and Indigo was Wade's supplier of Blue. Wade, Bredda, and Viktor had been taking Blue and having sex mere hours before Viktor's death. There had to be a connection. Noah had to admit that a drug dealer sounded pretty good as a murder suspect, then forced himself to stay open-minded. It would be a mistake to make assumptions without proof.

A short train ride brought Noah back to Dai Memorial Park in the Dome, where he did a quick visual scan of the area. People wandering, trees growing, water rushing. Someone had mowed the grassy areas, and the smell of fresh-cut lawn permeated the air. Noah called up Bredda's picture on his monocle again and continued checking the park. No sign of Bredda, and Wade's description of Indigo fit half the students currently in the Dome. Still, it was the beginning of a new semester, and it seemed likely Indigo would be out and about, meeting up with old customers and finding new ones. Noah thought a moment, then ducked into Xiao Yen Hall, where the security offices were located. He emerged a moment later wearing a light, flesh-colored glove on one hand and an earplug in one ear. A small pistol nestled in his pocket, and he carried what looked like a giant toy gun. The latter consisted of length of plastic pipe with a stock on it. Noah scanned the Dome again, and his eye fell on two young men walking down one of the paths, engaged in serious conversation. With a subtle gesture, he pointed his glove at them.

"... *have you known?*" said a male voice in his ear.

"*Since we were in grade school,*" replied a second. "*Geez, Rick, I'm your best friend. How could you think I wouldn't know?*"

Pause. "*I guess I didn't think about it. It's just . . . I was afraid to tell you.*"

"*Why? It's nothing to be ashamed of. Takes a little getting used to, but not a big deal. Long as you don't try to convert me.*"

Rick snorted and kicked at a rock. "*Not likely. I think you have to be born like this.*" Another pause. "*So it really doesn't bother you?*"

"*Nope.*"

"*What a relief,*" Rick sighed. "*Not everyone would stay friends with an admitted Barry Manilow fan. You know, there was talk of cloning him back in—*"

Noah dropped his hand and the voices faded. The directional mike in the glove was working perfectly. And as long as the conversations took place in a public spot like the Dome, he didn't have to worry about warrants or being accused of invading privacy. Legally, there *was* no privacy out here.

Noah picked out a bench, sat down, and kept a lookout for Bredda and brown-haired Caucasian males in their late twenties. Of the latter he saw plenty, though none of them were engaged in conversations of any interest. None of them mentioned the word Indigo or talked to anyone who called them by that name.

An hour passed, then two. Noah was getting hungry and he had to go to the bathroom. He grimaced. One disadvantage of not having a partner on a stakeout was that you occasionally had to leave the scene for biology breaks, and Murphy's law ensured that the moment you popped into a restroom, the person you were hunting would stroll down the street. Noah sat and waited, growing more uncomfortable as time passed. His bladder began to pulse, and it was hard to sit still. He shot a speculative glance at the copse of trees where he'd screamed into his sleeve. Maybe he could duck back there and . . .

Bad idea. He didn't know what the penalty for indecent exposure was on Luna City, but he doubted it would be any fun to find out, especially for a deputy.

Noah got up and drifted toward Xiao Yen Hall, trying to keep an unobtrusive eye on the park as he went. He was about to dash up the stairs into the building when something tugged at the corner of his eye. Less than thirty meters away, under the shade of an ash tree, was Bredda Meese. Her sharp, angular features matched her picture, and her spiky hair stood out like an angry pine tree. She was talking to a rather younger man—a freshman or sophomore, Noah judged. He had black hair and was too young to be Indigo. Who was *he?* Noah's heart raced, and choices flashed through his mind. He could try to grab Bredda and interrogate her right now. He could wait and follow her. He could bide his time and see if Indigo showed up.

He could run inside and use the restroom faster than he had ever done in his life.

Why does this kind of thing always happen when you have to hit the toilet? he thought, trying not to dance around on the building steps.

He discarded the restroom idea—too easy for Bredda to wander away while he was gone. Instead, he went back to his bench and sat down, bringing his head lower than the joggers, walkers, and lopers on the pathway, partially hiding him from view in case Bredda recognized him. He set his obie to record, then pointed his gloved hand at Bredda and her companion. Their voices instantly sprang into his earplug.

"*. . . so much better with Blue,*" Bredda was saying. "*You just go on and on. It's the biggest mind-fuck ever.*" She put her hand on the young man's shoulder in a gesture that reminded Noah of Ilene.

"*I've heard it's addictive,*" the young man said slowly. "*I mean, it's probably fun, but—*"

"*It's only addictive if you use it too much,*" Bredda countered. "*And it makes a woman* really *appreciative.*"

"*Is it expensive?*"

"*Don't worry about that, Todd. I can get you a taste for nothing.*" Bredda leaned in to Todd's ear and whispered something the microphone didn't pick up.

Run away, Todd, Noah thought. *Run far and fast.*

Todd, however shuddered, then flushed and grinned. "*Yeah?*" he said. "*You'd do that?*"

"*Oh yeah. But only with a guy on Blue. You won't believe how it'll blow your mind.*" She backed up a step. "*But if you don't want to, I'll understand. I know this other guy who—*"

"*No,*" Todd said quickly. He stepped forward and put an arm around her. "*I'm game if you are.*"

"*Then let me talk to my supplier,*" she said with a grin. "*He's just a phone call away.*"

Click. Pieces fell into place with a precision that set Noah's heart to pounding. This was what he loved. This was the *good* stuff, the moments that made the hours of scut work worthwhile. Noah's mind worked furiously as Bredda raised a hand to her ear, a common gesture for people making a call through an obie. Blue was highly addictive, and no matter what Bredda said, it didn't take long for the jonesing to set in. Three or four uses brought on strong cravings. Seven or eight guaranteed a full-blown addiction that was harder to break. A few people got hooked after a single shot. And this was clearly Bredda's angle. She—probably at Indigo's instigation—tempted new customers into her bed, but only if they used Blue. This provided Indigo with a steady stream of customers and gave both of them a tidy cash flow.

The problem with Bredda and Indigo's setup was the transient nature of Luna City's population. Eventually most of their addicted customers would graduate, transfer, or drop out of school, forcing Bredda and Indigo to continually recruit new buyers. Noah wondered if they tried to push Blue on women. He shook his head. Probably not. When it came to Blue, male addicts outnumbered females by something like ten to one.

Viktor, Noah realized, may have figured out this little scheme when he ran into Indigo with Bredda and Crysta the night of the murder. Maybe Viktor demanded a cut. Or maybe he just got pissed at being manipulated a step closer to addiction. After Crysta abandoned the group, Viktor and Bredda had gone down to the fishpond. Indigo went with them, or maybe he followed them. Viktor got angry at Indigo. They fought, but Viktor was already high on Blue. Indigo forced more Blue down Viktor's throat and drowned him, probably with Bredda's help.

Bredda was subvocalizing and the mike couldn't pick up what she was saying. Noah shifted again, trying not to think of the bathroom. If he left, Bredda might take Todd to meet Indigo somewhere else, and Noah would lose them.

He wished he had thought to grab a tracer from the Security office. It would be easy enough to plant one on Bredda and track her that way, but Noah, idiot that he was, hadn't thought of it until it was too late. So instead he had wait.

Not long after Bredda finished her call, a good-looking man in his late twenties strolled up to Todd and Bredda. Noah automatically noted his physical characteristics. Five or six centimeters shy of two meters tall. Hair a medium shade of brown. Eye color indistinguishable from this distance. Late twenties. Medium-to-stocky build. Maybe ninety kilograms, Earth weight. He fit Wade's description of Indigo, but that didn't necessarily mean . . .

"Todd, this is Indigo," Bredda said. *"How about a Blue sample for a friend of a friend?"*

A wide, friendly smile spread across Indigo's face. *"You got it, babe. Let's go someplace a little more private, hey?"*

That was enough to make an arrest. Noah got up and followed the trio as they turned to move down one of the walkways. As they walked, Noah pressed a hand to his ear.

"Obie, call Linus Pavlik," he said. "High priority."

Linus came on the line almost instantly. *"What's going on, Noah?"*

"I'm following two suspects in the death of Viktor Riza," he said. "I recorded them planning a drug sale so I've got enough to make an arrest, but I need backup."

"Where are you?"

"Dai Park. The suspects are leaving the scene, though, and I don't know where they're going."

Slight pause. *"There's no one in the Security office at the moment but me, and I can't leave it unstaffed. Nearest on-duty deputy is Marks, and she's ten, maybe fifteen minutes away. Can you wait that long?"*

"I don't know." Noah dodged around a group of chattering freshman and brushed against some bushes. Twigs scratched his bare arms. Bredda, Indigo, and Todd were getting farther away. "I'm afraid I'll lose them."

"Stay on them," Linus said. *"Marks should be there soon."*

Noah broke into a loping trot, trying not to bound above the crowd and draw attention to himself. He cursed his idiocy. Any fool would have known to call for reinforcements the moment Bredda showed herself. Instead he had gaped like a first-year rookie.

"Noah Skyler?" came a new voice in his ear. *"This is Valerie Marks. I'm tracking your signal and I'm on my way. ETA eight minutes."*

"Thanks," Noah replied. "I'm keeping the suspects in sight as best I can."

The trio vanished around the corner of a building into a wide alley. Noah took advantage of the situation and vaulted over the heads of several people so he could catch up. The people shied away. Noah hit the ground and jumped again, feeling like a superhero.

"Newbie!" someone shouted.

"Slow down!" yelled someone else. "You might hurt someone."

Noah ignored them. His third leap took him to the corner. He tried to halt so he could peer around the building, then realized he was still moving. His own momentum shoved him forward, forcing him to take another leap or fall down. Another building loomed ahead of him. It was surrounded by a fierce-looking hedge. Noah pushed sideways when he hit the ground. His ankle turned, and he tumbled into the alley. Cement scraped his elbows and tiny bits of stone tore at his knees. He bounced once, twice, then fetched up flat on his back. A fire escape made a lattice down the side of one of the buildings above him. Burning pain trickled over the scraped parts of Noah's anatomy. Warmth ran down his upper lip and he realized his nose was bleeding. How had *that* happened?

A trio of heads poked into view and looked down at him. Bredda, Todd, and Indigo. Shit. No hiding now.

"What the hell?" Indigo said.

Noah started to spring to his feet, then thought the better of it. He scrambled carefully upright. "Bredda Meese?" he said.

"Who are you?" she shot back.

"Noah Skyler, Security. You and your friend here are under arrest for—"

Bredda leaped straight up into the air. Halfway up the side of the building, she caught the fire escape and flipped onto it with the skill of an acrobat. Noah barely had time to register any of this because Indigo took a sudden swing.

Noah hated fighting. Still, it was part of being a cop, and Noah had never been one to shrink from necessity. His arm reflexively came up and blocked the punch even as he stiff-armed Indigo with the other. Indigo flew backward under the light gravity with a surprised look on his face. Todd gaped. Noah snatched the odd pistol out of its holster at his side and aimed up at Bredda, who was already gathering for another leap from the fire escape. He squeezed the trigger. The pistol coughed like a hippopotamus blowing a spitwad. A pellet spurted upward and pinged against the fire escape. Orange dye splashed over the black latticework. Bredda leaped clear of the fire escape and Noah fired again. The second pellet caught her in mid-flight. An orange flower splashed over her back, her neck, and her hair. The arc of her jump carried her over the top of the building and out of sight. Noah spun in time to see Indigo bounding down the alley. He took more careful aim and fired one more time. Orange dye splattered liberally over Indigo's retreating back. Noah holstered the pistol with a sigh, then remembered Todd. The young man was staring at Noah, his hands half-raised.

"Am I under arrest?" he asked.

"No," Noah said. "Get out of here. And stay away from Blue. These two were trying to get you hooked."

"Yessir," Todd said. He turned and fled.

Noah checked his scrapes with a grimace of pain. A drop of blood fell from his nose and fell slowly toward his shirt. Noah back away, and the droplet landed neatly on the ground, barely making a splat. Another drop started downward. Shit. He looked up at the orange splash on the fire escape. At least the day hadn't been a total loss.

An Asian woman in a brown deputy uniform rounded the corner in a hurry. Acne scars marked her face, and her hair had been buzzed short. "Noah Skyler?" she demanded, screeching to a halt in front of him.

"That's me," he said. "Before you ask, yes—they got away."

"Why didn't you wait for me?" Valerie Marks demanded.

"I . . . couldn't wait. Circumstances changed." He felt his face grow hot and prayed she wouldn't press for details. Although Noah lied to suspects all the time, he couldn't seem to do it well when it came to his colleagues. Not any better than he did with his family. His mother, in particular, was adept in picking up when Noah was stretching the truth, so he had given up trying to lie to her before he turned twelve.

"Are you all right?" Valerie said. "You're bleeding."

He touched his nose and winced. "I'm fine. Shit."

"No need to swear," Valerie Marks said primly. "We should set an example."

"Uh . . . right."

"So what happened?"

"I rounded corner into the alley and there they were," he said, keeping his tone even. "They knew something was up the minute they saw me. We fought, they ran, I fired. At least the suspects are marked, even if they got away."

Valerie nodded. "It's only a matter of time. Kind of hard to hide indelible dye, and as the Chief likes to say, 'Where are they going to go?' I'll put out an alert. You better get those scrapes taken care of."

"Thanks," he said, and checked his watch. A small pang hit his stomach. "Uh oh."

Valerie, who had pressed her finger to her ear, looked up at him. "What's wrong?"

"I'm running late for my show and I *really* have to go to the bathroom."

Several minutes later, Noah limped into the apartment he shared with Jake and Wade. His nose had stopped bleeding, but his cuts and scrapes still burned, and he must have twisted his ankle worse than he thought—it hurt quite a lot.

How the hell had he twisted it in low-g, anyway? He must have hit the ground just right. Or maybe that should be "just wrong." At least the moon's gravity made it easier to walk with the injury. Jake perched on the couch playing a flat-screen video game. The screen showed a lush prehistoric jungle. Jake waved his hands in complicated gestures, and a small carnosaur jumped over a log to dodge away from a *Tyrannosaurus rex*. The tyrannosaur roared in frustration.

"I haven't seen that game in years," Noah said. "I didn't even know they still made it."

Jake glanced at him, then pointed at the screen. The scene froze. "I loved dinosaurs when I was a kid and held on to my copy. It's still fun, sometimes." He blinked. "Jesus, what happened to you? Are you okay?"

"I'll be all right. Had a dust-up with a pair of suspects."

Jake's eyes went round. "Really? What happened?"

"It's an ongoing case. I can't really talk about it." Noah limped into the bathroom and pulled off his shirt to examine the damage. Both elbows scraped, nose half-clogged with dried blood, small bruise on his forearm where he'd blocked Indigo's punch. His ankle still hurt.

"Autodoc," he said, "I need help."

"Is this an emergency?" asked the computer.

"No."

"Please face the medicine cabinet and remain stationary."

Noah obeyed, and a green bar of light ran up and down his body. After a moment, the computer beeped.

"Diagnosis: small contusion on right forearm, slight inflammation of right ankle, scrapes on both elbows, ruptured blood vessels in nasal cavity partially healed. Treatment: clean scrapes with soap and water. Treatment: soak contusions in hot water. Treatment: analgesic to prevent pain and swelling. Treatment: mild antibiotic to prevent infection."

Noah held out his arm. A mechanical arm that ended in a wrist cuff extruded from the medicine chest on the wall and clamped gently around Noah's wrist. A slight hiss indicated the drugs had entered his system. The pain lessened considerably. Noah pulled off the rest of his clothes and stepped into the shower. The hot water loosened his stiffening muscles and he stood beneath it until his fingers shriveled into pink prunes. Wrapping a towel around his waist, he crossed the hall into the bedroom. His duffel bag lay in the corner. Both beds were made, and Noah made a mental note to pick up a sleeping bag as he rummaged through his duffel for something decent to wear on stage.

Jake poked his head into the room. "You sure you can't talk about it? I'm dying, here. Was it a big shoot-out?"

"Nothing that dramatic. I fell a couple of times chasing two people. I cornered them both. One of them ran and the other took a swing at me. He got away, too, but I marked him. Now I have to get ready for tonight."

"Oh yeah, your show." Jake leaned against the doorframe. "You nervous?"

"Strangely, I'm not." Noah came up with a bright blue shirt and a pair of dark trousers. They'd do. Most of his clothes, including his costumes, were in storage back on Earth. Fortunately, his show didn't really require much in the way of special clothes. He dropped the towel and pulled them on. "I think I've been too busy for nerves."

"What do you do, anyway?"

"Vaudeville revival. I make with some jokes, tell a few stories, maybe sing a little."

Jake shuddered, his dark eyes looking haunted. "I could never do that. I'd be scared that I'd forget the words or screw up in some other way with all those people watching. How do you do it?"

"By remembering what the audience wants." Noah sat on one of the beds to fasten his shoes. "They're not waiting for me to screw up—they want a good show. They're rooting for me, really."

"You ever get a bad audience?"

"Oh, yeah." Noah laughed. "One time a bunch of drunks started throwing nuts at the stage. I tried to make a joke out of it, but they just got worse. I finished the story I was telling really fast and got off the stage. The manager was pissed at me, but I told him I wasn't going to risk taking a peanut in the eye for him." He stood up and brushed the wrinkles out of the shirt. "How do I look?"

Jake made a frame with his hands and examined Noah through it with exaggerated care. "Pretty good. No bruises showing. What time's the show start?"

"Eight. I need to be there by seven, which gives me"—he checked his obie—"an hour. Just enough time for supper."

"I saw all the fish in the refrigerator and freezer. Where'd it come from?"

"My . . . uh, friend. Her name's Ilene Hatt."

"Ilene *Hatt*? As in—"

"Yeah. Them."

"Shit, man—you hit the gravy train. Hold on to her!"

Noah frowned. "Isn't it supposed to be the woman who's looking for a wealthy husband?"

"Who gives a shit? I'd be a kept man any day."

The phrase *kept man* made Noah feel suddenly strange, off-balance. He decided to change the subject. "Hey, you know how to cook fish? I'm not good at it."

"Yeah, I can cook. Wade sucks at it, but I'm not bad."

"Cool. How about I provide the food and you make supper?"

Jake agreed to this, and Noah watched his roommate put together a quick batter of beer and breadcrumbs. He dragged several fillets through it and dropped them into smoking hot oil, where they crackled and hissed. They ate on the packing crate, dipping the hot, crisp pieces into malt vinegar.

"You'll have to teach me how to do that," Noah said when the last bite had disappeared. "At home I eat out a lot, but that'll break the bank up here."

"Unless you get your rich girlfriend to treat you."

"Uh . . . yeah. Hey, where's Wade, anyway?"

Jake shrugged. "Haven't seen him lately. He comes and goes. I don't really pay close attention."

Noah helped clear the table, thanked Jake for the cooking, and headed down to the Dai Theater. He arrived exactly on time, and Judy Roberts, the stage manager, favored him with a curt nod at his promptness, and showed him to a tiny dressing room. A student whose name Noah didn't catch carefully slathered makeup on his face and hands and combed his auburn hair. When she was about halfway done, Wesley Yard popped into the room.

"I came across a couple glitches with the lighting," he said, "but they're fixed now. Everything should run perfectly."

Noah thought back to the debacle of the tech rehearsal and suppressed a grimace. Wesley's words didn't fill him with confidence. Wesley sketched a hesitant wave at Noah and disappeared.

The makeup artist, meanwhile, gave Noah's a hair a final flick, pronounced it "smashing," and left as well. Noah checked his watch. Quarter to eight. He wanted to venture onto the stage and peek at the audience, but restrained himself—not only was it unprofessional, it was bad luck. Besides, he had to figure out his lineup.

Noah pulled his monocle around and called up a newsfeed to skim the latest. A story about the John Doe now carried a computer-generated image of his face. Anyone who might know him was asked to call Security. Noah studied the image with interest, failed to recognize the individual, and continued reading the feeds. Back in the States on Earth, President Fred Bachman was trying to muscle another peace agreement through southeast Asia.

Yeah, good luck with that, Noah thought.

Three U.S. drug companies had successfully lobbied for legislation to open up various parts of South America to their market. A survey of Luna City occupations had turned up the fact that Luna had the lowest number of lawyers per capita of anywhere in the world—or solar system. Had to be a joke there somewhere.

Noah continued reading, falling into an old rhythm. First the government headlines, then a couple features, then editorials, if he had time. The jokes would write themselves, if he just let the words flow. The storytelling part of the show would have to be old, comfortable material, since he hadn't had time to rehearse anything new. "Paul Bunyan" was a good one, as was the German version of Cinderella.

Judy Roberts poked her head into the dressing room. "We're ready for you backstage."

Noah rose to follow her. Showtime.

CHAPTER TWELVE

Dr. Karen Fang waited in the theater lobby. She watched the people filing in and waited. She checked her fingernail watch and waited some more. She tapped her foot and waited yet again. *Technically*, Linus wasn't late. *Technically*, curtain for Noah's show was set for eight o'clock, and it was barely a quarter of. But although Karen could be perfectly patient when it came to examining a patient or running tests, she was decidedly *im*patient when it came to her social life. People who showed up late to dinner parties sent her around the bend. Friends who arrived tardy at parties drove her loony. And blokes who were late for dates . . .

Karen firmly tamped down that train of thought. This wasn't a date. At least, not as far as Linus knew. They were just two friends going to see a show together. And afterward, they would get a drink together, and Karen would have a nice talk with Linus about sending their relationship in a new direction.

Or maybe she would say something now.

People moved through the lobby, laughing and chatting. Most were students. The show was free to them. Professors and researchers paid a nominal fee. Visitors and tourists paid exorbitant rates. Noah was a new performer, a new face, and that always meant a heavy turnout. Karen, for example, had never been a fan of the vaudeville revival, but here she was. She supposed the theater was perfect for Noah's kind of show. Red carpet and wall hangings gave the place a hushed, old-world elegance Karen liked very much. Carefully tended green plants hugged the walls. Ticket-sellers—people instead of computer terminals—sat in glass booths. Very posh to look at, but not particularly fascinating when you were waiting for a particular someone. Karen checked her fingernail again. Ten minutes to curtain. Where the hell was—

"Linus Pavlik, reporting for escort duty," he said next to her.

Karen's heart jumped deliciously in her chest and she turned to face Linus with a smile of greeting. Genuine gladness at his presence flooded her.

"Hoy, love," she said, and stood on tiptoe to give him a peck. His cheek had that wonderful male smell, a combination of shaved skin and a tiny bit of cologne. He wore a button-down shirt open at the neck and dark slacks, and a few curls of chest hair peeped over the line of his collar. Karen suppressed a desire to wind them around her fingers and instead contented herself with looking at him.

"What?" he said.

She paused for a single heartbeat. "Nothing," she said. "Let's go in."

"I have something to tell you," he said with a small smile.

"Oh? What's that?"

"I'll tell you when we get inside."

"That's a cheat," she said. "Tell me now."

"Not knowing heightens the experience," he said.

She gave him a playful smack on one solid shoulder. He offered her his arm in response, and they joined the shuffle of people heading inside. Their tickets sent them to the center of the fourth row. Linus seated her with an automatic gallantry she knew he had learned in the Marines. The stage in front of them was bare except for a plain wooden stool and a small table with a pitcher and a glass of water on it. Karen glanced at Linus as he sat down beside her and experienced a delightful flutter.

It was only recently that she had realized how attractive Linus was. Stealth-handsome, she called it. She couldn't put her finger on the exact qualities. His dark hair was going silver, but it still contrasted sharply with his gray eyes. His nose, taken by itself, looked too large until you put it together with his mouth and eyes, and then it seemed strong and masculine. His shoulders were broad and powerful, his build square and reassuring. When the light caught him just right, as it did now, something in his face shifted from merely decent to surprisingly stunning. Linus would never turn heads the way Noah did, but that made it all the better—he could stay Karen's secret.

It wasn't just his looks, of course. Linus exuded a quiet strength and competence that made Karen feel like she didn't need to be so damned smart and good at her job all the time, as if she could be a human being instead of the ultra-proficient Chief of Medical Facilities in Luna City. She felt comfortable around Linus, no bullshit desired or required.

Karen also couldn't put an exact time or date on the realization that she was half in love with Linus Pavlik, but once she *had* realized it, she saw no reason not to tell him.

Except fear of rejection.

Karen had been married three times—divorced twice, and widowed once. Most people, she mused, would be soured on the idea of entering into another relationship, but Karen always kept the philosophy that you never knew until you tried.

The downside was that sometimes a try bit you in the ass.

"Any idea what Noah's going to do tonight?" Linus asked. His voice was low and sweet. Around them, the audience was settling into place, muttering to itself like a monster settling into its cave.

"Not knowing heightens the experience," she said.

"Ha ha," he said.

"Listen, love," Karen said. Her heart was beating fast and her mouth was dry. "There's something I wanted to ask you about, but I'm not sure how—"

"I know where our John Doe came from," Linus said abruptly.

Karen bolted upright and turned to face him, all thoughts of relationships driven out of her head. "You do? Where?"

"He was blown out of an airlock."

"I hope you can do better than that, love," she said with menace.

"Let me back up." His face was alight with enthusiasm now. "I was outside, following the evidence trail and thinking about our victim. He wasn't in any Luna City identification database. It was as if he had never existed here. And then I realized it was because he *didn't* exist here."

"Go on," she said. "You're clearly enjoying drawing this out. Just make sure you finish before the curtain rises or I'll drag you into the coatroom and beat it out of you."

"The victim wasn't in any of the Luna City databases because he never entered Luna City. He was blown out of an airlock, all right. But it wasn't a Luna City airlock. It was the airlock of a shuttle."

The solution landed on Karen like a second shoe hitting the floor. She smacked herself on the forehead. "I'm an idiot," she said. "Why didn't I think of that?"

"Because you weren't outside watching a shuttle come in for landing. It even explains the missing shoe and the bone Noah broke."

Most of the audience was seated and the talk was growing hushed. A small part of Karen wondered if Noah was standing backstage and if he felt nervous. "Go on. I assume you'll explain how the body arrived at the dump site even though the shuttles don't fly over that part of the landscape."

"That's what threw me, too," Linus admitted. "Except sometimes they *do* fly over that crater—if the pilot makes a mistake."

"A mistake," she echoed.

"Every so often a pilot gets the math wrong and the shuttle overshoots the landing pad. It's rare, but it does happen. In such a case, the pilot has to flip the shuttle around with the maneuvering jets and fire the main booster to reverse course. At the moment the shuttle changed direction, the killer blew an airlock. John Doe's body was still traveling in the shuttle's original direction, so it continued going that way while the shuttle reversed. The net effect was to fling the body clear of the airlock. No one saw it happen because the shuttle was well past any witnesses at the landing site. You wouldn't see the body fly out unless you were looking at the shuttle with binoculars. No one was."

"The body landed in the crater," Karen said, picking up the thread. "That's when all the bones were broken. But what about the missing shoe and the bone Noah broke? I mean, without an atmosphere to create drag, the shoe should have traveled right along with the body, even if it came off. It wouldn't change course in a vacuum."

"There's a communication antenna between the crater and the spot where I think the body was ejected. John Doe's leg hit the antenna, which knocked the shoe off and sent it in a different direction. The impact cracked the bone partway through, and Noah broke it off the rest of the way. When the body landed, it skidded, creating what we *thought* was a drag mark. We might have realized sooner that it was an impact mark instead if it hadn't been partially obscured by all those footprints. But now we have it."

"Brilliant!" Karen said. She started to grab him in a hug, then thought the better of it. "So what's the next step? We still don't know who he is."

"Well, Hector found a file on the victim's obie that had been modified six months ago, so we know John Doe was alive then. All we have to do is check the station's records and see if any shuttles overshot in the last six months. Once we know which shuttle overshot, we'll have our primary crime scene."

The audience was growing restless. Karen glanced at her fingernail. Five after eight. The show was running behind. Normally this would have annoyed her, but at the moment she couldn't have cared less.

"How many shuttles operate between Tether Station and Luna?" she asked.

Linus grinned. "Only two. And one of them is currently sitting on the landing pad at the port. We have a fifty-fifty chance that it's the right one."

"Shouldn't we get down there right now?"'

"We? You're a doctor, not a detective."

"You don't think I'm going to sit this out," she said. "Besides, you'll need an assistant, and Noah is working on the Riza case."

"I have other deputies," Linus said, but she could see he was teasing.

"Perhaps I should schedule your physical for tomorrow morning," she said. "You know—the one you're required to take at *my* discretion. I'm thinking a nice long stress test followed by a lower-GI series."

He laughed. "All right, all right. I can certainly use your help. But we can wait until tomorrow. It's been several weeks since the murder—perhaps even six months. Any evidence that's survived this long will survive until tomorrow morning. And I need a break with my best friend."

Karen's heart sped up again. She had to say this, get it out into the open before she burst. "Speaking of friends," she said slowly, "I was thinking . . ."

The house lights dimmed, then went out, leaving the audience in darkness. Several people made shushing noises. Karen trailed off.

"You were thinking what?" Linus murmured.

Karen considered blurting it out to him, then tossed the idea aside like a newly removed appendix. "Nothing, love." She patted his hand. "I'll tell you later."

The stage lights came up, illuminating the apron with false sunshine. "Ladies and gentlemen," said a female voice over a loudspeaker, "please give a warm welcome to Luna City's newest entertainer . . . Noah Skyler."

The audience erupted into applause. Two rows down, front and center, a blond woman raised her hands over her head and clapped wildly. Noah loped onto the stage and waved to the audience with a wide, white smile.

"Hello, Luna City!" he boomed. "Home of the smartest crowd in the solar system!"

This comment drew more applause and some cheers.

"I was reading the newsfeeds backstage," he continued when the noise died down. "And I learned something. Luna City has a lower number of lawyers per capita than any-where on Earth." He paused. "I *told* you we were smart."

Laughter.

He told a few more jokes about the news, then settled back onto the stool and took a sip of water. "I grew up in Wisconsin, a place that has a fascinating history—unless you have to read about it in a high school history class. And we have stories, too. Grandpa told me lots of them, and I'll tell one or two to you." The stage lights dimmed slightly, then abruptly went out. The auditorium was plunged into blackness. The audience remained quiet, but the darkness went on. The exit lights created a thin, dim glow that only served to make the shadow seem deeper. People began to fidget, and the restless sounds of their movements sounded like snakes whispering in the dark.

"I don't think that was part of the show," Linus whis-pered, and Karen wondered if she could get away with clutching at him in pretend fear. She decided not.

Noah's voice—unmiked—came out of the blackness. "Folks, I think the lawyers didn't appreciate my humor and they got a court order to kill the lights."

Small amount of laughter. Karen awarded him silent points for a nice recovery.

"But since a story takes place in our heads, we can keep on going. I was going to tell you one of my favorite Paul Bunyan stories, but I think the mood has been set for . . . murder."

His voice dropped into a harsh whisper that somehow carried across the entire audience. As Karen sat there in the dark, she became aware that her knee was touching Linus's. She could feel the warmth of his skin through the thin fabric of her trousers. Was he aware of the contact? He wasn't moving away. Her heartbeat quickened just a little. Maybe she should press back, see what he did. Or would that embarrass him?

Noah, meanwhile, slipped into a story about an old woman, recently widowed, whose only companion was a small black dog. The dog sometimes slept on the floor beside the old woman's bed and sometimes on a rug before the fireplace. On nights when she felt lonely or afraid, she could put her hand down to the floor, and the dog would lick it in reassurance. One dark, stormy evening, the woman read a news report of an escaped madman who killed his victims and ate the flesh from their bones. Noah's hoarse description of the howling wind and crashing thunder made Karen shiver. Linus moved his knee away. Karen wasn't sure if she should be disappointed or not.

Frightened, the old woman locked her doors and went to bed. But she couldn't get the news story out of her mind. She tossed and turned as the storm raged outside. At last she dozed off, then jerked awake from a terrible nightmare about a man picking open her back door—scrape, scrape, scrape—and creeping into her bedroom on cold, icy feet. Karen and the rest of the audience sat spellbound. The theater felt chilly.

The old woman told herself it had been nothing but a dream, but she was too afraid to get out of bed and check the house. Instead, the old woman slipped a hand out of the covers toward the place where her little dog slept. His tongue licked her fingers as they always did, and she felt better. Then a stroke of lightning flashed outside the window. In its light, the old woman caught a glimpse of her living room through the open bedroom door. Before the fireplace, curled up on the rug, lay her little black dog. The tongue beside the old woman's bed gave her fingers another long lick.

The lights burst back on. Everyone jumped, including Karen, and several people screamed. A few sprang upward several centimeters and had to drift back down to their seats. Noah was sitting on his stool with a perfectly innocent look on his face. The audience laughed and broke into applause. Noah raised his water glass to them. Karen and Linus clapped their hands with equal amounts of enthusiasm.

The show continued. Noah told other stories, joked some more about what he had read on the newsfeeds, and even sang two songs. The second one was a bawdy one about a blacksmith and the ladies who examined the size of his hammer. The blond woman down in front cheered the loudest after that one. Karen clapped and laughed aloud, amazed at how much she had enjoyed herself.

At last Noah announced he was finished, and the theater rang with applause. Noah was persuaded to give an encore— the Paul Bunyan story he had tried to tell before the lights went out—and the show ended to more applause. Karen noticed Linus slide his monocle over his eye as they rose and edged toward the aisle with the other theatergoers.

"What are you doing?" she asked.

"Checking the flash reviews," he said. "It never takes long for the bloggers and slaggers to—hmmmm."

"What?" Karen leaned closer, as if she could check the text on Linus's ocular display. "What do they say?"

"They love him." Linus grinned. "The kid's going to be insufferable after this."

"If you think that," Karen told him, "you're the worst judge of character I've ever seen."

"Joke, K. You missed it."

They moved slowly toward the exits, keeping pace with the crowd around them. Karen's arm stole into the crook of Linus's elbow, and he accepted it without comment. They walked like that, exiting the theater and moving up the wide corridor in comfortable silence. Karen enjoyed the warmth and solidity of Linus's arm around her hand. The lights of Tourist Town glittered around them, and the smell of popcorn drifted on the air. Karen looked at Linus's face and saw a faraway, almost dreamy expression. Feeling swelled for him. What had she been so scared of? Now was the perfect time to take their relationship a step forward.

"Where are you, love?" she asked. Her heart beat faster. "You look a million miles out."

"Hmm?" He turned toward her, still looking a bit lost. "I guess I was wishing Robin could have seen Noah's show. She would have loved it."

Karen cocked her head. "Who's Robin?"

"My wife."

Cold water crashed over Karen in an icy wave. The scene around her blurred. Voices of the pedestrians smeared into an unrecognizable mass of noise. Her knees actually went a little weak, and she stumbled. Linus caught her wrist and steadied her.

"Are you all right?" he asked.

"You never—I didn't—" She closed her eyes for a second and forced herself to get a grip. Iron will shoved her backbone upright and cleared the pain from her face. "You've never mentioned a . . . a wife."

"I don't often talk about her," he admitted slowly. "It's . . . painful."

"She doesn't live in Luna City, does she?" Karen's mouth was dry, and she could barely speak. It felt like she was disconnected from her body. She was outside herself, manipulating her voice and legs from a distance like a marionette. A small part of her was amazed that she could still walk beside him.

"She lives on Earth," he said, "with my daughter, Vicky."

That stopped Karen flat. Her legs refused to carry her forward. Linus didn't notice at first, and her hand came free of his elbow before he realized it.

"You have a *daughter*?" Karen's voice rose a notch.

"Yeah."

"Good god, I need a sit-down," she muttered, and made her way to a heavy planter full of rhododendrons. She perched on the edge, feeling the hard concrete beneath her. Linus, his face full of concern, sat beside her.

"What's wrong?" he demanded.

"It's . . . you've shocked me, love," she said. "You never mentioned a wife or a daughter. Not once. You don't even wear a wedding band."

He held up his empty left hand. "Too dangerous in my line of work. Rings get caught on weapons or in tight places. Robin doesn't wear one, either."

"She's a cop, too, is she?"

"No. A Marine."

She waited, but he didn't say anything else. Abruptly she wanted to hit him, crack him a good one across the jaw for deceiving her. She knew it was irrational, that Linus had no reason to tell her about a wife if he didn't want to, but the feeling of betrayal remained.

Her emotions must have invaded her expression because Linus gave her an odd look. "What?"

"If you don't give me more details, love," she said through gritted teeth, "I'm going to pry them out of you with a crowbar or cut them out with a scalpel."

"Oh." He scratched his nose. "What do you want to know?"

Everything, she snarled silently. *I want to know the little minx who stole you from me even before I knew I never had a chance.*

"Why isn't this . . . why isn't *Robin* up here with you?" Karen asked.

"I was only supposed to be up here for eighteen months, getting my masters," Linus replied. "We decided it would be difficult to separate for that long, but worth it in the long run. Robin's in the United States Marines, so we were used to going a few months without seeing each other. Then I got . . . sick. When Dr. Piltdown told me my heart valves were permanently damaged and I couldn't go back to Earth, we thought about bringing Robin up here. Except Luna is an independent nation. There's no U.S. military presence here, so she can't exactly transfer—or commute."

"Why doesn't she just quit?" Karen asked, more snidely than she had intended.

"The Marines are her life," Linus said. "Just as police work is mine. And she's in the middle of an eight-year contract. She can't up and leave."

"How did you have a child, then?"

Pain crossed Linus's face, and Karen was suddenly sorry she'd asked. He said, "Robin's visited a few times. Lunar trips are expensive, and it's hard for her to get away. Vicky was conceived up here, just before I got sick. She's eighteen months old now, and I've never held her."

Karen closed her eyes, unable to imagine the pain the situation must cause him. Her anger melted away, but that only made it worse—it was easier to distance herself from someone who had pissed her off. Feeling sorry for him only made him more attractive to her.

"I sometimes use my contacts to access satellite imaging," he said softly. "When Robin and Vicky go outside, I can see them, once in a while. Robin doesn't know. I think it would make her uncomfortable, the idea of me looking down at her from above like some sort of angel voyeur. When her enlistment is up, we'll have to decide what to do. It would kill Robin to leave the Marines, and it would kill me to leave Luna. We've got a couple years before that happens, though. Maybe we'll find a solution."

"Like a heart transplant," Karen said.

"We can hope," Linus sighed. "But since I'm at the bottom of all the lists . . . Well, better for me to lose my family through separation than for someone else to lose their family through death. It's still . . . I still wish . . . well, you know."

Karen knew she should say something comforting, but she couldn't bring herself to do it. Thank god she had kept her mouth shut about her attraction to him. Her face flamed hot at the thought of what she had almost done. Quickly, she patted his hand and stood up. "I should be getting home," she said.

"I thought we were getting coffee or something." His tone was hopeful.

"I can't, love," she said briskly. "I've got to get an early start tomorrow."

"Don't forget about checking the shuttle," he said. "I'll meet you at the port at eight, if you're still interested."

She had completely forgotten about the investigation. Her first impulse was to make an excuse and back out, but she realized it would sound weak and inane. And the scientific part of her mind admitted to continued curiosity about the murder. So she nodded at him, not trusting herself to speak, then turned and strode quickly away.

Noah stood backstage in a small crowd of people, shaking hands and smiling and trying to keep from committing murder. He had dealt with his share of technical screw-ups, but tonight . . . tonight was the worst. Lights and sound going out at the same time, leaving him stranded on stage with a full house. Did *anything* go right in Luna City? Wesley Yard was a dead man. Noah scanned the crowd. No sign of him. Yard was probably doing the smart thing and hiding in a closet somewhere.

"Great show," said an older man. He wore sharply tailored, expensive-looking clothes and he had a hard handshake. "Worth a trip to Luna all by itself."

"Thanks," Noah replied. "It was fun to put together."

"Do you always make up your jokes on the spot?" asked a woman. Her handshake was limp and cold as a dead fish.

Noah smiled at her, falling into the old rhythm of post-show conversation. Some entertainers hid in their dressing rooms after a show, or even fled the theater. Noah preferred to hang around and meet people, talk to them. He supposed part of it was ego-stoking—praise was always fun to hear—and part of it was just that he liked talking to people. Most cops did, he supposed. Noah loved watching people, seeing how they moved, how they reacted. It was fun to fill in the blanks. This one looked shy and withdrawn. Had his girlfriend dumped him? That one carried herself stiff and rigid. Maybe she was on her way to interview for a job she desperately needed.

The woman—probably a professor—talking to him right now leaned a little too close, her voice a bit too cheerful. Probably overcompensating for something. Or maybe she was just one of those overly friendly people.

"I have a few jokes I keep in reserve just in case," he said. "But most of them I make up when I read the newsfeeds just before I go on."

"How do you *do* that?" the woman said. "Just make them up, I mean."

"Are you kidding?" he replied lightly. "How can anyone look at the newsfeeds and *not* laugh?"

That got a laugh all its own, for all that it was a joke Noah had told a hundred times. For a minute he felt like he was back in college. And then he realized he *was* back in college. It felt strange, as if he had walked backward through his life and arrived on Luna by mistake.

Roger Davids, the entertainment coordinator for Luna City, pushed his way through the group to shake Noah's hand. His blue eyes sparkled with enthusiasm, and delight lit his sharp, handsome features. "Noah, that was a great show. We'll want to have you back as a regular!"

"Thanks. Uh . . . how often? I mean, I start classes soon, and I keep getting these cases to investigate."

Roger waved this aside. "It'll only be twice a month, like I told you. Maybe more, though. The reviews are coming in, and they're great, just great!"

Noah had forgotten about the reviews—odd, really. When he'd done vaudeville revivals the first time, he'd rushed to the feeds after every show. Now the reviews didn't seem that important. Probably because he wasn't getting money for his shows up here, while down on Earth he'd depended on them to pay rent and buy groceries. Bad reviews meant poor attendance, and poor attendance meant less money. Up here, he could play to a totally empty house or a completely full one and it wouldn't matter in the slightest. He kind of liked that, actually. The lack of pressure made it easier to enjoy himself.

A pair of arms caught him from behind in a wild hug. Noah tensed and automatically drew up an elbow, ready to ram it into the person's gut. Lilac perfume wafted over him.

"That was so much fun!" Ilene said in his ear. "A great show, and believe me, I've seen *lots* of vaudeville revival."

He turned around and, before he could say anything, she kissed him. Scattered laughter ran through the crowd. Noah felt abruptly naked and exposed. He backed away from Ilene with a patently false smile on his face.

"What's wrong, guy?" she asked.

"You just startled me," he said, and wondered how many images of this would land on the feeds. GAZILLIONAIRE SMOOCHES VAUDEVILLE ACTOR. He felt at once uncertain and attracted. Ilene's outgoing, vivacious personality, he was learning, was a sword with two edges.

She smiled at him, then raised her voice. "Okay, everyone—our star is exhausted and needs to go home. Thanks for coming! Bye, now!"

Noah started to protest, but Ilene grabbed him by the hand and towed him away. A moment later, they were out the back door and heading into the domed area of Tourist Town. The Tourist Town dome was much smaller than the one that enclosed Dai Memorial Park, though it contained its share of trees and shrubs. Side corridors led to various entertainment facilities like the Sueyin Dai Memorial Theater, while other facilities were housed in dome itself. Now that it was evening, the place was crowded with students, visiting parents, and university faculty looking for something to do. Lights glittered on the dome overhead, advertising places like the Loony Casino and the Fluffy Bunny restaurant. In the distance, Noah heard the faint rumbling of a roller coaster and the accompanying shouts and screams of the riders. Smells of fried food hung on the air. The place reminded Noah of a county fair back in Wisconsin.

Ilene tucked her arm under his as they walked. "You didn't thank me."

"Thank you?"

"You're supposed to say it as a statement, not a question," she said with mock severity.

"I mean that I don't understand why I should—"

"I got you away from those people who wanted to paw all over you. And I did it in such a way that you came off looking nice while I looked like the bitch." Ilene smiled winsomely at him. "Saves your reputation."

"Oh. Well. You know, I kind of *like* talking to people after the show."

"Really?" She leaned in and lowered her voice to a breathy whisper. "Would you rather talk backstage with them or go home with me?"

A delicious shudder ran through him and all his previous uncertainties vanished like a candle flame caught in a thunderstorm. "*Am* I going home with you?"

"In a while you are," she said in a voice that dripped promise like melted chocolate. "Ever ride a roller coaster in low-g?"

"What kind of roller coaster are we talking about?" he asked warily.

Ilene gave him a playful slap on the shoulder. "That's not until later, dear boy. I mean a *real* roller coaster. Come on! We can be little kids for a while."

She took his hand and towed him toward the rumbling noise. Wincing slightly at the tiny, dull ache in his injured ankle, Noah gave in and ran with her. They bounded and weaved through the crowd, and Noah became proud of the fact that he didn't trip or fall even once. Noah whooped as he leaped and ran. His feet left the ground and touched down again, light as feathers and snowflakes. It was like running in a dream, with no restraint, no boundaries. Once in a while he jostled someone, but he barely paused long enough to give a laughing apology. Ilene skipped around people like a leaf swirling on a summer breeze. Calliope music swelled around them both, and the dome overhead just barely held back a trillion stars.

Ahead, the roller coaster bulged and looped against the sky. A long car started up the first hill and made the familiar clattering sound as the chain caught and towed it upward. The riders chattered and laughed. It was, Noah knew, entirely possible to make a silent roller coaster, but the quiet ones invariably died for lack of popularity. The clattering of chains and gears heightened the anticipation, and anticipation was half the ride.

An impressive line of people threaded their way steadily through a queue maze made of fake wooden slats cut to resemble rough fence rails. Overhead, an arched sign gave the roller coaster's name: MOON SHOT. The car reached the top of the hill and slid down the slope trailing shouts and screams. Noah headed for the line, but Ilene caught his wrist. She was getting pretty good at halting him dead in his tracks.

"Not that way," she said. "Come on."

She loped to the roller coaster's exit and pulled aside the hinged slat that made a symbolic gate. The slat was marked LINE JUMPERS WILL BE EXPELLED FROM THE PARK. Ilene held it open for Noah.

"Come on," she repeated.

Noah was about to point out the obvious, then thought, *What the hell,* and joined her. Ilene trotted toward the stairway that led down from the roller coaster's main platform. A group of riders streamed downward and around them. Several gave Ilene and Noah dirty looks, but no one said anything. Ilene climbed the stairs and Noah followed, wondering how much trouble he could get into for this. What would Linus say if he got thrown out of Tourist Town? But he stayed behind Ilene.

An attendant was standing guard at the top of the stairs. "Did you lose something?" he asked, though his tone said, *Line Jumpers Will Be Expelled From the Park.*

"We're good," Ilene said, and held up a plastic card. The attendant looked at it, then stood silently aside. She flashed him a friendly grin and brought Noah up onto the platform. It was divided into sections a bit like the starting gate of a racetrack. Riders could choose which seat they wanted. The roller coaster's front seat was the most popular.

"What was that card?" Noah asked.

"What's the fun in being stinking rich if you can't buy a few perks?" Ilene countered. "Come on—I want to sit in back."

There was no wait at all for the rear seat, and they got on the very next car, which was two seats wide. A padded safety harness dropped across Noah's upper thighs the moment he sat down, and a computer voice rattled off safety precautions. Childlike excitement made him bounce a little in his seat. He hadn't been on a roller coaster in years, and now he was going to ride one on the damned *moon*. Not only that, he was doing it with a beautiful woman who was obviously interested in him. As if reading his mind, Ilene shifted beneath her own harness and put her hand on Noah's knee.

"I feel I should warn you," she said. "I'm a screamer."

The car jerked into motion. It scooted around a bend in the track, then clattered up the first hill. A few people raised their hands over their heads. Something occurred to Noah—something besides the fact that Ilene was sliding her warm hand higher than his knee.

"How does this thing go so fast?" he asked. "Roller coasters get their speed from gravity, right? Up here, we shouldn't go faster than a baby buggy."

"They cheat," Ilene said. "It's motorized. You're supposed to pretend, silly."

Noah noticed something else. The higher the coaster climbed, the higher Ilene's hand climbed. For the second time that day, his groin grew tight and a coppery taste tanged his mouth. Ilene's hand caressed the inside of his thigh. Noah realized now why Ilene wanted to sit in the back—no one could see them. His excitement grew as the front of the car reached the summit, and he put an arm around her shoulders. Ilene's fingers made a quick, jerking motion, and Noah felt cool air wash over newly exposed skin. His heart pounded in his ears, and he shot a glance at the people in the seats ahead of them. The seat backs were high, but he could the see the tops of their heads. If either of them turned around, they wouldn't see much, but it would be obvious what was happening right behind them. The thought should have horrified Noah, but he was so hard and Ilene was so close that the situation only made him more excited. Her long hair brushed over his arm. The car continued to climb toward the top of the dome.

"What happens when we hit the top?" he asked hoarsely.

"We go down."

The car slid over the peak and rushed down the steep slope. Noah's seat dropped out from underneath him and he was weightless. Only the safety bar kept him in place and pulled him down the hill with the roller coaster. Wind rushed past his ears. And then Ilene bent her head into his lap. Her warm mouth closed over him, her tongue moving like a caduceus, round and round. Noah groaned out loud, but the sound was covered by the shouts of people and clatter of wheels. The roller coaster car swept up one hill and plunged down another. Ilene brought Noah close to his own peak, then backed away at the last moment. Her tongue moved, first light as a feather, then heavy as velvet. He squirmed in his seat as gravity came and went. He heard himself babbling, begging Ilene to either finish or stop entirely. She acted as if she didn't hear, bringing him closer and closer, then pulling away yet again. He was a prisoner of the roller coaster, of gravity and momentum, of the pleasure Ilene gave and withheld. Now the car was plunging down the final hill. It would rush around a final curve and reach the platform in a few moments. Ilene's mouth slid up and down and Noah felt a familiar upsurge begin. But the car was close to the end of the ride.

"Wait!" he panted. "Stop!"

Ilene ignored him. Her mouth remained in soft suction around him. His knees went weak.

"Please!" he said. "No!"

In a moment he was going to hit the point of no return. The car rushed toward the platform, seconds away from arrival. Noah groaned in mixed terror and pleasure.

And then Ilene sat up. Noah grabbed himself, willing his body to subside. His groin throbbed, threatening to burst. He held his breath, bit his lip, and the feeling abated. With a swiftness he didn't even know he possessed, he readjusted his trousers just as the car reached the platform. It stopped with a series of jerks in front of the next set of people waiting to board.

"Welcome back, shooters," the computer said. "When your safety bar disengages, please exit to your right, and thank you for riding the Moon Shot."

Noah untucked his shirt with a yank as he stood up. The tail dropped below his belt line, hiding a prominent fact he'd rather not make public. Ilene took his hand as they exited the coaster. A small smile played around the corners of her mouth.

"Want to do it again?" she asked.

He started to refuse immediately, then, to his amazement, found himself giving the idea serious consideration. Desire, fear, and excitement all mingled in a strange ménage à trois. He couldn't deny it had been a major rush, and he wondered if Ilene might let him . . . finish. Putting himself completely into her hands—if that was best way to phrase it— was frightening and thrilling at the same time.

"I don't . . . I'm not . . ." he began.

"I was joking," she said. "There's only so much in it for *me*, you know."

"Sorry," he said quickly. "I didn't even think that—"

"It's all right." She slid a hand under his shirt and into his back pocket. "You can pay me back at my place."

Noah barely remembered the train ride to Ilene's apartment. Usually he didn't go in for major public displays of affection, but Ilene seemed to have broken through a barrier. They kissed and nibbled and stole touches all the way back, ignoring the people around them. They finally reached Ilene's door and went inside. Desire surged and pounded through Noah's body in heavy, thunderous waves.

"What about your roommate?" he asked, though by now he wouldn't have cared if Ilene's bedroom turned out to be onstage at the Sueyin Dai Memorial Theater.

"I don't have one," she said. "Another perk."

They entered her bedroom, which was set up exactly like the one in Noah's apartment. Ilene raised her hands over her head as if she were riding the roller coaster, and Noah slid her soft blouse over her head. She wasn't wearing underwear. Her breasts were small, with large areolae. Noah caressed one lightly and Ilene shivered. She stepped out of her slacks, then pulled off Noah's shirt. Her fingers were a little cool. He drew off his own trousers as Ilene lay back on the bed and crooked a finger at him.

"I want you on top of me," she said. "I want to feel you move."

Noah was shaking with the intensity of need and desire. Moving carefully, he slid over her, his skin warm on hers. She arched her back to meet him.

"You're so light," she whispered. "But so solid. Come on, story-boy. Perform for me."

This struck Noah as an odd thing to say, but at this point he wouldn't have cared if she had spoken Sanskrit. He entered her with a groan. Ilene moved with him. The fantasies Noah had about low gravity all turned out to be true. Neither of them had to worry about the other's weight. Positions that would be awkward or painful on Earth turned graceful and erotic on Luna. Ilene shuddered beneath him, then rolled over to take a position on top. Noah cupped her buttocks under his hands and lifted her up and down. Ilene moaned. Noah marveled—she weighed nothing. He thrust faster, unable to slow down. He was pulling her to him and pushing her away, becoming one with her and separating from her. Sweat broke out all over his body. Ilene's breath came faster and Noah felt the buildup again. This time Ilene didn't pull away. He pulled her body to him and exploded inside her with a rush. She threw back her head and howled.

I feel I should warn you, I'm a screamer.

When it ended, they rolled apart. Noah started to reach for her, but Ilene skipped out of the bed and nipped into the bathroom. He sat up on the bed, the sweat drying on his body. That had been incredible. Ilene was a truly amazing woman. He wondered what it would be like to stay with her, have her steadily in his life. Her wild nature was unpredictable and little scary, but that was what made her so attractive. Noah couldn't remember ever meeting anyone like her. Maybe he should—

"You're not dressed?" Ilene was standing in the doorway, wearing a red silk bathrobe. "Don't have to be in early tomorrow to work on those cases?"

"I suppose." Noah reached for his trousers, a little startled. "I mean, I'd figured on spending the night."

"Maybe another time." She wagged a finger at him. "I'll call you sometime, all right?"

"Surprise and anger tightened Noah's jaw and the words popped out before he could stop them. "I'll just leave the money on the nightstand, then. You must have a couple mill in there by now."

Fury spread across Ilene's face. Before she could react further, Noah grabbed the rest of his clothes and fled.

CHAPTER THIRTEEN

Linus rose early, brushed his teeth, and shuffled to the coffee maker, which had already switched on and filled the tiny kitchen with the familiar rich smell. Black with lots of sugar—that was the only way to wake up. Cream was for wimps. Linus perched on the sofa, bare-chested and boxer-clad. He sipped the overly sweet, dark brew, felt caffeine and sugar fire up his brain, and sighed with satisfaction.

The fake sun that rose on the vid-screen finished rising over the ocean. Recorded seagulls called out with a thin, lonely sound. The vid-screen and a few framed pictures of Robin holding Vicky were the only decorations in the entire apartment. He raised his mug to his wife and daughter in silent salute as he did every morning. Every so often he thought about making his place less austere so it would be less like his office. Some holograms in the corners, house-plants, new furniture. Hell, Julia Espinoza could probably browbeat one of her grad students into installing floor-to-ceiling vid-screens and putting together a spiffy little theme for him—Underwater Caribbean or Merrie Olde England or whatever. But something always put him off.

The coffee had cooled a bit, and Linus took a heftier swig. Something. He knew himself well enough to understand exactly what the something was. Decorating his apartment and his office would be an . . . admission. People who decorated, who brought in houseplants, who put up holograms and vid-themes—these people planned to stay for a long time. Even forever. Linus had other plans.

No. Not true. He didn't have other plans—just other hopes.

Being both a realist and a cynic sucked moon rocks. You couldn't cushion yourself with the usual warm, happy delusions that everything would somehow work out in the end.

Linus unconsciously rubbed his chest. No scar marked the place where Dr. Piltdown had sliced him open, but he felt one just the same. It felt rough and puckered beneath his fingertips, like a worm left beneath his skin. Sometimes he even felt blood. At times, it seemed like his heart was a rotten balloon inside his chest, one that could collapse any moment, *would* collapse if he ever set foot on a shuttle and blasted back to Earth.

His gaze wandered to a picture of Robin holding baby Vicky on one hip. She was smiling beneath regulation-short honey-brown hair. It looked like Vicky was going to have dark, straight hair like her father. Linus pursed his lips, feeling an ache of separation mixed with a pang of guilt. Robin hadn't been so sure Linus getting his masters from Luna University was such a great idea. Separation for eighteen months would be hard on both of them. Robin's duty to the Corps had never taken her away more than three months. Would their marriage survive it? What if they changed and became incompatible after so long apart? The risk, Robin said, frightened her. But Linus had argued and cajoled. Luna was the most prestigious place to study, bar none. A degree in criminal science from Luna U would let him work anywhere in the world, which meant he'd be able to find a job no matter where Robin might be transferred. In the end, Robin had finally given in.

The decision had stranded him like a castaway on a stale, gray beach.

Why hadn't he listened to her? If he hadn't pushed so hard to come up here, he would never have gotten sick. He would be home right now, drinking coffee with his wife and watching his daughter scamper across the floor.

He drained his coffee, set the mug in the sink, and fished his workout clothes from their usual place under the bed. Best to keep moving when these moments hit. Work out, then bury himself in the investigation. There was always something going on in Luna City, and getting himself involved in it was the best medicine. Who cared if he was turning into a workaholic? He had no family—not up here, anyway—and he didn't date. Hell, the only person he'd met that he'd consider going out with was—

—Karen. He pulled on gym shorts, T-shirt, and tennis shoes, then caught up a small carryall. Okay, while he was admitting stuff to himself, he might as well admit that there was something there. Last night at Noah's show, he'd felt it strongly enough. When the theater had gone dark, he had felt an almost irresistible urge to put his arm around her, hold her close, smell her hair. Kiss her lips. When he was with Karen, he forgot loneliness and being a castaway. When she announced her intention to stay on Luna permanently, he had all but jumped to the ceiling for joy.

Linus knew full well that Karen felt the same attraction. Last night had confirmed it. Only a fool could miss the signs that she wanted more than friendship—the excuses she made to touch him, stand close to him. The tiny, overly subtle innuendos. Thank god he had solved the mystery of where John Doe had come from—it gave him an excuse to chatter at her and prevent her from saying anything about it. He had dropped his marriage on her as soon as he had been able to figure out a way to work it into the conversation. A little twinge of guilt had followed. He should have mentioned Robin and Vicky long ago, but mentioning a wife and daughter Earthside inevitably brought up the need to explain the separation, and that only made his invisible scar bleed again.

A little voice inside him whispered that he could safely have a fling with Karen. Robin, more than forty thousand miles away, would never know, could never find out. Karen might be up for it. She made no secret of the fact that she enjoyed men. No one would know.

Except me, he told himself, and stepped smartly out into the corridor. A few minutes later he was at the rec center. Time: six-thirty A.M.

Linus headed straight for the spider gym, weaving his way down the sloping ramps and blue-carpeted corridors of the center like a big cat moving through the jungle. At this time of morning, the rec center was nearly deserted. By seven, it would start getting crowded, and by nine it would be insufferable. The spider gym was one of the more popular workout spots, and early morning was the only time it wasn't backed up like a clogged drain.

The outline of a palm print stood guard outside the spider gym door. Linus pressed his hand to it. A green light winked on indicating there was room inside, and the door opened. Linus entered a small changing area that smelled of sweat. He removed a matching set of black gloves, socks, and kneepads from his carryall along with a bicycle safety helmet. After stashing the carryall and his tennis shoes in the locker, he pulled on the equipment. Tiny Velcro hooks on the soles of his socks skittered at the tile floor without gaining purchase as Linus entered the spider gym proper.

The walls, ceiling, and floor of the enormous, three-story room were padded with blue material made of Velcro eyes. Moving pillars and cubes with rounded corners randomly extruded from all surfaces like whales breaching the surface, then slowly sank back flush with the wall, ceiling, or floor. A huge sphere, also padded with Velcro, hung suspended in the center of the gym. Even at this hour eight or ten people were using the gym. Linus made a mental note of their locations, then crouched and *leaped.*

He left his stomach behind as he soared straight toward the sphere in the gym's center. It was like flying, or the closest thing to it. Just as his momentum began to slow, he hit the sphere. Linus slapped it with both palms and brought his knees up. The Velcro on hands and knees easily caught and held him in place. The light gravity allowed him to cling to the side of the sphere like a human spider. Barely pausing to gather himself, he leaped again. This time he hit the wall and clung there with palms and toes. Linus climbed, scampering upward with dozens of tiny ripping sounds until he reached the ceiling. A young woman was just ahead of him, and she made the corner without even pausing. Linus followed, crawling upside down like a fly. A pillar oozed out of the ceiling to reach down for the floor, and Linus yanked himself free. He dropped lazily downward and snagged the moving pillar one-handed as he fell past it, then swung himself around and climbed back upward. Another jump took him back to the central sphere. Sweat beaded on his face and gathered under his arms as he leaped, skittered, crawled, and scampered around the gym, avoiding the other climbers and having a hell of a good time. The pressures of the investigation, the Mayor-President, and his difficult relationships fell away. He was like a kid transformed into a comic book hero.

The spider gym admitted more people, and Linus had to pay more and more attention to where he was going. Two other climbers collided in mid-air and dropped to the ground, though neither of them was hurt. Linus tensed for a moment, thinking one might start a fight with the other, but the pair shrugged it off and went back to their workout. Eventually, Linus's obie announced in his ear that it was a quarter to seven. Time to leave. He made two more leaps and reluctantly landed near the door. Back inside the entryway, he stripped off the climbing equipment and helmet, retrieved his carryall, and headed out the door. A line of people already snaked up the corridor, and the person at the front immediately moved in to take the workout slot Linus had vacated.

Linus exited the rec center and broke into the light, loping jog that passed for running on Luna. This second half of his workout took him back to his apartment, where he peeled off his sweaty clothes. He shoved them under his bed, showered, shaved, and dressed in the tan slacks and white shirt he usually wore to work. Breakfast consisted of two pieces of tofu toast, instant oatmeal, and more coffee. He dumped the dishes in the sink and checked his watch. Karen was supposed to meet him at the shuttle at nine. Linus prayed it wouldn't be awkward working with her now.

It was for the best, he told himself as he left for the train station. Linus was happily . . . he was . . . well, he was married, even if he didn't see his wife more than once a year. And one day he would be with her and his daughter. Somehow.

The spaceport was nearly deserted. Yesterday's shuttle had long since disgorged its passengers, and it wasn't scheduled to take off until tomorrow afternoon. In the interim, it would be serviced in meticulous detail. Linus grimaced. Vanessa Maygrave, manager of the spaceport, probably wouldn't be happy when Linus told her the shuttle wasn't going anywhere until he had thoroughly processed everything. Well, police work rarely made you the life of the party. At best you got annoyed cooperation. At worst, you got demands for warrants and court orders.

Linus arrived at the port at two minutes after nine. Karen was waiting for him just inside the main doors looking coolly pissed off in a white lab coat and dark coveralls. Linus groaned to himself. Karen hated tardiness of any stripe, and it was likely she didn't feel well disposed of him right now to begin with. He braced himself and wondered how it would feel to walk around with his head ripped off.

She said nothing, merely accepted one of the scene kits he handed her.

"Morning," he said a little too brightly. "Ready to catch a killer?" *Oh, great dialogue*, he thought.

"Sure, lo—sure," she said. Her tone was brisk. "Let's go."

Linus led the way through the nearly deserted gray corridors of the spaceport to the office of Vanessa Maygrave. Like most rooms on Luna, the spaceport manager's office was small, though this one felt big. It might have had something to do with the floor-to-ceiling picture window that looked out over the gray sandscape. The window currently lay in shadow, and stars shone down like hard jewels. A hundred meters away, Linus could make out the landing pad and the bulbous shuttle that lay on it like an abandoned Christmas ornament. The view, Linus mused, would be pretty spectacular during takeoff and landing. Vac-suited technicians swarmed over the shuttle, busy as silver-coated bees buzzing around a hive.

To one side was Vanessa Maygrave's desk. Vanessa came around it to greet Linus and Karen, eyebrows raised. Her white hair, trapped in a neat bun, contrasted sharply with a dark Asian complexion. A spidery network of wrinkles creased her face with a quizzical expression, and a pair of reading glasses hung from a chain around her neck. Vanessa wasn't a citizen of Luna City. She didn't even work for the University or for the Lunar government. Her employer was International Flyways, Inc., the company that maintained a controlling interest in Tether Station, flat-out owned the shuttles, and possessed a chunk of the spaceport to boot. International Flyways rotated spaceport managers through Luna City every six months. Vanessa was on her third posting up here, and Linus had dealt with her many times over the years. She had shown him around the port when he was a just a Lunar rookie, and they had occasionally run into each other at social functions. Linus liked her well enough, though she wasn't someone he'd invite over to his apartment for his famous crepes.

Which reminded him—Linus owed Hector a crepe supper. He made a mental note to call the man later.

"What brings you two down here?" Vanessa asked after a few pleasantries.

"We need access to a few records and possibly to the shuttle," Linus said. "I'm hoping to do it without a warrant."

"You can indeed hope," she replied with a small smile. "But I'll need a little more information first. Have a seat. Can I pour you some tea?" She gestured at a red ceramic teapot that squatted amid a set of round, Asian cups like a mother hen surrounded by a brood of chicks.

Linus declined, Karen accepted. They both took up spots in two guest chairs that Vanessa had managed to squeeze into the cramped space. The office was neither clean nor cluttered, but fell somewhere in between. Vanessa poured herself and Karen cups of tea, and the room filled with the sweet smell of cinnamon.

"Now," she said, "tell me everything. I assume this has something to do with that body that turned up outside? Or maybe you're investigating the death of Viktor Riza. That poor boy. He's going back to Earth when this shuttle leaves. International Flyways offered him a free ticket, and he accepted."

"Do you do that for all your murdered customers?" Karen asked.

"Karen!" Linus said, a little aghast.

Vanessa waved this aside. "The company isn't planning to milk the publicity, if that's what you mean. I recommended the ticket, and the company accepted the idea—with a little muscling."

"Sorry," Karen mumbled into her cup. "I'm just . . . well, I'm sorry."

"I need to know," Linus said quickly, "if you had an any accidental overshoots in the last six months."

"You mean, did any of our pilots screw up and overshoot the landing pad?"

"I'd be more polite, but yes, that the gist. Only in the last six months, though."

Vanessa cupped her hands around her tea. "I know we have a few now and then. The pilots who mess up like that take a great deal of ribbing when they finally land, you know. There are the usual jokes about taking the cost of fuel out of their pay and all that. I think we did have one four or five months ago. Let me check the records."

She muttered to her obie and put her reading glasses on. Linus saw text skitter across the lenses, though it was backward to him. Vanessa's eyes tracked as she read.

"Ah!" she said at last. "I was right—we did have an overshoot. Just four months ago, in fact."

Linus leaned forward, all senses on full alert. "Which shuttle was it?"

"The *Anna May*." Vanessa gestured toward the window. "She's on the pad right now."

"And who was the pilot?"

"Her name is Adrienne Miao. Quite competent, actually. This overshoot is her only one."

"I don't suppose she would be . . ." Linus began.

"She is," Vanessa interrupted. "Adrienne piloted the *Anna May* in. We only have so many qualified pilots, you know. I suppose you'll want to talk to her."

"You bet," Linus said. "I'll also need copies of the flight path the shuttle actually took, the flight path it was *supposed* to take, and any sensor data from the shuttle itself."

Vanessa tapped a long finger on the side of her cup. "This is a sensitive area, Linus. I'm not supposed to release that kind of data without authorization—or a warrant."

"I know." Linus kept his voice low and earnest. He knew Vanessa. She wasn't stubborn, she didn't go on power trips—unless she was pushed. Linus knew that if wanted quick results, he needed to convince her she was in charge. Getting a warrant would take time and would just piss Vanessa off. He opened his mouth to speak.

"We're hoping," Karen said abruptly, "that this could be easy. It's your station and you make the rules. But we're trying to catch a killer—one who doesn't care about the rules and who shoved an innocent man out into vacuum. Can you help us?"

Linus shot her a quick look. Karen's face was the picture of earnestness. Vanessa set down her cup and, after a moment, waved a dismissive hand.

"Of course, of course," she said. "I don't want a killer running around the city any more than you do." A glint came into her eye. "But this doesn't come free, Linus Pavlik. It's the Luna rule, you know—you have to trade for everything."

"What do you mean?" Linus asked warily.

"I hear from Hector Valdez that you make a mean crêpes suzette?"

Linus laughed at that. "You got it."

"Good. I look forward to your invitation. Meanwhile, you can kill two birds with one stone—Ms. Miao is out on the shuttle as we speak, probably in the crew quarters. I'll forward you those records as soon as I can put them together. Do you know your way to the landing pad?"

Linus said he did while Karen deposited her empty cup on Vanessa's desk. They left the office, crime scene kits in hand, and loped down hallways and across wide receiving rooms to the entry bay. Neither of them spoke. Linus felt awkward and wondered what he should say. It was stupid—Karen was his best friend, and he had never had trouble talking to her before. His admission of marriage changed everything, exactly what Linus had hoped to avoid. It wasn't fair. Telling her made things awkward between them. Not telling her would have been a lie and led to even more awkwardness in the long run. It was stupid, but he didn't know what to do about it. For her part, Karen seemed content with the silence, so Linus stopped trying to come up with something to say.

A quick walk down an off-white corridor took them to the airlock that connected to the shuttle. The shuttle crouched on its rocket boosters like an autographed baseball resting on a stand with four stumpy legs. It was divided into several levels and bays designated for fuel, passengers, luggage, and cargo. Airlocks, both emergency and everyday, dotted the shuttle's surface. When the shuttle was full, passengers and crew swarmed the bays and hallways like students crowding high school hallways. At the moment, it was quiet as an Egyptian tomb. It even smelled empty. Linus slid his monocle around and asked his obie how many airlocks the *Anna May* had.

"Forty-two," his obie told him. "Ten everyday and twenty-two emergency."

"Great," said Karen, who had overhead the exchange. "What was that you said yesterday about using other deputies?"

"Maybe we can narrow things down a little," Linus said. "Let's talk to Ms. Miao first."

The area just inside the airlock led into a large passenger bay. The seats were all empty, and the bay had a curious feel, as if it were holding its breath in anticipation of more passengers. Linus adjusted his monocle.

"Obie," he said, "link with the *Anna May*'s computer and give me directions to the crew quarters."

A red directional arrow popped up on Linus's readout. He followed the arrow and Karen followed Linus. They threaded their way through another passenger bay, up a set of stairs, through a kitchen, and down a short corridor to a door marked CREW ONLY. Karen knocked. A moment later, the door slid open, revealing a woman so plump that she was nearly spherical. Her brown eyes threatened to disappear into folds of flesh. Her hair was hidden by a black skullcap that only emphasized the roundness of her body. The green jumpsuit she wore made her look like a Granny Smith apple.

"Yeah?" she said. Her voice was flat, with a hint of sandpaper.

"I'm Chief Inspector Linus Pavlik." He flashed his identification. "This is Dr. Karen Fang. We're looking for Ms. Adrienne Miao."

"Why?"

"Are you Ms. Miao?" Linus asked.

She paused. Linus waited patiently. People often hesitated before giving their names to the police, as if by admitting who they were, they were confessing to some crime. Either that or they were reviewing recent questionable behavior, something that might bring a cop to the door. Linus thought about reassuring her that she wasn't in trouble—she'd been piloting the shuttle at the time the body was tossed out, so she couldn't be the killer. Still, it was probably better to keep her a little on edge. Nervous people tended to babble, and babblers were always useful.

"I'm Adrienne Miao," the woman said at last. "What's this about?"

"Could we come in and sit down?" Linus said.

Adrienne stood aside. The room beyond was a common-area lounge for the crew. Chairs ringed a pair of rectangular tables, all of which were bolted to the floor. Closed cupboards of stainless steel lined one wall near a full-sized refrigerator, a sink, and a small stove. A hand of solitaire lay face-up on the table next to a bag of red licorice whips. Adrienne wedged herself back into the chair and picked up the remaining pack of cards. Linus and Karen took up chairs of their own, and Linus set his obie to record.

"What's up?" she asked, fiddling with the deck. "I'm on a winning streak here."

"You play with cardboard cards?" Karen said. "Pretty rare these days."

Adrienne fished a stick of licorice from the bag, bit it in half, and stuck one piece into her mouth like a cigarette. It gave off a sweet, childhood sort of smell that made Linus think of Halloween bags and Easter baskets.

"Computer cards are for sissies," Adrienne said. "My dad was a blackjack dealer in Beijing, and he taught me and brother how to handle a *real* deck. Watch." She swept the solitaire hand together into a single pack, tapped it once on the table, and flicked the entire deck into a perfect fan. Her plump fingers danced as she expertly shuffled a few times. She flipped the top card over to show the queen of spades, flipped it back over, and dealt half a dozen cards to Linus and Karen. The cards floated into place like butterflies. A flick of Adrienne's fingers exposed the top card again—the queen of spades. She dealt more cards, then showed the queen again.

"Lady stays on top," Adrienne said. "The best way all around."

"Pretty good," Linus said, impressed. "Do you cheat when you play solitaire?"

"Of course. How do you play?" The licorice whip dangled from her mouth like a snake's tongue.

"We wanted to ask you about your overshoot four months ago."

Adrienne blinked at him. "You're here about that? Weird."

"What's weird about it?" Karen asked.

"It was a weird overshoot, that's what." Adrienne bit the end off the licorice whip and chewed on it, all without removing the whip from her mouth. The remaining piece bounced up and down like a conductor's baton. "What do you want to know?"

Linus reminded himself not to lean forward, though his interested was piqued. "Can you tell us what happened?"

"I was taking the shuttle in on its final approach to the spaceport. After a minute I realized something had gone wrong and I was going to overshoot." She tapped the cards on the table. "Per procedure, I alerted the captain and the crew to the problem and recalculated. Once I'd triple-checked the numbers, I flipped the shuttle around and gave a gentle blast to get us going in the right direction. Landed just fine after that, though the rest of the crew won't let me forget any of it."

"Okay," Linus said. "What was so weird?"

She took another bite of licorice whip and chewed noisily. "God, I need a cigarette. These things are a fucking poor substitute for a good unfiltered. None of that menthol shit, either."

Smoking was illegal on shuttles, of course. Aside from the attendant health problems brought on by second-hand smoke, cigarettes sucked down oxygen like a half-starved pig at a trough. They were illegal on Luna for the same reason. Air was too expensive to waste on bad habits.

"Quitting?" Karen asked sympathetically.

"Hell, no. I'm just on hiatus until I get back Earth-side." Adrienne reached for another licorice whip. "These make the time go by faster. They're low in fat, too."

"What was weird about the overshoot?" Linus repeated.

"The computer had fucked up."

"What do you mean the computer?"

"We always check the reason for overshoots," Adrienne told him. "Can't let it go, you know—overshoots are expensive enough, and the bosses don't want 'em happening more than once. Anyway, when I saw the computer data, it showed numbers I didn't remember entering. They were *close*, but not the same. I went back and checked the keystrokes, and they showed me entering the wrong numbers, too. But I triple-checked like I always do, and I *know* the numbers were fine when I entered them. The crew got a fuck-all of a laugh out of that, let me tell you. Thank god I caught the problem early on or we might have ended up halfway to the dark side."

"You're sure the numbers you entered were correct?" Linus said.

"Positive. The official report has it down that I made a mistake because I can't prove it was the computer, and it burns me, you know?" The pilot held the licorice whip between two fingers and blew out a short breath, as if she were smoking it instead of eating it. "Are you investigating this for the company or something? Am I in trouble?"

"Not so far as I know," Linus said. He hitched the chair a little closer to the table. "Look, can you tell me which airlocks would have been facing away from the spaceport at the time you hit the burners to reverse direction?"

"Easy. The ones in the lower quarter, closest to the boosters. What's this about?"

"We're investigating a death," Linus said. "Did you hear any talk of a stowaway on that trip?"

Adrienne gave a laugh like wood going through a chipper. "Joke, right? You have to know the exact mass of everyone and everything on this tub before it leaves Tether Station so we know how much fuel we're gonna need. A stowaway would show up on the sensors within five minutes. Doesn't stop people from trying, of course—some of these college kids will try anything—but security routs them out fast enough."

"One more question, then. Did you get any reports of an airlock being blown while you were in flight?"

"Nope. And the boards would report that pretty damn quick."

"Thanks for your time," Linus said, rising. "If you think of anything else, please let me know, day or night."

They left her dealing out another hand of solitaire and reaching for more licorice. Karen turned to him once the door was shut.

"If an airlock blew," she said, "the computer would have recorded it."

"The same computer that didn't screw up Miao's numbers?"

"So you think someone messed with the computer," Karen said.

"That's my theory. Come on—let's find the airlock. The one that didn't blow."

"There's an innuendo in there somewhere, love, if you'll give me a minute to find it."

"No thanks. Come on."

Their obies provided maps and schematics of the *Anna May* and highlighted the airlocks in the lower quarter, per Adrienne's information. Linus furrowed his brow.

"Eight down here," he counted. "Five emergency, three everyday. Any ideas which one we should hit first?"

"I trust your judgment, love," Karen said. She sounded much closer to her old self. "Hit whichever one you like."

"Assuming you're a computer whiz who doesn't have to worry about setting off alarms," Linus said, thinking out loud, "you'd want to avoid airlocks near high-traffic areas. That narrows it down to the emergency locks, since the main ones are all near passenger and cargo bays. An emergency airlock is down that flight of stairs."

Karen hefted her kit. "Off we go, then, Mr. Holmes."

"After you, Dr. Fang."

The banter did much to relieve Linus's tension as they loped down the steps. Maybe he'd been mistaken about Karen. Maybe she'd just been in a bad mood earlier. Maybe . . . maybe she'd never felt anything toward him at all.

The thought made his stomach tighten, and the reaction surprised Linus. He wasn't supposed to feel anything for her but friendship. He *didn't* feel anything for her but friendship.

Right, he told himself. *Keep telling yourself that. Why don't you write a nice letter to an advice columnist while you're at it and see if she agrees?*

Emergency airlock 5A was an empty room big enough to hold about ten people—fifteen if they were friendly. It was painted pale green. Both the outer and inner doors sported a thick, round window that reminded Linus of a porthole. The outer window looked out over the gray lunar landscape. A sensor node the size of a light bulb jutted out from one wall at head height above a control panel near the inner door.

Karen set her kit down and glanced around. "The walls are the same color as the paint I found beneath the victim's fingernails. But then, so's half of Luna City."

Linus set his own kit on the floor, produced a flashlight, and got down on his hands and knees to examine the floor and the jamb around the inner door. "No scratch marks that I can see."

"I'm getting DNA." The green bar of light from Karen's scanner hummed slowly over the walls and floor. Every so often she paused, swabbed a section of ceramic tile, and fed the end of the swab into her scene kit's computer. Each time, the results that flashed across the display made Karen shake her head and go back to scanning the floor. Linus realized he was admiring her quick, efficient movements and forced himself to concentrate on the search for scratch marks. He found nothing.

"I'm getting maintenance workers and other crew members," Karen reported after an hour, "but nothing that matches the victim."

"I'm coming up empty, too." Linus rose. "Let's try the next airlock."

They did, and again turned up nothing. The two of them quickly fell into a pattern. Linus checked for scratches first around the doorjamb, then on the floor, then around the walls. Karen scanned for DNA first on the floor, then around the walls, then around the doorjamb. It was a dance. They moved around the airlocks, not quite touching, able to stay out of each other's way with ease, like a long-married couple cooking together in the kitchen without stepping on each other's feet. It should have been cool and clinical, but Linus found it oddly intimate, knowing how and when Karen would move and timing his own movements to coincide.

By the time they arrived at the fourth emergency airlock, they didn't even need to speak, and Linus found it disconcerting when his flashlight beam ruined their pattern by revealing faint scratch marks around the airlock's inner door. His heart jumped.

"I've got it," he said excitedly. "Scratches. Right here." Linus aimed his obie at the marks and captured the image. They were only a few millimeters deep and barely visible, but present nonetheless. He got a swab from his kit, ran it down the frightened scratches left in the paint, and inserted it into the kit's computer. Linus held his breath. After a long moment, the display flashed.

"Oh my god," Linus said, not daring to believe it. He grabbed Karen by the wrists and danced her around, almost stumbling in the light gravity. "The DNA matches! Our John Doe was in this airlock, and he made the scratches. We found him!"

"Very good, love," Karen said, laughing. "Don't bump my head on the ceiling now."

He quickly released her and swallowed hard. "Sorry."

"Can't blame you," Karen replied with a pretty smile. "And at the risk of sending you through the roof, I found something strange over here. Take a look."

Linus came up behind her. She was pointing with gloved fingers at the sensor node.

"What is it?" he asked.

In answer, she touched a spot just below the node. Her finger encountered faint resistance when she tried to pull her hand away.

"It's sticky," she clarified. "Some sort of adhesive. There's a ring of it all the way around the sensor node."

Now that Linus knew what to look for, he could see it— a faint circle about twenty-five or thirty centimeters in diameter all the way around the node. He stared at it for a long time while Karen swabbed a sample. Linus snapped his fingers, not an easy trick in crime scene gloves.

"Got it. Come on."

While a puzzled Karen followed, Linus ducked into the hallway just outside the airlock and opened one of the lockers that stood there. Just as in Luna City, the lockers contained vacuum suits. Linus pulled out a helmet, returned to the airlock, and fitted it over the sensor node. The ring of the helmet's base had exactly the same diameter as the ring of adhesive. Karen made an *ahhhh* noise.

"That's how the killer kept the alarms from going off," she said. "Sealing the helmet around the sensor node fooled the computer into thinking the lock was still full of air, even after the lock had been evacuated."

Linus set the helmet on the floor and ran a gloved finger around the inside. No stickiness on this one, but they'd have to check the others. "It doesn't explain why the computer didn't record the airlock being opened, though. And it—"

Behind them, the airlock door rolled shut with a heavy *clunk*.

CHAPTER FOURTEEN

The sun rose on the vid-screen ocean, filling the living room with gentle orange light. Noah Skyler quietly awakened and rolled over on the couch to stare at the ceiling. It was amazing he had gotten any sleep to begin with, considering the well-deserved berating he had been giving himself for most of the might. Stupid, stupid, stupid! What had he been thinking, making a crack like that? On the other hand, everyone knew that people who said "I'll call you" mentally added "after hell gets over that warm spell." Who did she think she was, putting him in this position?

His position. Maybe that was what the problem had been from the beginning. No matter how attractive she was, no matter how kind she had been, he had automatically assumed she thought she was better than him because of her money. And of course *he* had been the real snob all along. An insecure jerk, whose masculinity was threatened by a little—OK, a lot of money.

Noah tried to call her for the seventh time since he had returned to his apartment the previous night. For the seventh time, she didn't pick up, and for the seventh time he felt he felt a mixture of disappointment and relief.

After all, he didn't really know what he would say if and when she ever spoke to him again. "Sorry I stepped over a line I didn't know existed"?

He put his head his hands for a moment, then forced himself to get up and moving. Best to stay busy. He took a hot shower, dressed, and was debating whether or not to skip breakfast when the bedroom door opened and Jake emerged, dark hair tousled, eyes still heavy with sleep. He wore only a pair of old shorts, and his body was well-contoured with defined muscle.

"You *did* sleep out here," he said, running a hand over his face. "Why didn't you use the other bed?"

"I got in late and assumed Wade was in there."

"Nope. I think he's crashing with some friends." Jake yawned. "You scared the shit out of him. I'm betting he doesn't come back."

Noah groaned. "He's not dead, is he?"

"Doubt it." Jake trudged toward the bathroom. "But we better enjoy having the apartment to ourselves while we can. We'll have a new roommate before the week's out, promise you that."

While Jake busied himself in the bathroom, Noah left the apartment and took the train down to the security offices. His stomach hardened with tension when he saw Gary Newberg sitting behind the duty desk. Behind him sat more desks, and it occurred to Noah that one of them was probably his. At the moment all of them were empty, and Noah's footsteps echoed slightly in the large room. Gary gave Noah an even stare.

"What's up?" Gary demanded.

Noah leaned his fingertips on the duty desk and kept his voice steady as a leveled pistol. "You want to explain what the hell you were doing?"

"You want to explain what the hell you're talking about?"

"We both know I didn't screw up at the crime scene. We both know that *I* didn't lie to Linus. We both know that—"

"I don't know any such thing," Gary replied hotly.

"What did I ever do to you?" Noah said, abruptly changing tactics. "Why the hostility?"

"Fuck you."

Noah reined in his temper. "Fine. At least tell me if those two perps I marked yesterday afternoon have been apprehended."

"I'm pleased to say they haven't." Gary smirked. "No collar for you."

"And unless you get off your fat ass, you won't have one, either," Noah snapped.

Gary bolted to his feet, face red, fists clenched.

Noah jutted out his chin. "You gonna hit me, Gare? I don't think you have the balls."

Gary drew back his fist and Noah tensed. The pain would only last until he got to an autodoc, but it would be worth it. Hitting a fellow deputy might be enough to get Gary Newburg tossed from the force. At minimum he'd be temporarily suspended. But Gary paused and dropped his hand.

"Get the fuck out," he said.

"Make me."

"Then stay. I don't give a shit anymore." Gary swiveled his chair so his back was to Noah. Feeling a bit confused, Noah left the office, got a crime scene kit from the storage area, and headed down to the fish farm.

What the hell was up with Gary? The guy's reactions made no sense. Noah hadn't done a single thing to him, and then, out of nowhere, he had lied to Linus about Noah's ineptitude. It couldn't be an attempt to cover Gary's own mistakes—Noah hadn't reported anything. The scene they'd played out in the office also made little sense. Sure, Gary would deny lying in case Noah was recording the conversation, but the abrupt change from angry aggression to weary acceptance struck Noah as very odd.

The fish farm crime scene was still sectioned off with holographic tape. The holographic generators reported that no one had crossed the lines since Noah had last visited the scene. Around him, filter motors hummed in concrete tanks, fish splashed beneath the screens, and the smell of scales and algae permeated the air. Employees dressed in blue coveralls wandered among the square tanks. One of them worked a control, and the screen covering one tank winched up to the ceiling. He worked another control, and another screen, this one perpendicular to the tank, scraped downward to line one wall. Machinery hummed as the screen slid forward, herding the fish ahead of it until they were a squirming silver mass pressed up between the screen and the far wall of the tank. Two other employees armed with hand nets swiftly ladled the wriggling fish into the back of a cart. Harvest time.

Noah glanced warily around the chamber to see if Irene was lurking anywhere. He didn't see her, so he turned his attention to the crime scene. The air down here was extremely damp, and it had taken two days for the floor to dry completely. Setting up heat lamps would have changed the water temperature in the tanks and had an adverse affect on the fish, and fans would have moved the water around, destroying footprint patterns. So Noah had been forced to wait for natural evaporation to do the job. Not that he'd had time to come back any earlier than this, in any case.

From his scene kit, Noah extracted a large spray bottle filled with a clear liquid and approached one end of the crime scene. He sprayed the liquid over a section of floor, then got the light bar for the kit's scanner. Noah changed te frequency of the bar so it would emit a healthy dose of ultraviolet radiation and switched it on.

Although the workers did their best, the water in the fish tanks was far from sterile. Various forms of bacteria easily survived the filtration, as did a certain amount of fish scales and lots of microscopic algae. The chemical marker Noah had sprayed down latched onto the cytosine component of the organic material's DNA and RNA. When Noah ran his ultraviolet light over the area, the marker reacted with it and made everything glow. Noah nodded in satisfaction as several sets of purple footprints appeared beneath the light bar. Working carefully, he sprayed the rest of the crime scene and ran the light bar over the area, moving slowly toward the fish tank Viktor Riza had died in.

Some of the footprints were blurry or smeared, and none of them contained tread marks, though Noah would be able to check shoe sizes with them. Taking images as he went, Noah meticulously examined the entire area. Two sets looked like boot prints to Noah and probably belonged to the paramedics. A big splotchy area near the concrete tank marked the spot where the killer had pushed Viktor's face into the water above the screen and where the paramedics had let Viktor's body slide to the floor.

Noah also found three sets of footprints that didn't seem to belong to the paramedics. One of them obviously belonged to Viktor. Another, the smallest set, probably belonged to Bredda, and Noah was willing to bet the third set belonged to Indigo. He pulled his monocle around and told his obie to seek out contact information for shoe stores in Luna City. There were only two. Noah used his authority as a deputy to access the sales records. Bredda had bought a pair of shoes there five months ago, and her size was on record. It matched one of the sets Noah had found. Another set of prints matched Viktor's size. That left one more set— Indigo's. But since Noah had no way to know yet who Indigo was, the shoe size wasn't much of a clue. Any number of people might wear the same one. He made a record of it, in case another lead turned up.

Next Noah started trying to piece together what had happened by following the pattern of prints. Three sets— non-paramedic ones—headed toward a different fish tank, not the one Viktor had drowned in. There was an area of splashing around this tank, and the third set of prints— presumably Indigo's—left. The remaining two sets of prints wandered toward the tank where Viktor had met his death. The prints got smeared as they neared the tank. Further away from the tank, the third set of prints reappeared without drawing near. Bredda's small footprints went toward them, and both sets headed away. The paramedics came in from another direction, and their prints mingled in the smeared section near the drowning tank.

Noah stared at the glowing purple footprints, inhaling damp air laced with smells of fish and algae. He had to figure this out. It would show Linus that Noah knew what he was doing, that he was an experienced investigator who didn't make stupid mistakes. It would also be a fine thing to hand Linus a solved case and thereby get the Mayor-President off Linus's back. He could already see the smiling, grateful look on Linus's face.

Noah set his jaw. He was faced with a puzzle, one that he knew he could solve if he went over it step by step. Or footprint by footprint. Noah cursed the fact that he had never gone hunting. This was a job for a tracker. Maybe he should call over to Security and see if anyone with that skill could come down. Then he remembered that Gary was on desk duty and all such requests would go through him. Noah would rather have gnawed his own leg off in a vac suit.

So. The prints were there, and so was their story. All he had to do was think logically. Noah furrowed his brow. It looked like Bredda, Indigo, and Viktor had all three come to the fish tanks together. Something had happened and Indigo had left—or he had pretended to. Bredda and Viktor had wandered toward one of the tanks. Viktor was high and horny thanks to a massive dose of Blue. There had been a brief struggle—the source of the smearing—and Bredda had shoved Viktor's face into the water that topped the screens and held him there until he had drowned while Indigo cold-bloodedly watched.

The only question was *why*. Why kill Viktor? Indigo and Bredda's goal was to addict new customers to Blue, not kill them off. Killing new customers accomplished nothing—dead people didn't buy Blue.

Maybe Viktor had tried to force himself on Bredda, and Bredda had killed him in self-defense. No, that didn't work. Viktor's blood work had shown enough Blue to stun a horse. There was no way he would have been able to force anything on anyone. And if Bredda could claim self-defense, it was unlikely she would have run away from the police. Maybe Viktor had realized what Bredda and Indigo were trying to do and had threatened to report them. But why, then, had Indigo left?

The final pieces of the puzzle lay with Bredda and Indigo. Someone should have seen the orange dye on them and called Security by now. They should have been arrested within hours, even minutes. So why hadn't they shown up anywhere?

Because someone was hiding them. All Noah had to do was figure out—

Noah smacked himself on the forehead with the heel of his hand. Idiot! He had been overlooking an obvious lead.

Before running back to Security, however, Noah forced himself to finish processing the crime scene, checking for fingerprints, DNA, and other trace evidence. He didn't find anything of interest. The concrete tanks were too rough to accept fingerprints, and there were too many DNA traces left from hundreds of workers, maintenance people, and general passersby to be useful. Indigo's DNA might be here somewhere, but Noah wouldn't be able to figure out which bits of genetic material belonged to him.

Noah did find several hairs on the edge of the tank where Viktor had drowned, and they turned out to belong to Viktor. He also found Bredda's DNA in the form of skin flakes left on the lip of the concrete. More proof of Bredda's involvement in Viktor's death.

Noah packed his kit, left the crime scene boundary up in case he thought of something else to look for, and headed back to the Security office. Carefully he refilled the crime scene kit, then went to the weapons room, where he signed out another ink pistol, a needle pistol, and a can of Sticky-Foam. Noah slid the three weapons into an equipment belt around his waist, then gritted his teeth and went in to see Gary.

"I need backup," he said without preamble. "I have an arrest to make, and I'm pretty sure I know where the perps are."

"Pretty sure?" Gary echoed. "Pretty sure doesn't get you very far, pretty boy."

Noah stared at him. "Are you going to get me backup, or are you going to make me call Linus about it?"

At that moment, the main door opened and Deputy Valerie Marks came in, her acne-scarred face looking serene and calm beneath her buzzed hair. "Hey, Gary. Sorry I'm late, but you wouldn't believe what just happened to the Chief. I'm here now, though, so you can go—"

Gary made frantic shushing gestures.

"—on walking duty," she finished. "What's wrong?"

Noah closed his eyes for a long moment. If Gary was on walking duty, he was the number-one candidate for backup. "Okay, Gary," he said. "Let's get this over with. And try not to get shot in the ass."

A long, silent train ride later, Gary and Noah were standing in front of an apartment door. Birds sang merrily among scented blossoms, unaware of the police action just below them. Noah rang the bell, and a moment later, the door slid open to reveal Crysta Nell. Her expression froze for a moment before forcibly relaxing.

"Did you find Bredda and that guy yet?" she asked, a little too brightly. "I still haven't seen either of them, not since that little party we had with your roommate."

"Didn't your mommy teach you it's bad to lie?" Noah said. "Especially to a policeman."

The bright tone left her voice. "Fuck you."

"That wasn't nice, either. May we come in?"

She planted herself firmly in the doorway. "No. Not without a warrant. And I know you don't have one because you'd have shown it to me already."

"We don't have a warrant," Gary said. "We don't any right to search this nice lady's apartment, Skyler. Let's go."

Noah, however, was looking hard at Crysta's right hand. "Ms. Nell, is that a fleck of orange paint I see on your hand?"

Crysta whipped her hand behind her back.

"That's the exact shade we police use to mark criminals who flee a crime scene," Noah said matter-of-factly, "and it abrogates the need for a warrant. Step aside, or I will move you aside."

Crysta face changed from defiant to frightened to defiant again. Still she didn't move. Noah stiff-armed her and she stumbled backward into the apartment, her feet backpedaling in midair for a long moment in the low gravity. Gary followed Noah inside.

"Don't blow this, Gary," Noah said. "It's a collar for you, too."

"Fuck you," Gary muttered. He was already handcuffing Crysta. Noah pulled the can of StickyFoam from his belt and kicked the bedroom door open. He wasn't the least bit surprised to find Bredda and Indigo inside. Although their clothes were clean, various parts of their skins were blotchy with orange dye. They had a raw, scrubbed look, as if they'd tried to remove the dye with sandpaper. Bredda had dyed her hair a fake-looking black, but the dye was designed with this possibility in mind, and orange streaks were showing through the dark color.

Bredda screamed when Noah burst in, and Indigo swore. Noah aimed the can at Bredda, who was closest, and pressed the release. White foam gushed out of the can in long strings, covering Bredda with tentacles that clung to her body, her clothing, the floor, and to the wall behind her. The foam set in less than a second, becoming slightly flexible but unyieldingly sticky. Bredda screeched and clawed at the foam, but she couldn't tear free of it.

Indigo, meanwhile, surged toward the door. He managed to shove Noah aside and make it into the living room, where Gary stood guard over the cuffed Crysta.

"Don't let him get away!" Noah shouted, scrambling for balance in the wretched gravity.

Gary shot Noah a hostile look, then grabbed for Indigo. He managed to get his arms around Indigo from behind. Indigo struggled for only a split-second before breaking free and leaping for the apartment door like a superhero. Swearing, Noah snatched his needler from its holster and loped into the hallway. Indigo already had a good lead, and he ignored Noah's order to halt. Noah aimed and fired. The pistol snapped a barrage of needles at Indigo's retreating back. Several went wide and shattered harmlessly against the corridor walls, as they were designed to do. Several more, however, embedded themselves in Indigo's back. He twitched, managed a few more steps, them stumbled to the ground in a drugged haze. Noah cuffed him and dragged him back into the apartment, where Gary was still standing over Crysta.

"That was deliberate!" Noah snarled. "You let him go on purpose, you son of a bitch!"

Gary shrugged. "No such thing, Skyler. Guess I just need to hit the gym a little more. Too bad you'll be up to your eyebrows in paperwork now that you've fired on a civilian."

Noah set his teeth, then used his obie to call for a pickup. A few minutes later, an electric wagon glided up to the door and two deputies got out. They sprayed the cursing, snarling Bredda with an enzyme to dissolve the Sticky-Foam, cuffed her, and put her in the wagon along with Crysta and Indigo. Gary smirked at Noah.

"See you down at the station for the paperwork," he said, and vanished out the door.

Noah stood there in the empty apartment for several moments. Then he buried his face in the crook of his sleeve and howled until some of the rage subsided. That done, he calmly sealed the apartment and boarded a train back to Security. It was blessedly uncrowded for once, and Noah actually got a seat. When he was settled, he pulled his monocle around.

"Obie," he murmured, "access Security personnel database."

His eyes tracked as he read for several minutes. Then realization dawned on his face. He reread the information to make sure it wasn't a mistake, then severed the link and rode the rest of the way to the station in thoughtful silence.

At the station, he found Gary at a desk in the main room, tapping madly at a computer. Bredda and Indigo sat in separate chairs, their hands still cuffed behind them. Indigo still looked woozy. Valerie Marks was talking to Crysta in a low voice. Noah slipped down to the storage area and grabbed another spray can, this one marked PEEL ADHESIVE. Gary was still typing when Noah came back upstairs. He looked up when Noah approached the desk. The hostile smirk was still on his face.

"Shame about that lousy collar," he said.

Noah hooked a foot under Gary's chair and yanked. For once, the moon's light gravity made something easier. The chair came up and Gary flew backward with a yelp. He fell slowly, landing flat on his back. Before he could react further, Noah hosed the front of his shirt with the contents of the spray can. Valerie, Crysta, and Bredda all stared. Indigo drooled. The chair continued upward, hit the ceiling, and drifted back down to the floor like a wooden feather.

"What the fuck are you doing?" Gary screamed.

The liquid in the can formed a clear, flexible film over Gary's shirt. In a single sharp gesture, Noah grabbed one edge of the film and jerked. It tore free with a Velcro ripping sound. Threads and tiny bits of fabric clung to the other side. Noah checked to make sure the film was dry, then rolled it into a translucent scroll like a medieval monk with a precious parchment. Gary scrambled to his feet.

"I said, what the fuck are you doing?" He was panting, his face red with outrage.

Noah favored him with a tight smile. "Let's go see Linus."

CHAPTER FIFTEEN

Linus tried to wedge his fingernails between the airlock door and the seal, knowing it was futile, having to try anyway. Beside him, Karen beat with frantic fists on the ceramic. Panic gripped Linus's throat, and he had to choke down a scream. Somehow he kept his head long enough to punch frantically at the control panel next to the door. It didn't respond.

A faint hissing sound slid through the room like a cobra, and Linus's ears popped. The air was evacuating from the chamber. Karen's eyes went wide with terror. The analytical part of Linus's mind told him that in a few short moments, the air would be gone, the opposite door would open, and he and Karen would have perhaps ninety seconds before they died. Between ten and fifteen of those seconds would grant them useful consciousness. Linus desperately tried to remember where the closest emergency airlock was. Could he reach it in less than fifteen seconds? Ten? What about Karen? Already the air was growing thin, and Linus couldn't draw a full breath.

"If you're going to make a run for it," Karen gasped, "don't hold your breath. Let it out or you'll rupture your lungs like our John Doe."

He reached out and grabbed Karen's hand. She squeezed it gratefully. Linus had never been so glad to feel another human being, and he had never been so glad it was Karen.

"Karen," he panted. "Karen, I—"

"Don't!" she interrupted. "Not now. Just don't. Let's exhale and run and hope."

Linus didn't have the air to respond. Ahead of them, the outer door started to roll aside. A crack of bright sunlight appeared, and Linus's heart almost stopped. He'd forgotten about the sun. If the vacuum didn't get them, the radiation would. But he had to *try*, dammit. Karen's hand was cold as iron in his. Linus forced himself to exhale, let the life-giving air out of his lungs before the tiny molecules shredded the delicate tissue like a billion tiny needles. Terrible pain lanced his head as both his eardrums burst, and his remaining air rushed out in a scream of pain. The crack around the outer door widened, letting in more deadly radiation, indicating the vacuum in the airlock was complete. Linus thought of Robin and Vicky, and he wished he could talk to them for just two seconds, or even one. How would they hear of his death? And when? What were they doing right now, while he stood dying in an airlock forty-four thousand miles away? Would Vicky even understand what had happened? Black spots danced in front of Linus's eyes, and he leaned forward, ready to run despite the pain, despite the radiation.

And then a blast of wind caught him from behind. It nearly knocked him over. Abruptly he could breathe again. He sucked in a gulp of air and spun around, Karen still at his side. The door to the shuttle behind them had rolled halfway open. Adrienne Miao, a red licorice whip in her mouth, stood in the doorway. Wind whipped her short hair around her head. Alarm lights flashed, but Linus couldn't hear the klaxon. Adrienne clung to the doorway with one plump hand and held out her other. Karen lunged for it.

Adrienne hauled her out of the airlock. Linus managed to take another breath. It was like standing upwind in a hurricane. Abruptly his feet slipped out from under him and he was both falling forward and flying backward. He tried to scream and couldn't tell if he had succeeded.

A steel-hard hand grabbed his. Karen. She had Adrienne's arm hooked through hers, and Adrienne maintained a death grip on the doorjamb. Linus wavered in the wind like a frantic flag. With excruciating slowness, the two women hauled him out of the airlock. At last, all three of them were inside the main door. Adrienne slapped a button, and the door rolled shut. Linus collapsed, panting, on the floor. Every breath was sweet as new honey. His ears continued to throb, and he could already see the bruising on his skin from blood cells yanked out of their vessels to burst in the low pressure. He and Karen would both be black and blue by morning.

Karen, on the floor next to him, sat up and moved her mouth. Linus couldn't hear her. A wave of panic swept him, and he forced himself to calm down. Ruptured eardrums were easy enough to fix, an hour or two at most. Linus pointed at his ears and shrugged. Karen abruptly flung her arms around him. Her body shook, and he realized she was crying. Linus put his arms around her and held her until the storm subsided. It was a long moment that Linus wished would last until the sun went dark. At last Karen pulled away from him. She held him at arm's length and said something else Linus couldn't make out. He managed a weak smile. His arms felt limp, though whether from the ordeal or from the embrace he couldn't tell. To his consternation, he discovered he was hard.

Adrienne helped them to their feet. With great exaggeration, she mouthed "Medical bay" at them and pointed toward the stairs. Karen nodded, and the two of them followed Adrienne through the shuttle to a small but efficient-looking sick bay. Two examining tables could be sectioned off by curtains, and cabinets filled with medical supplies lined the walls. Karen gestured at Linus to sit on one of the tables while she rifled expertly through them in eerie silence. Adrienne stood in the doorway, her plump arms folded across her chest. Linus's ears still hurt like hell, and his skin was turning a reddish purple. His entire body ached.

Karen fastened a cuff around Linus's elbow and injected it first with a clear fluid, then with a yellow fluid. The pain instantly eased. She did the same to herself, and relief crossed her blotchy face. Next she took an earplug from a drawer and slid it into her left ear. She handed one to Linus, and he did the same.

"Can you hear me?" Karen said. Her voice sounded high and tinny, as if she were talking through helium, but she was perfectly understandable.

"Yes," he said gratefully. "Thank you."

"You sound like a cartoon character," Karen told him. "I can regrow our eardrums in a couple hours back at the medical center, but these neural simulators will do for now. The pain's easily manageable, of course, though I can't do anything about the bruising except recommend long, hot baths. Besides all that, how do you feel?"

"I think I'm all right. How about you?"

"Other than terrified, I'm fine."

Linus turned to Adrienne Miao. "Thank you. If you hadn't shown up, we'd be dead now."

"Hey, it was my pleasure." The licorice whip moved around her mouth like a cigar. "I heard the alarm go off and ran down to see what the hell was going on. I don't think anyone else was onboard, to tell the truth. You got lucky."

"So what the fuck happened?" Karen demanded in her new squeaky voice.

"I'm guessing it was something to do with the computer," Linus said. "Let's take a look."

A few minutes later, they were bending over Adrienne Miao, who was in turn bent over a terminal the connected directly to the main computer bank.

"Here it is," she said, pointing to the display. "An order to open emergency airlock 5D."

"Who authorized it?" Linus squeaked.

Adrienne started. The licorice whip fell from her mouth and drifted toward the floor. "Oh, Jesus. It says I did. But I didn't do it. You have to believe me."

"I do believe you," Linus said grimly. "But I'm afraid I'm going to be cooking a lot of crepes for poor Vanessa."

"Why is that?" Karen asked.

"Because the shuttle's entire computer bank is now evidence in a case of attempted murder, and I need to take it with me."

"I think I'll just pop down to the medical center and start on our eardrums then. I don't want to be anywhere near ground zero when Vanessa gets the news. Furious won't begin to describe it."

"Can I go with you?" Adrienne asked wistfully, and Linus sighed.

Vanessa was indeed furious. She raved, she screamed, she shouted, and she threatened. She shattered two teacups, no small feat in low gravity. And it didn't help that to Linus she sounded like Minnie Mouse throwing a temper tantrum. But in the end she was forced to allow Valerie Marks and Linus to remove the databanks and haul them back to Security for analysis. Linus only partly mollified her by promising to have them back by the next day.

While Marks escorted the computers to the security station, Linus stopped at the medical center and found Karen in one of the examination rooms. Her face was purple by now, as were Linus's arms and legs. He'd have to take a long, hot bath tonight. Karen held up a covered petri dish.

"It's ready, love," she said in her squeaky voice. "You're just lucky that regrown tympanic tissue isn't at all prone to cancer, unlike cardiac tissue. Otherwise you'd be hearing Disney voices for the rest of your life."

He ignored this and lay down on the table on his side as she instructed. Linus always kept his eyes closed during any medical procedure, unable to stand watching it come near him. He felt Karen's cool fingers brush the side of his face, and his groin tightened unexpectedly as it had back in the airlock. His face flushed as he felt the erection grow down the side of his leg. It pulsed warm with every beat of his heart, demanding immediate attention. His mind burst with images of Robin and Karen together on the examining table with Linus himself sandwiched between them. Their bodies writhed and twined together. Linus clamped his teeth together. A tiny touch, a faint pressure, would make him burst. He had never felt so horny in his life. More than anything in the world he wanted to snatch Karen (Robin?) into his arms and feel her warm mouth on his, slide into her, feel her moist heat around him.

"All done with that side," Karen said. Linus winced. He'd gotten her voice in weird stereo—normal in one ear, squeaky in the other. He pulled the plug from his other ear, then rolled over, side-to-stomach-to-side in order to hide his arousal, and let her complete the procedure with his other ear. He almost came the second time she touched him, and he bit his lip until he tasted blood to keep control.

"You're shaking," Karen said as she finished up. "Are you all right? I didn't hurt you, did I?"

"No," he said hoarsely, sitting up with his back to her. His erection ached as it rubbed softly against his underwear, and he felt close to the edge. "Everything's fine. Just some post-trauma jitters, I think."

"It's okay, love. You survived, and everything's fine."

Unexpectedly, Karen hugged him from behind. Her breasts pressed into his back, and Linus came. A wave of pleasure washed over him, and he shuddered hard under the intensity of it. Warmth flooded his groin.

"It's okay," Karen whispered in his ear. "I'm here. You can cry. I won't tell anyone. Promise."

Linus almost laughed. She had mistaken orgasm for tears. Story of his life. He grabbed her wrist, squeezed, then gently disengaged himself.

"Thanks, Karen," he said. "I just need a minute alone."

She gave him a long look, then nodded and withdrew. The minute the door had shut, Linus scrambled out of trousers and underwear and managed a quick cleanup with a washcloth he found in a pile of linens and dampened in the sink. The sticky underwear he thrust deep in the wastebasket, the damp trousers he pulled back on. Jesus, what had gotten into him? Linus couldn't remember the last time he had creamed his jeans. He was acting like a horny teenager or something. It was certainly abnormal in a man of forty. The whole incident scared him half to . . .

. . . half to death.

Linus grimaced. Near-death experiences made lots of people horny. It was either an adrenaline rush, or the result of a subconscious desire to leave children behind in case the next such incident turned out rather worse. That was all it had been.

Had Karen felt the same thing? Maybe she'd had the same reaction when he touched her wrist.

Jesus. The thought of Karen having a spontaneous orgasm was making him hard again. He firmly reined in this line of thought, finished doing up his trousers, and splashed cold water on his face. A glance in the mirror told him he looked like shit. Multicolored blotches were splashed across his face, and his eyes looked like the aftereffects of a three-day bender. Sexy he wasn't.

Once he had made himself as presentable as possible, he exited the examination room and asked a passing nurse where Karen might be found.

"She's undergoing a procedure, Chief," the young man said. "Do you need to see someone?"

Linus gave himself a mental shake. Of course—someone would have to restore Karen's ears as well. He'd check back with her later. Right now he had to track down a killer.

Back at Security, he realized he had switched his obie off. He had several messages waiting for him. One was from the Mayor-President, demanding an update. Linus thought about that. Calling her was a calculated risk. Linus could call her back later, which would increase the chances of pissing her off but also increase the chances that he'd have something to tell her. Or he could call her right now, decreasing the chance of pissing her off but also decreasing the amount of information he'd have for her.

He decided to wait.

Down in the evidence room, he found Valerie Marks hooking up the shuttle's computer bank to a police terminal. The bank itself was a gray box the size of a small briefcase. Valerie left once she was sure everything was set properly. Linus accessed the shuttle's main computer and was about to check the airlock records when his obie trilled. The alarm indicated a top-priority call, and it was coming from the Mayor-President's office. Linus sighed and pulled his monocle around. Ravi Pandey's expression was dark and chilly as a crate on the far side of the moon.

"What's this I hear about you making off with the entire computer bank of a Tether Station shuttle?" she said in a controlled voice. *"Vanessa Maygrave just called me in a fine temper."*

"Did she tell you why I confiscated the computer?" Linus asked mildly.

"I couldn't get much out of her, to tell the truth," said the Mayor-President. *"I assume you have a good reason, Chief Inspector, but I need to know what it is."*

"Someone sabotaged the computer so it would open the airlock Karen and I were processing for evidence in the John Doe case," Linus said. "He or she almost killed both of us. Since there's a good chance the person who arranged that is the same one who killed our mystery man, I took the computer bank to see if I can figure out who it was."

"I see. Keep me informed, then." And she signed off.

"Thanks for your concern," Linus said to empty air. "It's not like I nearly died or anything."

He turned back to the computer with a sigh and started searching. He readily found the order to open the airlock, but as Adrienne Miao had said, the order appeared to come from her. Linus didn't think for a second it really was Miao, of course. If she had really tried to kill Karen and Linus this way, it seemed highly unlikely that she would also have saved them at the last minute—or used her own, easily traced access codes to open the airlock in the first place.

Linus tapped the table with his fingertips. Too many things didn't match here. The body had appeared to come from a Luna City airlock, but it had actually come from the shuttle. The body had been missing one shoe. The airlock had been opened, but not by the person who matched the access codes. The John Doe's DNA didn't match the DNA of anyone registered on Luna. What else didn't match?

On impulse, Linus checked the shuttle computer to see if it contained the biometric data of its crew. It did. Another checked showed that it still contained a list of the crew who had been on board the day Adrienne Miao had overshot the landing. None of them had been reported missing, but wasn't it possible that something wouldn't quite match? Linus called up John Doe's DNA and told the computer to check it against the DNA of the shuttle's crew. The computer ran the check, and Linus held his breath.

No matches. Dammit!

"What's going on, love?"

Linus jumped. He hadn't heard Karen come in. Her expression was lightly quizzical, though her skin was blotched and purple with bruises. Linus realized he was leaning toward her for a hello kiss and pulled back in confusion. Karen appeared not to notice.

"I'm looking for matches," Linus told her. "But I'm coming up empty."

Karen looked over his shoulder at the computer data winking on the holographic display. "It seems to me that only a member of the crew could pull of something like this," she said. "I mean, even assuming you were a world-class hacker, would *you* know how to order a space shuttle's computer to open an airlock?"

"No," Linus admitted. "I wouldn't even know where to start."

"So the killer has to be someone on the crew roster," Karen said, pointing. "Logic would also say that the same goes for the victim."

"The victim could have been a passenger," Linus said. "Though none of the passengers from that flight have been reported missing."

"Did you check John Doe's DNA against the passenger data, just to be sure?"

Linus nodded. "Long ago. That's the weird thing, Karen. Everything matches perfectly, except for the victim. He doesn't match anything or anyone. We know he was on the shuttle because we found his DNA in the airlock, but the computer doesn't have a record of him among the crew or passengers. Miao said stowaways are impossible, so where the hell did John Doe come from?"

"Maybe we need to challenge the premise," Karen said. "How do we know John Doe was on the shuttle?"

"We found his DNA there," Linus replied promptly.

"Can we assume it wasn't planted there?"

"I think that's safe to assume. It would be ungodly difficult to create those scratches and plant Doe's DNA in them without leaving your own DNA behind as well, and the computer only found Doe's DNA."

"And how do we know Doe's DNA doesn't match the DNA of anyone who was on the shuttle the day Miao overshot?"

"I checked Doe's DNA against the DNA of everyone who was on board. It didn't match."

"Let's be specific," Karen admonished. "*You* didn't check the DNA yourself."

"What are you talking about?" Linus said, surprised. "Of course I did."

"No. *You* didn't do it."

"Yes, I did. I fed the DNA into the computer myself."

"So you didn't check it yourself," Karen maintained with a mischievous glint in her brown eyes.

Linus began to feel like he was trapped in an Abbott and Costello sketch. "Yes, I did."

"Did you compare every strand of DNA yourself? Hold up a chart of John Doe's DNA and compare it to a chart of everyone else's DNA?"

"Obviously not. That would take decades. I fed it into . . ." He trailed off.

"Yes, love?" Karen asked, and he knew she'd had the answer from the beginning.

"I fed it into the computer," Linus said slowly. "And the computer told me nothing matched."

"The computer told you," Karen echoed.

Linus disconnected the shuttle's computer bank, snatched it up with one hand, and grabbed Karen's wrist with the other. "Come on!" he said, towing her toward the door.

"Where are we going?" she demanded, putting up no real resistance.

"To see Hector."

They found Hector Valdez in his immaculate office, his waxed mustache quivering with anticipation at the look on Linus's face. As always, a cluster of grad students hovered around the computer terminal in the corner, playing god with computer code.

"Well?" Hector said. "You still owe me crepes from your first visit, Linus. And what in the world happened to your face? And yours, Doctor?"

"We had an accident," Karen said, "that wasn't really an accident."

"I need you to check this computer bank for tampering," Linus told him. "First see if you can trace an order to open an emergency airlock."

The grad students were giving Linus and Karen sidelong glances and their voices dropped. Linus made a note of their presence, then ignored them. Hector, meanwhile, connected the shuttle computer to the terminal on his desk and set to work. The holographic display that hovered over the keyboard flickered and flashed like a dancing genie.

"Crude," Hector muttered. "Very crude. Look at this. The order appears to have come from this Adrienne Miao woman, but it couldn't have—the datastream didn't originate from the terminal Miao appears to have used."

"Where did it come from?" Karen asked.

Hector typed quickly. "It came from off-site. Someone accessed the shuttle's computer remotely, ordered the computer to open the airlock, then used a small virus to mask the origin of the order. It was crudely done, and I suspect whoever did it had to work fast."

"Can you trace the real origin of the order?"

"Let me try." Hector's fingers flew over the board and he muttered technical commands to the terminal. Data flashed by, most of it meaningless to Linus. He stood by while Hector worked, trying not to show his impatience. At last Hector dropped his hands with a sigh.

"I'm afraid I can't trace it," he said reluctantly. "The order to open the airlock came quickly, but the person clearly took his time scrubbing away any line leading back to him—or her. I'm sorry I can't tell you more."

"Actually, you've told us quite a lot," Linus said. "You've told us the killer is a computer expert."

Hector brightened. "This is true. The average person would have no idea how to go about this. Did you have something else you wanted me to check?"

"I want you to see if anyone has tampered with the biometric data of the passengers or crew," Linus said. "Especially the passengers."

"Ah! A challenge." Hector cracked his knuckles. "Let me see."

He set to work. Linus and Karen leaned silently against the wall and waited. The room became warm and stuffy as grad students cycled in and out of the office, always clustering around the terminal in the corner. Linus wondered what the attraction of that particular terminal was, but didn't want to distract Hector or call attention to himself by asking one of the students directly.

"This one!" Hector almost shouted, making Linus jump. "Here. This one. Look at this. All the biometric data files, including DNA files, were uploaded and created on the shuttle on this date here." He pointed at the display. "But this one—this passenger's data file was changed several hours later and resaved. Whoever did it forgot to change the time stamp."

Linus looked down at the display, and everything clicked. A rush of exhilaration thrilled through him, making his skin tingle and filling him with an urge to leap up and punch the ceiling.

"So that's our victim?" Karen asked, leaning in to look.

"No," Linus said. "It's our killer."

"The killer?" Hector echoed.

"Explain," Karen said.

Linus muttered to his obie for a moment, then began to pace, too restless to stand still. "While the shuttle was flying from Tether Station to Luna, the killer got the victim alone, hit him hard enough to stun him, and shoved him into an airlock. Hell, the killer may have thought John Doe was already dead. Then the killer fastened a space helmet over the sensor node and got to work on the shuttle's computer. He replaced the victim's biometric data with his own, then altered Miao's flight plan to make her overshoot the mark. When she corrected, he cycled the airlock, though the victim woke up at the last moment and tried to escape. The shuttle changed direction, but the victim's body wasn't held down, so it kept going in the original direction. Once the airlock was clear, the killer reset it, removed the helmet, and erased the incident from the computer. He was even able to change the record of keystrokes to make it look like Miao had entered the wrong flight data."

"That seems terribly complicated." Hector stroked his mustache. "Why didn't the killer murder his victim back on Earth and dispose of the body there?"

"Because DNA databases back on Earth are almost impossible to hack," Linus said. "Security is extremely tight.

But the killer had access to the shuttle's computers and could easily replace the victim's DNA records with his own, and that's what the killer wanted in the first place."

"He wanted to take his victim's place?" Karen said.

"Exactly. Once the killer arrived on Luna, he assumed his victim's identity. He gave his assumed name and a DNA sample to immigration. They checked both against the records *on the shuttle*, and of course, everything matched. He was granted entry to Luna City under his new name, and everything was both hunky and dory. Except for one little thing."

"One little thing," Karen said. "I assume the great detective has already figured out the one little thing?"

"He has," Linus replied. "The victim, you see, was coming to Luna City University to study, and all students have to take a secondary job. That job is assigned long before the student arrives, and it's already logged into various Luna City computers. The killer wouldn't necessarily be any good at the victim's secondary job, but there would be no way for him to change it without blowing his cover."

At that moment, the door opened and Wesley Yard came into the office. Everyone turned to look at him.

"There's some kind of problem with my schedule for the new semester?" Yard said. "I got an urgent message telling me to come down here about it."

"Well, Mr. Yard, technically speaking, I suppose that's true." Linus moved smoothly between Yard and the door. "There's definitely a problem with your schedule next semester. You won't be finishing it."

Yard looked wary and worried. "I don't understand."

"You work tech for the Dai Memorial Theater, is that right?" Linus asked. "How's that working out for you?"

"It's okay," Yard said. "What's that got to do with my schedule?"

"It's okay, love?" Karen came around from behind Hector's desk. "There were some pretty horrendous problems with the lighting at Noah Skyler's show last night. And you were listed as the lighting technician. A little barmy, that. Your record says you have several years experience working theater and lighting back on—"

Yard lunged. Linus had been ready for him to break for the door, and was caught off-guard when Yard went for Karen instead. In less than a second, he was standing behind her, one hand around her throat, lifting her nearly off the ground. Karen made a small choking sound. Her bruised, purple face made it look like she was choking to death. The cluster of grad students gaped.

"I'll break her neck," Yard snarled. "So help me."

Linus broke into a cold sweat. Calling Yard down to the office had been an impulse—and a mistake. He should have sent a pair of deputies down to Yard's apartment to arrest him quick and quiet. Instead he had turned the entire affair into a circus and put Karen's life in danger. Fear for her squeezed his stomach into a tight ball.

"No one wants anyone to get hurt," Linus said, voicing a calm he didn't feel. "Why don't you just let her go and we'll talk, okay?"

"Fuck off," Yard barked. "Move away from the door, or I break her. You know I killed the real Wesley Yard. One more kill won't matter."

Linus edged slowly away from the door. "It's okay, son. I'm not going to—"

"I'm not your son," Yard shouted. "Now open the—"

And then Karen moved. Yard doubled up. Air whooshed out of him like a spent balloon and he dropped slowly to the ground. Karen kicked him on the way down. Twice.

"Idiot," she spat. "What kind of fool takes a doctor hostage? I know all the tender bits."

"You have sharp elbows," Linus said weakly.

"Damned nice of him to bring himself within range of them," Karen said. She ran her hands over her neck. "Did he bruise me?"

Considering the black-and-blue condition of her skin, Linus wasn't sure if she had meant that as a joke or not, so he didn't respond. Instead he savored the relief he felt and suppressed the urge to sweep Karen into his arms for a kiss. Then he slid plastic handcuffs on the gasping man lying on the floor and put in a call to the station.

CHAPTER SIXTEEN

"**W**esley Yard's real name is Donato Giacci," Linus said. "Once I got that much out of him, the rest was easy to piece together. Took a little research, though."

"So Yard—Giacci—is keeping his mouth shut?" Karen asked. She was sitting opposite Linus in his cool office, her face still bruised. The holographic stream continued to rush over stone and ice.

"He isn't saying a word. They only confess to everything in the vid-feeds." Linus ran a hand through his hair. It was barely an hour after the arrest, but he felt like he'd been working all day. "Giacci's application to study at Luna City University as a grad student is on file. Can you guess what field he wanted?"

"If it's not computers, I'll buy you lunch every day for a month."

"Safe bet," Linus said. "Giacci didn't make it in, but his undergrad roommate did. Can you guess the roommate's name?"

"Same bet, and it was Wesley Yard."

"The doctor wins again. Giacci's a little . . . off, though. I talked to a couple of his professors at Cambridge, where he did his undergrad work. They said Giacci was obsessed with studying at Luna U. Talked about almost nothing else. He even got a job working for International Flyways right after he graduated in order to be closer to Luna. Giacci is a great programmer, and he was fairly quickly assigned to work the Luna shuttle. It must have been some kind of torture for him, seeing the place just out of reach, and it must have pushed him over the edge when he was turned down but his old roommate got in."

"So he decided to take Wesley's place?" Karen said. "Sick bloke."

"Sick, yes, but not stupid." Linus leaned back in his chair. "Giacci planned the entire murder carefully and carried it off perfectly. Even the choice of victim was careful. Yard's parents are dead, and he has—had—a much older sister who he hadn't spoken to in years. No extended family he kept contact with. No girlfriend or boyfriend. In other words, no one would miss Wesley Yard or try to find him if he dropped out of sight. No one would try to call him and be surprised when someone with a different face answered the phone. No one would invite him to the annual family picnic and wonder why he didn't show.

"Giacci approached Yard on the shuttle flight from Tether Station and pretended to be surprised to see him. Old roommate! Old friend! Hey, let's talk, get caught up. How about someplace more private? I know—we can try that emergency airlock. No one goes down there, and we can talk all we want."

"So then Giacci cracks Wesley over the head to knock him out down by the airlock," Karen said. "That explains the wound I found in his skull."

"Exactly. Giacci uses his imp gun to erase Wesley's obie, though he's unaware the erasure isn't complete, allowing us to find the partial file that set Wesley's arrival at less than six months ago. Next, Giacci seals the vac suit helmet over the airlock's sensor, goes to his work station, and hacks into the piloting program, easy enough for someone who helps oversee the shuttle's computer systems. He changes Adrienne Miao's numbers so the shuttle will overshoot and makes sure the keystrokes are traced back to her instead of him. When she notices the mistake and fires the burners to correct the course, Giacci orders the airlock to cycle. He also erases the computer's record of the event. But Wesley wakes up before the cycle is complete and claws at the door, trying to escape. It doesn't work. Wesley dies, and when the shuttle reverses course, his body continues going in the original direction. It goes out the airlock door in a long arc and eventually falls into the crater where those two students eventually find it. On the way, the body hits a communications antenna. One leg cracks and a shoe flies off in a different direction.

"Meanwhile, Giacci is busy at the computer again. As a computer technician, he has full access to passenger records. Giacci erases Wesley's DNA, his image, and everything else from the passenger file and replaces the information with his own. Later, when he hits immigration, the worker checks Giacci's identity against the file from the shuttle, and of course everything matches. Giacci simply gives his name as Wesley Yard, and no one here knows the difference. If he hadn't missed that time stamp when he replaced the files, we might never have caught him."

"And I assume he was the one who tried to cycle the airlock on us," Karen said.

Linus nodded. "Hector confirmed it. I don't know yet how Giacci found out we had learned about the crime scene, but he still has friends in International Flyways, so maybe he found out that way. Or maybe he just saw you and me heading for the shuttle and figured it out on his own. At any rate, Giacci used a University computer terminal to access the shuttle's computer. He still knew his way around the system, though he had to hack his way past the security, and he didn't have time to silence the alarms or erase his digital footprints very well. Hector said it was good work, considering how little time Giacci had, and then he complained that I owed him extra crepes for arresting one of his most promising students. Go figure."

"Except what did Giacci plan to do when he was done with his graduate work?" Karen asked. "He'd have problems continuing on as Wesley Yard back on Earth, wouldn't he?"

"Maybe so, maybe no," Linus said. "After spending two or three years here, he would have built up quite a history of himself as Wesley. The only people who'd check his biometric data would be doctors and law enforcement people. The original Yard didn't have a criminal record, so his DNA wasn't on file with the law, meaning Giacci would be safe there, even if he were arrested. And he'd have a few years of medical records from Luna to take to a new doctor back on Earth, so no worries there, either. Or maybe Giacci was planning to apply for Loony citizenship. After everything he went through to get here, it seems likely he wouldn't want to leave."

"So how come no one missed Donato Giacci? He couldn't just vanish from his job."

"Actually that's exactly what he did. Once he arrived on Luna, he notified International Flyways that he was resigning to attend grad school at Luna University. International Flyways didn't bother to check up on that. Why would they? It happens every now and then—someone gets a job on the shuttle for the sole purpose of getting a free ride to Luna. International Flyways has a policy of not rehiring such people and of giving them poor references, but that didn't matter to Giacci. He was going to spend the rest of his life as Wesley Yard, Loony U graduate. He was all set."

"Except that Giacci knew nothing about lighting systems," Karen pointed out.

Linus smiled. "Yeah. Giacci had put in a request to transfer to a different secondary job, but Roger Davids wouldn't let him go without a replacement. So Giacci was stuck pretending he knew what he was doing. Poor Noah caught the brunt of that."

At that moment, Linus's obie chimed with an incoming call from a familiar source. "Speaking of the kid," he said, and put the call on speaker.

"Linus, it's Noah," came the familiar voice. *"Are you down at Security?"*

"Sure am," Linus replied. "What's up?"

"I've solved the murder of Viktor Riza."

Holograms and flat images lay spread across the white evidence table, along with sets of reports and summaries. Gary Newburg stood seething in one corner but said nothing. Noah ushered Linus and Karen into the room like a butler showing guests into a dining room.

"Gary was involved in the arrest?" Linus asked.

"Yeah," Noah said, "but not in any way you might think."

"You've had it in for me ever since I caught you screwing up," Gary snarled.

Noah kept his temper without even trying. "You're so cute when you're angry, Gary. Maybe we can get some coffee together after this is all over."

"Fuck you, Skyler."

"Have a seat, Gary," Linus said. "You'll have your say."

"What's going on, then?" Karen asked.

"All right, let me start from the beginning. I was actually one of the last people to see Viktor alive after I threw him out of my apartment, along with Crysta Nell and Bredda Meese. Crysta told me the three of them went down to the Dome and hooked up with a stranger who seemed to be selling Blue. We later learned the dealer goes by the name Indigo. Crysta said Indigo and all the Blue creeped her out, so she went home. Bredda and Indigo, meanwhile, went to work on Viktor. They have a little scam going. Bredda comes on heavy to men but only agrees to go all the way if the guy uses Blue, supplied by Indigo. The plan is to get the guys addicted to the stuff and provide Indigo with a long-term customer.

"Viktor hadn't used any Blue in the orgy back at my apartment, but my roommate Wade had, and Bredda used that to persuade Viktor—see what a good time Wade had, and all that. Indigo gave Viktor the Blue, probably for free or at a greatly reduced price, and the three of them headed down to the fish tanks, which is one of the few places you can find privacy around Luna City."

Noah thought about Ilene and her private apartment. She still hadn't returned his call. A twinge whipped through him, and he hurried to continue.

"Down at the tanks, Viktor got high on Blue. One of the trio walked away—" Noah pointed at an image of purple footprints "—and the shoe size matches Indigo's feet. I'm guessing Indigo and Bredda staged an argument that would give him an excuse to leave Viktor and Bredda alone. Bredda would then persuade Viktor to take more Blue. That was when things went wrong. Viktor was high and horny, but he apparently kept his head enough to refuse more Blue. Bredda eventually lost her temper and forced more on him. They struggled at the edge of the tank, causing these water splashes." Noah indicated another image, this one showing purple smears all over the floor around the tank. "Normally Viktor would have had the advantage, but he was on enough Blue to slow down a football team. Bredda shoved him over the edge of the tank—I found her hairs there—and held him under until he drowned. Then she walked over to join Indigo, who watched the entire thing. You can see that his footprints reappear here, at the edge of the crime scene, and Bredda's join him. They left him to die, but a late-night maintenance worker found Viktor and called the paramedics.

"Bredda was staying with Indigo, which is why her roommate hadn't seen her in weeks. Later, when I slapped paint on Indigo and Bredda in the park, they ran to Crysta and hid at her place. She lied about not knowing where they were, gave them new clothes, and helped them try to get the paint off. That was when Gary and I showed up, and when Gary deliberately screwed up the arrest."

Gary jumped to his feet. "What the hell are you talking about? *You're* the fuckup, Skyler! *You're* the—"

Linus held up a hand. "That's a stiff accusation, ki— Noah. Especially when you consider the history between you two."

"I don't have *any* history with Gary," Noah said. "But he has one with me. He claimed that I made mistakes out at the crater crime scene when *he* was the one who messed up—and yeah, I know it's my word against his. But I *do* know that either Gary doesn't know a thing about restraining someone or he deliberately let Indigo go."

"Explain," Linus said before Gary could shout again.

Noah allowed himself a small bit of triumph as he picked up the plastic sheet and unrolled it flat. Little flecks and fibers were scattered across it, backlit by the lighted table. "I sprayed Gary's shirt with evidence film and tore it off right after Gary fought with Indigo. The only fibers on it are from Gary's shirt. None from Indigo's. I also couldn't find any significant DNA traces from anyone but Gary. This indicates that Gary held Indigo so loosely that no fibers or DNA were transferred to Gary's clothing. Either Gary is laughably incompetent at restraining perps or he deliberately let Indigo get away."

Gary opened his mouth, then clamped it shut, hard.

"I understand what you're saying," Linus said slowly, "but the obvious question here is why Gary might do such a thing."

"I wanted to know the same thing," Noah admitted. "I'd never even met Gary until we processed the crater scene together, and he seemed to have it in for me from the start. So I did some digging and learned something very interesting. Did you know that Gary applied for the Aidan Cosgrove Memorial Grant?"

Linus shook his head. "But I only judged the final round of candidates."

"I know." Noah shot Gary a penetrating look, and a flash of anger tightened his chest. "He was eliminated from the candidate pool in the semifinal round. Gary doesn't hate me specifically—he'd be just as pissed off at anyone else who got the Cosgrove grant. I don't know whether he's trying to sabotage me because he's hoping I'll lose the grant and he'll get another chance or if he's just holding a grudge, but he *is* trying to sabotage me."

"I see." Linus turned to the seated deputy. "Gary? Your response?"

"He's making it all up," Gary said tightly. "The so-called evidence Skyler gathered is all circumstantial. He screwed up at the crater, not me. I fought with that Indigo guy, but I was caught by surprise and just didn't have a chance to get a grip. It happens to everyone. Yeah, I was turned down for the Cosgrove grant, but that doesn't prove anything, either."

Another wave of anger washed over Noah, surprising him with its intensity. His hands curled into fists that itched to smash Gary in the face. He forced himself to turn his back on Gary and stare at images of fish tanks and purple footprints while Linus considered.

"Gary seems to be correct," Linus said at last, and Noah's heart sank. "I don't see any hard evidence that he's attempting sabotage."

Gary smirked at Noah and rose to his feet.

"However," Linus continued, "I should the matter investigate more thoroughly. While this is going on, Gary, you'll be assigned to desk duty."

"Desk duty?" Gary squawked. "For how long?"

"Until the investigation is completed," Linus replied calmly. "It shouldn't be more than a few weeks."

"But I don't get as much field credit behind a desk," Gary objected hotly. "You can't—"

"Don't tell me what I can and can't do in my own department," Linus snapped. "You'd better get to your desk now. Tell Marks she'll be picking up your field time until further notice."

Gary shot Noah a look of pure hatred before storming out of the room. Noah couldn't help smiling.

"Thanks," he said to Linus.

"It's departmental procedure," Linus replied in a neutral voice.

"I wouldn't walk down any dark alleys if I were you, Noah," Karen said. "He looked madder than a shark with a toothache."

"I didn't ask for him to be an enemy," Noah said. "Maybe he'll calm down after a couple weeks." Though even as he said it, he doubted it would happen. He sighed. "Anyway, I should probably start writing the report on Viktor Riza's murder."

"Actually, I think you should hold off a bit," Linus said.

Noah blinked at him. "I should? Why? Am I being suspended or something?"

"Nothing like that." Linus gestured at the evidence table. "It's just that your conclusion about Viktor's death doesn't match the evidence."

"I don't understand."

Linus sighed. "You've missed a few important facts, Kid. First, the water smears at the tank were almost certainly caused by the paramedics, not by a fight between Bredda and Viktor. All you can say for certain from these footprints is that Bredda walked away from Viktor."

"Maybe," Noah said doubtfully, "but it still could have—"

"There's more," Linus interrupted. "Blue is administered orally. It comes in ampoules, but the users squirt it into their mouths and swallow or mix it in a drink. It's unlikely in the extreme that Bredda could have forced Viktor to take enough of it to get his blood levels that high. He must have taken it on his own. Also, according to Dr. Rose, the only material under Viktor's fingernails was fish scales and algae. In your scenario, Viktor struggled with Bredda up close and personal, and that would have left her skin flakes under Viktor's nails, maybe even blood. I'm sorry, Kid, but there's only one solution to this case."

Noah started to object, then halted the words before they could escape. It was hard to admit it, but Linus was right. There were holes in Noah's case, big, obvious ones. He had just not wanted to see them. Now that Linus had pointed him the right direction, Noah saw the correct solution. He forced himself to look Linus in the face.

"Viktor's death was an accident," Noah said slowly. "Bredda persuaded Viktor to take more Blue, and, as an inexperienced user, he took so much that he wasn't any . . . fun to Bredda, and he was too high to buy any more Blue. So Bredda left and rejoined Indigo. Viktor tried to get up and follow them, but stumbled against the tank and fell face-first into it. The worker noticed him in time to call the paramedics, who smeared the water around."

"That's how I read it," Linus said.

Karen patted his shoulder. "It wasn't your fault that Viktor died, Noah."

Noah stared at her. "What? How did—?"

"It's not hard to see, love," Karen said gently. "The way you saw it, if you hadn't thrown Viktor out of your apartment, he'd still be alive and undamaged. You were thinking that if you could find his killer, it would balance the scales—there'd be someone else to blame."

"Yeah," Noah said. "That's kind of . . . yeah."

"It wasn't your fault," Karen continued. "Viktor decided to overstay his welcome at your apartment. Viktor decided to go off with Bredda and Indigo, and Viktor decided to take the Blue. I wouldn't wish his current position on anyone, but he doesn't have anyone to blame except himself. No one can blame you."

"Maybe," Noah said. "I'll have to think about it for a while." But he felt rather better.

"And you cracked a major case all on your own," Karen finished.

This startled Noah. "I did?" he asked.

"Well, yeah," Linus said, clapping him heartily on the back. "Weren't you paying attention? Indigo clearly has a line on Luna's illegal drug trade, and I'm sure he'll have a lot to say once we get him talking. You blew the lid off the whole thing single-handedly. Pretty good for your first time out."

"Hey, yeah," Noah said. "And my show got some pretty good reviews, too." And he'd gotten to try sex in low gravity.

"Go home, Kid," Linus said. "Get some rest before classes start. Then you'll learn the *real* meaning of the word *pressure*."

"I'm going to have to come up with a nickname for you," Noah muttered. "Old man, old fart, ancient one. If you're going to call me *kid*, anyway."

"I've never called you *kid*," Linus protested.

Noah sighed and left.

"I didn't call him *kid*, did I?" Linus asked Karen as they entered his office.

Karen gave a light laugh and leaned over to kiss him on the cheek, then thought the better of it, then decided *What the hell* and bussed him soundly. He smelled good, even if his face was bruised.

"I'm sure you'll get over it love," she said.

Their eyes met for a long moment. Karen remembered the heat she had felt in the medical center and the affect she'd had on Linus. He'd had the same effect on her, and the intensity of it had surprised her. She had held him close, telling him he could cry, to cover her surprise and confusion. Now, with his gray eyes meeting hers, she wondered how she could ever be confused about anything.

A chime sounded, and Linus broke eye contact. "That's probably the Mayor-President calling," he said, reaching for his desk. "I'll have some good news for her."

Karen hovered behind him as Linus's display popped up. His face went impassive.

"Actually it's Robin," he said. "My wife."

The moment ended. Karen headed for the exit. "I'll just give you some privacy, then." She shut the door and leaned against it, wishing she could hear the murmurs from within but also feeling glad she couldn't. Love wasn't supposed to be a dichotomy, but it was. Dr. Karen Fang stood in the hallway for a long moment, then nodded once to herself and walked firmly away.

Noah arrived at his apartment, wishing he could take a bath but willing to settle for a hot shower. Jake lay stretched out on the living room, reading textbooks on his obie. A bowl of fluffy white popcorn sat next to him, and Noah smelled the butter. Fake butter, probably, but who cared?

"Oh man," Jake groaned when Noah came in. "I don't know how I'm going to survive this semester."

"Harsh reading?"

" 'Harsh' doesn't even start to describe it. This book makes hydrochloric acid look like a milkshake." He saw the tired expression on Noah's face and sat up. "Hard day?"

"Yeah. Wade here?"

Jake shook his head and stuffed a handful of popcorn into his mouth. One kernel got away from him and drifted to the floor like a malformed snowflake. "Got the official notice a couple hours ago. Wade's moved out."

"So it's just you and me, hey?"

"I doubt it. We'll probably get someone even worse."

Noah tried to plop down on the sofa, but the low gravity turned it into more of a gentle plunk. "Let's be optimistic," he said. "It might be someone better."

"Define 'better.' "

"Someone who won't hold all-night orgies without inviting his roommates," Noah said, and Jake laughed.

The door opened. "Hello? Anyone home?"

"In here," Jake called out. He shot Noah an apprehensive look, but Noah just smiled back at him. They'd gotten the Roommate from Hell out of the way. Whoever it was would only be an improvement.

The young man who entered reminded Noah of an Asian grasshopper—all knees and elbows and nervous energy beneath thick black hair. He carried an old-fashioned suitcase. One thumb tapped an odd rhythm against the handle.

"Dudeguys," he said, holding out a long-fingered hand. "Stan Ping."

"Hi," Jake said, reaching up to shake Stan's hand. "I'm Jake Jaymes. This is Noah Skyler. Computer said you're the new roommate."

"That's me. Nice to meet you both, dudeguys." Stan parked his suitcase next to the sofa and glanced around the tiny space. "Um . . . do you both live here?"

"Yeah." Noah felt a sudden and overwhelming sense of déjà vu. "It's a two-person apartment with three people assigned to it. Happens all the time up here."

"That's cool." Stan dropped to the floor next to the coffee table crate. His hands moved restlessly, drumming on his knees, his shins, his body. He nodded his head in time to some internal song—or maybe his obie was playing music for him. "How do we sleep?"

"First two to hit the hay get the beds," Noah explained as Stan continued to drum on himself. "Last one gets the sofa."

Stan's hands wandered from thumping his thorax to tapping on the table. He didn't even seem aware he was doing it. The constant rhythm set Noah's teeth on edge.

"Sounds fair," Stan said. "I'm a late-night sort of dudeguy, so I'll probably get the couch a lot." *Tappity tappity tap tap tap.* Noah heard a beeping sound that indicated he was getting a call.

"Right," Jake said. He couldn't seem to stop staring at Stan's constantly drumming hands. "So are you a music student? I didn't even know Luna U had that kind of program." Noah ignored the beeping. It was probably Linus. Or Richard. Or maybe his advisor.

"Nah. Psycho-genetics." *Tappity tappity tap tap tap.* "I'm looking at the impact of gene therapy on unconscious repetitive behaviors. Cool stuff, dudeguys. It's amazing the shit people do without even realizing it." Whoever it was, Noah wasn't going to take the call. He had enough to deal with talking to this Stan joker. Unless . . . "I hope you dudeguys are spiffy-cool, you know?" Stan said. "My last roommate— shit. He defined the term *roommate from hell,* know what I mean?"

"Can you hold that thought?" Noah asked. "I've gotta get this." He took the call. It was Ilene.

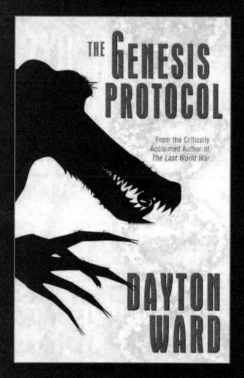

PHOBOS IMPACT

An Imprint of Phobos Books LLC, 200 Park Ave South, New York, NY 10003
Voice: 347-683-8151 Fax: 718-228-3597
Distributed to the trade by National Book Network 1-800-462-6420

PHOBOS
IMPACT

Sandra Schulberg
Publisher

John J. Ordover
Editor-in-Chief

Carol A. Greenburg
Executive Editor

Matt Galemmo
Art Director

Terry McGarry
Production Editor

Andy Heidel
Marketing Director

Hildy Silverman
Webmaster

Chris Erkmann
Advertising Associate

PHOBOS
IMPACT